WOLFSKIN

Wolfskin

LARA MORENO

Translated from the Spanish
by Katie Whittemore

Curated by Katie Whittemore for the 2022 Transaltor Triptych

OPEN LETTER

LITERARY TRANSLATIONS FROM THE UNIVERSITY OF ROCHESTER

Originally published in Spanish as *Piel de Lobo* in 2016 by Penguin Random House Grupo Editorial, S. A. U., Barcelona

Copyright © 2016 by Lara Moreno
English translation copyright © 2022 by Katie Whittemore
First published in English in 2022 by Structo Press, Witherslack
First Open Letter edition 2022

Library of Congress Cataloging-in-Publication data: Available.
PB: 978-1-948830-71-3
Ebook: 978-1-948830-72-0

Support for the translation of this book was provided by Acción Cultural Española, AC/E

AC/E
ACCIÓN CULTURAL
ESPAÑOLA

Printed on acid-free paper in the United States of America.

Designed and typeset in Karmina by Euan Monaghan
Cover artwork based on an original photograph by Liza Summer

Open Letter is the University of Rochester's nonprofit, literary translation press:
Dewey Hall 1-219, Box 278968, Rochester, NY 14627

www.openletterbooks.org

To Beatriz, my sister

I USED TO SLEEP under a pile of stuffed animals that triggered my allergies. Sometimes, my eyes and nose would swell shut from the dust mites, but I slept buried among those felt sacks of synthetic cotton stuffing with plastic eyes and bushy whiskers because I was afraid. I was afraid, for instance, of the Holy Spirit: a grim dove with a dirty beak and sharp talons stealing into a dark hayloft, beating its menacing wings, robbing you of something very valuable inside, something irreplaceable. It was a threat, more than a mystery of faith. And when I thought about infinity, I experienced a vertigo that turned my stomach. Infinity was everything up above, it was us humans on Earth, plus the other planets, the stars, the universe, the widest black expanse, limitless, and there my mind would go, trying to grasp either the beginning or the end, I'm not sure which, but something forbidding that hurt my head because behind all that immeasurableness was God, the only theory, the only unknown, a truth that gripped me to the point of insomnia. I would lie very still between the animals, pull the sheet over my head, shut my eyes. Sleep wouldn't come. My sister's skinny little body rested silently on the other bed, her mattress free of stuffed animals, her breath inaudible. For a child, there comes a moment in the night when turning on the light is utterly impossible. My only salvation, the hallway: at the end, my parents' bedroom.

Eventually, I would make up my mind and leap out of bed, leave the room, and creep barefoot down the hall, as if my little-girl feet might be heard on the tile. The trip was interminable—not because it was an especially long hallway, but because I wavered with every step, my figure in the middle of the night feeling its way forward, freezing myself in time, since at any given moment it was possible that I would be fine, everything would settle inside of me and maybe I could turn back, leave my parents undisturbed, not do anything unnecessary, return to bed, and sleep until morning. But there was the open door to my parents' room, the light from the moon or streetlamps filtering through the balcony curtains, the two nightstands and their books, my father's giant body lying face-up, taking up all the space, his heavy breathing that wasn't quite a snore that hung suspended within my own breath, a taut thread, a treacherous wingbeat, and my mother's body beside him, forming a triangle in the corner of the bed, her hand bent at her shoulder. The smooth hand of a mother at rest.

With the finesse of an aerialist, every muscle strained, I would make my way around the big bed until I reached my mother's side. I stood watching her, still and spectral. I didn't dare do anything else, I didn't whisper mama or touch her arm, I just watched her, because my father and his heavy breath slept on the other side, and if my father were to wake with a violent start, sit up in bed and find me there—well, that was something that just couldn't happen. Sometimes, I was very lucky. After a few minutes my mother would open her green eyes, startled by my presence—how did she know, as she slept, that I was watching her?—and mutter a few words, what are you doing there? a half-hearted scolding, and let me in under the covers. And there, between my parents' bodies—so different, my mother's and father's—careful not to bat an eyelash for fear that time would reverse and I'd be sent back to my own room, I could finally sleep: uncomfortable, hot, still, until the next morning.

THERE IS A SMALL plastic horse in the corner of the modest fenced-in yard. It looks like it's been there for eternity, yet it's not actually old. That particular corner is the only part of the yard that has been conserved as a garden, that wasn't sealed with cement and tile and made into a patio. Grass now grows in dirty clumps around the rocking horse. The grass has never been tended by a gardener, but, at one point, something like a lawn used to sparkle on sunny winter days.

Two sisters walk through the gate. They aren't unsettled by the sight of the abandoned plastic rocking horse, blue and white. Maybe they've shut their eyes, maybe they've entered that space blindly. They know the way by heart. Nevertheless, one of them—the youngest—walks over to the corner, resolute, while the other woman unlocks the door. Without thinking, as if she'd planned it, she grabs the horse by one of its handles and lifts. The dirt stirs with ants and woodlice, the only damp spot in the yard. The woman exits back through the gate with the rocking horse on her back and drops it next to the dumpster on the front sidewalk. The plastic creaks, defeated by sun and heat. Unfettered by nostalgia, the woman enters the house and doesn't look back.

Clothing and keepsakes have begun to pile up on the bed. Old pairs of dark trousers, hems hand-sewn and ironed, the crease on the trouser leg still intact. White shirts, an occasional light blue, winter plaids, fine-knit vests, leather belts, the changing shape of the buckle holes through the passing years. Thin socks, the elastic worn. A couple of jackets, no ties, a stiff raincoat, a thickly lined winter coat, mismatched pajamas with pitiful patterns from the 1990s, white briefs, some of them with holes. The sorry trousseau of a man on his own. No jewelry. His wedding ring isn't there, no pair of cufflinks with engraved initials, no little gold chain from his first communion. Sofía and Rita work thoroughly, impatiently. Almost everything they find they put in big plastic bags; sometimes one will stop to smell a piece of clothing, the folded cloth handkerchiefs, a throw pillow squashed down on the rocking chair. It all smells of dust, of damp, of closed rooms, but still, there's a remnant of a memory, the presence of the man, a light whiff of cologne or aftershave.

Their father died a year ago. He was fortunate: it wasn't cancer, nothing degenerative. A simple, efficient brain aneurysm felled him one June morning, just after breakfast. His overturned teacup had still been on the table. Instead of rolling to the floor, it knocked against the plate of toast and there it had remained: the butter knife on one side, a crumpled paper napkin on the other. The TV on. The windows open. The body on the floor, the leg of a chair pressing on his abdomen. He was like that for two days.

Sofía sifts through the books. Some she's read or heard of, but others are new to her, likely purchased at flea markets or from big overstock warehouses. They don't interest her. She puts them in boxes, without bothering to wipe off the dust. Nor does she look for any writing on the first pages, either: a date, a dedication, her father's signature. He didn't love books enough to write in them. She fills two boxes and seals them with packing tape, then places the few volumes she has set aside back on the bookshelf, next to some ugly, abstract porcelain figurines and framed photographs. She lays them facedown; they'll divide them up later.

It's beginning to get hot and Sofía is hungry. She goes through the rooms looking for her purse and finds her sister moving the kitchen furniture, coming and going with electric appliances covered in grease, a blender, a juicer, and dishrags, too, bought a decade before and never used. Are you hungry? Rita asks. I am, but I need to make a call first. Sofía finds her bag and goes outside. A green plastic table and two chairs sit next to the door on a little outcrop that can't quite be called a porch. They're dirty. The tabletop bears the marks of several glasses: fossils of fruit juice, a two-liter bottle, an inopportune whiskey, red wine from the odd family meal. Sofía sits in one of the chairs and stretches out her legs, spreading her feet wide. She's not sure if she's tired, bored, or simply ill at ease. Practically nobody is on the street at this time of day, just the occasional car, someone coming home from work for a mid-morning break. The house is in an old development outside of town, on the way to the beach. Not a uniform group of row houses, but a development from the 1970s, made up of libertine, unesthetic homes. But she likes it. Many of the neighbors have renovated the original structures, added another floor, a pool, raised the fences and covered them with ivy or bamboo cane. There had been other owners, but her father had left the house exactly as it was. He was responsible for that disaster of a yard, however, spreading cement over everything and laying tiles, just so there wouldn't be anything to maintain: convenience over beauty. She likes the house anyway. It makes her feel uneasy, but she likes it. Deep down she doesn't want to get rid of it; in the end, it's the only place she has to go back to. She opens her bag and grabs her phone, dials. She takes a deep breath, she wants to sound calm and confident when he picks up, maybe even a little distracted. No one answers.

Hey, are you done? I'm ready to eat. A minute later, Rita finds Sofía in the same position, seated on the chair on the porch. Sofía turns, the phone still in her hand. She's called twice more. Nothing. There's no reason to be afraid, just irritated. No reason

5

to worry. She shifts in the chair, looks at the sky. Rita observes Sofía's hands lying tense on her lap. Yeah, all set. Let's eat. Sofía pulls herself up, leaning her weight on the arms of the chair; her movements seem too slow, like something isn't working right, like she's aged. That's how she feels, actually. Old.

She put the bag full of food she prepared the night before in the unplugged refrigerator when they'd arrived at the house, and now she takes it out. She's starving. Resentment gives her an appetite. But Rita has other plans. She's wearing her canvas sneakers and carrying her handbag, has put on lipstick. She looks at Sofía, surprised. Please don't tell me you think we're going to eat here, in the house. There's nothing here, we're emptying it out ourselves. Why would you want to eat here? Sofía knows Rita's right: the normal thing to do is go out. I don't know, because I don't feel like wasting money at a restaurant. Because I made rice salad last night and that's what I feel like eating. Yeah, but you make rice salad every night. Don't you want to have lunch at one of the places on the beach? Sofía's face is already darkening, her own particular shade of weariness. I'd rather eat here, but you go. Rita sighs, turns, and drops her bag in one of the rooms, takes off her shoes, wipes off her lipstick. She does want to go out, get some air. But she'll stay. She'll eat with her sister in the empty house and she'll rush to finish packing so she can get out of that place before nightfall. Fine, we'll eat here, but I'm not eating on the porch because it's way too hot, and there's no way I'm sitting at papa's table or in one of those chairs. Move them and we'll eat on the floor. I have to pee.

Sofía has always looked a little heavy next to her sister, though she isn't, really. She's not big-boned, not a robust woman. She's tall, a little curvy maybe, but her curves are smooth, premeditated, as if they'll stay in the same place forever. But since she's the oldest, she's bigger. She weighs more, it takes more effort for her to move. She's always preferred to sit and watch her little sister—light, fibrous, lively, agile—dance around her, run down those sandy paths, almost flying. The wind carrying her off. It's still like that, now.

They've moved the table where their father was eating when he died, and the chairs, too. Sofía has managed to find a decent, unstained tablecloth, because a plain oilcloth wouldn't do. She spread it on the floor in the middle of the living room and set two pillows across from each other. Two plates, two glasses, a glass jug filled with tap water, two identical forks. In the center of the tablecloth, her brown rice salad: carrot and brown apple, a little olive oil, salt, and sesame seeds. Sofía no longer looks so defeated; this simulacrum of a picnic has cheered her. It wouldn't have bothered her to eat at the table where their father died because she suspects that he actually died on the floor. In fact, it's more likely that he died in the exact spot where her sister Rita now sits with her pretty legs crossed. Moreover, no one knows how long he was there, writhing on the verge of death. The doctors said no time at all, not even a second; he collapsed and it was over, but who knows, no one was there. No one came for two days. She'd like to tell Rita what's just occurred to her, but now isn't the time. Better to say nothing. Serve the salad. Eat.

And so they do. Sofía chews with the enthusiasm of a militant. Her eyes even shine. She's forgotten the phone, the unanswered calls, the hot little restaurants on the beach, her father. She chews and swallows with concentration, she likes the taste of olive oil on the brown rice. She knows it's good for her, good for the world. Rita watches her sister, her straight back, the solidness of her shoulders, her presence. She watches in amazement as she chews—a thousand and one times—those hard, bland grains of rice. Rita would almost say that the rice was raw, that Sofía took it out of the package like that, one handful then another and another, drizzled on the olive oil and there you go, lunch. She tries to swallow quickly, aided by big sips of water. This sisterly performance needs to end as quickly as possible. Her posture betrays her indifference. A somewhat despotic laxity, inherent to the eternal adolescence of her limbs, her delicate back, even her cheekbones and the high, clear reptilian forehead, beautiful, cold. She wants to wrap this all up. Sofía has proposed they rent out the house instead of putting it on the market, but Rita wants to sell, even though she's not necessarily the one who needs the money. Sofía finishes her meal and looks directly at her little sister, sinks into her big eyes: gray, brown, changeable, set in their dark circles. The look lasts only a few seconds. Just an instant, when neither sister has anywhere else to be, nothing waiting for them in the world outside. It's as if the years haven't passed, or better still, as if the two sisters have arrived at the place where everything comes to an end and all that's left for them to do is spread their wings. But this opportunity, it vanishes also.

IT'S PAST MIDNIGHT BY the time the bus pulls into the silent station. Bus stations are all the same at that time of night, with their air of violence, desolation, freedom. The people passing through after midnight look like keepers of sacred stories, or tales of grief. The buses slumber like giant worms, the ticket counters are shuttered, time crawls on. Sofía leaves the station and breathes deeply. As she exits the bus bay, she feels like she's gone back twenty years in time, back to when she used to make that trip on the weekends. She even hears the phantom wheels of the beat-up suitcase from her university days, rolling across the tile floor.

She's carrying just a large handbag and a wrinkled jacket. It's very late, but she had preferred to catch the last bus instead of staying and sleeping over in town. Her phone hasn't rung all day. It doesn't matter now, she's almost home. She starts off in the direction of the bridge, but a hundred yards later raises her arm and hails a cab. She gives her address, and as the car accelerates, she relaxes into the seat, trying—yet again—to determine the appropriate feeling or posture required by the moment.

She takes a deep breath, inserts the key in the lock, opens the door to her apartment. A light is on in the living room. She leaves her keys on the table, hangs up her bag, takes out the plastic bag with the rice salad container—empty and washed already—and leaves it on the kitchen counter. The kitchen is tidy, nothing has been left for her on a tray, no plate set aside with dinner, just in case, no sign that anyone else has eaten, either. She lays her jacket on a stool and is about to sit down again, to think again about how she should compose her face, as if she hadn't thought about it a thousand times already on the bus ride. She hears voices in the living room, a movie playing. The door is closed. She opens it.

Hey, how's it going? Good, I'm watching a movie. How are you? Tired. I bet. How did it go? Did you guys finish? I don't know, I'm not sure if we're done yet. Is there anything for dinner? You haven't eaten? It's so late, why haven't you eaten? I would have missed the bus. Well, you could have bought a sandwich at the station. I'd rather eat something at home, anything. We went out to dinner so there isn't anything ready. Ah, how nice. Where? A new Greek place downtown. A Greek place? Why did you go out to eat? It's Tuesday night. Yeah, it's Tuesday, so? Well, I'm going to make myself a salad. There's no lettuce left. Wow, okay. I guess I'm not that hungry anymore. Can I sit here a minute? Are you serious? Don't start. What, I don't know if you want me here, you were watching a movie. What's that got to do with anything? Well, just that maybe you didn't feel like talking. Oh, so you want to talk—you aren't really asking if you can sit on the couch, but if I want to talk. I obviously don't, and I don't know why you're asking. It's almost one in the morning and I'm watching a movie and I have to get up early tomorrow and I'm tired, too. Yeah, I know it's late, and it's not like you were waiting up for me. Come on, don't go there. I think I'll go to bed now. You're not going to finish the movie? No, I'm not going to finish the movie. And you don't want to talk? There's nothing to talk about, Sofía. I called you two or three times. I wasn't paying attention to my phone, I had a lot of work and then we went downtown and out to dinner, I already told you. But you could have called me back. Shit, you left early this morning, not two weeks ago. Did you need something important? If it was important you would have left a message, right? I'm so tired of these conversations. I'm tired too, we're both tired, and we've said that twenty times, we're always tired of something. But I called you to talk to Leo and you could have at least picked up the phone. I'm not going to argue. Did you guys go out to dinner just the two of you? Sofía, enough. I told you, I'm going to bed. I told you I don't want to talk. And I told you there's nothing to talk about, so don't even think about giving me a hard time just because the one fucking day you're away I don't return a couple of your calls. Eat something and go to bed. You'll be with Leo tomorrow, just like every other day of his life. I'm not hungry. And don't talk to me like that. Sofía, don't cry, please, it's so late. Don't cry. Well, I had a hard day and now this. Now this, what?! I'm going to bed. You didn't even ask me how it went. I asked you as soon as you got here, as soon as you came in the fucking door! No, you asked if we had finished, and I don't know if we've finished, there's a lot to clean, there's a ton to do, it's the whole house, and on top of it the market is slow and it's going to need some work, I think quite a bit of work actually; I don't know, I don't know what we're going to do, well, I do know, I suggested we rent it but she won't, she wants to sell, so we'll sell because I don't have the money to buy her out—I'll lose the house and that's it. I think that's good, you've only been going there because you've had to for years, and you could use the money. *I* could use the money? Not both of us? Well, I think you need it more than I do. Shit, Sofía, is this what you wanted to talk about? About the inheritance from your dad and stuff with your sister? Haven't we gone over this a thousand times? No. No, we haven't gone over it a thousand times, but actually I wanted to talk about us. About us? Ugh. I'm going to bed. I'm done.

It isn't an option to chase him down the hallway. To follow him into the bathroom, watch while he brushes his teeth, pees. Go on at him as he puts on his pajamas and gets into bed, rolls over, falls asleep, starts to snore. None of that is an option. She has to stay there, on the couch, sitting on the edge, with her straight, compact back, her hands on her lap, a pair of hands she won't use to do anything daring. She isn't crying, now. She stopped as soon as he told her to. Not out of obedience, but because deep down she really doesn't feel like it. She doesn't cry but she is hungry; she's been hungry ever since she was in town and they left the boxes and bags organized and ready to be split up, donated, thrown out, passed down—locking up the house as they left. Rita brought her to the bus station and they said goodbye. She was hungry but she didn't want to say to her sister, let's have dinner together, it's a beautiful night, June nights are always beautiful here. They said goodbye quickly; each was ready to go their separate ways. The sisters hadn't really shared much, in the end. Hadn't asked much. Neither had really wanted to know anything vital about the other at that moment in their lives, and the cordial, stifled conversation started to turn a little sour. Better just to get out of the car and walk with dignity to the platform, catch the last bus home.

Standing at the kitchen counter, Sofía wolfs down two bananas. Then she does something worse: she drinks a giant glass of whole milk, the milk she buys for her son. It's been years since she drank a cold glass of milk, barely stopping for breath, standing before the open refrigerator door in the middle of the night. She doesn't usually allow herself so much dairy, but she has absolutely no energy to fix anything else. She brushes her teeth and washes her face and finds a clean T-shirt in the basket of clothes waiting to be ironed. Leo's room smells like Leo. Like sleeping Leo, spilled into sleep. Sweaty Leo, warm and sweet. She buries her nose in his neck and his hair and breathes until she's dizzy. She picks him up carefully and moves him over, making space for herself in the little bed. Beside him, she falls right to sleep.

I REMEMBER IT WELL. Me and my sister clinging to the balcony railing, watching the dumpsters on the sidewalk just in front of the house. I could see over the railing, but my sister, who was quite little then, looked through the gap between the bar and the panel. I remember that it was in the afternoon, that it was sunny. I don't know why, but in childhood the sun doesn't seem as punishing. I'm sure it was hell on the balcony at that time of day and that our heads were roasting, but all that mattered was that we had to stay there, that we couldn't move until it happened. I remember the sun, but not the heat. This is what had to happen: we were to wait until someone took several of the toys next to the dumpster. They were on the sidewalk side so that passers-by could see they were still in good shape and usable. They *could* still be used, and they *were* in good shape. They were supposedly our favorite dolls.

My sister and I had been playing earlier that afternoon. I don't remember what we were doing, but we weren't in the playroom, we were on the rug in the living room, and there were toys scattered all over the floor. We started a fuss over something, we both wanted the same toy, and maybe, just maybe, one of us pulled the other's hair, but I could be exaggerating. We might have growled and squealed—sometimes we behaved like little animals. At that moment, my father came home and saw us. It's completely natural for siblings to fight, but my father couldn't stand it. It was simply beyond him, as were other such natural things. From up above he separated us, brusquely, and asked what had happened. I suppose we sputtered something about

13

the toys. The toys were to blame, not the simple fact of our coexistence. One wanted what the other had, something like that. I don't remember the details. But I do remember exactly what happened next.

My father said: Go get your favorite dolls and bring them here. You're going to put them next to the dumpster and then you're going to stay on the balcony until someone comes and takes them. You are not to move until someone has claimed your toys.

We obeyed. We went to the playroom. My heart was clenched like a fist and I cried thick tears. I couldn't stop thinking about my favorite doll of the moment. She was going to be taken from me; someone was going to carry her off from right under my nose. She was still new, a gift from a friend of my parents. She had blonde hair and bendable arms and legs and a bicycle she could sit on and pedal if I moved her. I could pose her wire limbs in any position and she was so entertaining with her bright-colored clothes and little elfish face. I loved her. I looked for her in the playroom and took her in my hands. I wanted to pass out, but a young child doesn't know that feeling, doesn't even know *how* to faint, and so all I sensed was the trembling in my arms and legs and how frightened I was. My behavior was straightforward, predictable. *Do this and suffer for it*, and so I did. Subtext didn't exist for me as a little girl.

My sister's behavior, however, was staggering. Even now, I'm humbled by the memory and find it hard to believe. Even now, I struggle to understand how that sharp wasp-brain worked, that strange little bird: intelligent, calm, drama-free. She was very small. I don't know how old we were at the time, but her body was thin, and her hair shone when she ran past me, flashing, leaving me dazzled and unsettled. I cried and hiccupped, clutched my blonde bicyclist. But not my sister. She entered the playroom, determined, without the slightest hint of suffering. Immersed in my own agony, I did stop briefly to think about her, about my little sister who at any moment would recognize the tragedy about to befall us. As I watched her climb up on a chair to reach one of the wide shelves of the bookcase, I felt pain, pain for her and pain for me, separate pain, because she was younger and was going to suffer, too. On tiptoe, she sped through her search of the dolls and the boxes, and from the bottom of one pulled out her "favorite doll." This turned out to be a fairly large rubber cat, passing for one of the characters from *The Aristocats*. We never played with it. It came to us in a box of toys passed down from another child and—this I swear—we had never as much as touched it, not once. I didn't even remember that it existed. A completely meaningless object. I stopped crying abruptly when I saw my sister serenely leave the room and go to where my father was waiting. I followed, carrying my beloved new doll. She was serious and calm. I was forlorn. We brought the toys outside and set them next to the dumpster. Then we went back inside to watch from the balcony.

It is—I repeat—staggering that my sister would devise that sort of scheme. I don't understand where she got her cold-bloodedness, her common sense, the nerve to take the shortest route and avoid the pointless. She was so small. So intelligent. It never crossed my mind to trick my father, not even after I saw her do it. It would have been easy, of course: my father had no idea about our favorite toys. My mother might have, maybe, but it wasn't our mother who was punishing us. Why didn't I do it, too? Our father was satisfied with the big lesson he was teaching us. And it had worked perfectly—on me, at least. But on her? She had soared over it, smoothly, ably, a flying fish vaulting over an imaginary pole in the middle of a calm sea, avoiding authority. An elegant feat.

Sometimes I stop and consider why I didn't tell on her. True, a shared punishment can bring siblings together and it's easy to imagine that I stayed quiet out of simple loyalty. But I could be a petty child, and I wasn't always loyal. I believe I didn't give her away because I knew that she—a little thing, barely three feet tall—was teaching me an important lesson, too, one I still haven't learned. I clutched the balcony railing and waited, tortured and terribly sad, for some strange girl to walk by the dumpster and carry away my doll. Beside me, her black hair shining more than ever, a stone in a river, polished and wet, my little sister watched the street, bored, impatient for someone to come and take away that junk already. My sister, skinny little thing, calm, silent, watching life go past.

CLOUDS ON FRIDAY MORNING. The city contains the June heat like a treasure it will hoard until it bursts. Sofía and Leo walk to school, hand in hand. The clouds aren't the flat bands typical of summer, running parallel through the sky and forming aerostatic designs at sunset. Today, the clouds are heavy, white, laden with dirty water. Sofía is as half-asleep as Leo; she's slept badly for three nights now. Last night she slept in her own bed, but the pressure not to move, not to touch, to breathe slowly and silently, was so great that she woke up with a cramp in her neck and back. Finally, it's Friday. She'll make a nice dinner and pick out a good movie. Maybe then they can finally chill out.

She says goodbye to Leo at the door to his school. He doesn't complain, he gives her a hug, and promises he'll eat well and that at recess he'll have the biscuits with no added sugar that he carries in his backpack, instead of the little industrial cream-and-chocolate-filled cakes his friends take for their snack. He doesn't say that exactly, just: Yes, mama, I promise, and gives her a kiss and goes inside. Sofía watches him walk away and feels a stab somewhere in her body; it's so fleeting, she can't say where. It always happens when she sees her son from the back. Leo's hair is black, like Rita's. He didn't inherit Sofía's hair, which isn't like anyone else's. Hair made exclusively for her, the first in the family, hair the color of dark wheat, wavy and coarse. Leo's hair is fine and straight like her sister's, but not as shiny, not a waterfall brilliant in the sun. He doesn't look like Rita in any other aspect; he's a mix of the two of them, Sofía and Julio. They both have full lips, a straight nose, a rather square jaw, dark eyes, cool and lively. Julio and Sofía look a bit alike, and this intrigued them when they met; another reason to think that they were destined to love each other. Now it's deeply disturbing; each rejects the reflection offered by the other.

The clouds have held back the heat, suspended it in the air above. Sofía walks through the streets in the city center, close to the school. She doesn't feel like going home, doesn't want to start work on anything. She sits in the plaza next to the new market, in front of the cinema, and orders green tea and a glass of ice. She doesn't try to imagine how she will begin tonight's conversation. She breathes through her nose, deep, feeling her ribs and belly and bladder expand, like they say to do in class. She only does this three or four times; she doesn't really have the motivation. She drinks her tea and watches people: their skin still pale in June, their sandaled feet still pudgy from winter shoes, their faces. She wouldn't mind running into someone, talking a bit. She gets up and goes to the bar and gets a newspaper. She looks over the headlines but sees nothing she wants to read and finally checks what movies are showing. It would be good to go to the movies, the three of them, on a Friday night. Even better, leave Leo with the babysitter, whom they haven't called in months, and go as a couple. In the theater, in the dark, sitting together, watching the same thing, a ceasefire.

Back home, she makes the beds, takes the clothes off the line, puts them in the ironing room, takes a few mullet fillets from the freezer and puts them on a plate, showers, washes her hair well, conditions it, scrubs herself with an exfoliating sponge, removing the dead skin cells from her legs. She scrubs her belly, too, bulky around the belly button, and her arms, her ribcage. She scrubs her breasts less intensely, taking care not to brush the nipples. Her small, fair nipples. Two little coins. They didn't really grow even when she nursed Leo, and afterward they went right back to their usual shape, possibly the only things to have returned to normal. As she stands in front of the mirror and smooths on an ethanol-free lotion, she notices Julio's toothbrush is gone. Her own toothbrush sits alone in the cup with the toothpaste and floss, next to the mouthwash. She feels a slight dizziness that lasts only a second or two, and remembers that today is Friday. Julio will go to the gym after work and must have put the toothbrush in his gym bag because maybe he'll eat out today, maybe he has a work lunch. Julio is scrupulous about his teeth and he'll certainly want to brush them when he showers after his workout so he'll be clean and can show off that smile, those big, bright white teeth, rooted so solidly in his gums. That must be it.

On the big table in her workroom, Sofía spreads a pattern over the new fabric. She stares at it, then picks up a cold, pink piece of chalk and grips it between her fingers. Re-inforces a straight line and a few marks. She looks closely at the fabric, which extends from under the pattern. And she observes the pattern, too, its whiteness, the markings, the masterfully traced lines. She stares intently, or is it with apathy? Her large, silver scissors are the best sewing scissors in the world. Julio gave them to her as a gift several birthdays ago, with other sewing tools of the highest quality, professional grade. Her toolkit for a new life, he and Rita called it. It had been her thirty-third birthday present. She grips the chalk between her fingers again and pulls the stool up to the table, threatens to make changes to the pattern. Her vision is blurry. The whiteness of the paper is now the cloudy morning sky, the airy sheet on the mattress, barren territory. Her eyes fog over. She stands and leaves the room.

Leo enthusiastically helps her set the table. He carries one thing at a time and limits himself to what is easiest: the silverware, the basket of spelt bread, clean cloth napkins, a candlestick with a new taper, water glasses, and the salad bowl, because he insisted and because it's a wooden bowl. He walks very carefully down the hall from the kitchen to the living room and his mother helps him put it on the table and then places it in the center. Everything is almost ready. The mullet fillets are waiting to be roasted, lined up on a board on the counter. You can wait, right, Leo? Or are you really hungry? I can wait. It's nine o'clock, the sky isn't yet dark. Sofía spreads butter on a piece of bread and gives it to her son. She tidies his hair again, gently, without hurting him. At nine-thirty she decides to roast some of the fish. Leo eats after his mother cleans the fillets of their curved, flexible bones, and watches a little TV, his eyes slow and tired. Sofía opens the bottle of wine chilling in the freezer. She pours herself a glass and drinks it quickly. At first, the cold wine isn't pleasant in her throat, but she pours another glass and enjoys it. She tucks Leo into bed, fibs when she says she called his father and it turns out he'd forgotten he had an important work dinner. Cartoons are still on the TV. Sofía downs her third glass of wine and eats a little salad. Then she turns off the television and does everything one usually does when they've waited long enough to know someone isn't coming home.

For the time being, calling him is not an option. It didn't work that day she went to the town with her sister. It hadn't worked when she told him off for not picking up the phone, for not calling her back. And although Sofía can't say that this is the most drastic event to ever have occurred in their relationship—that wouldn't be true—in some sense it is the sharpest stone, the best-aimed blow. On Friday, when she'd realized the reason Julio wouldn't be home for dinner was because he wasn't coming home to sleep, Sofía went rigid. She drank, put the fish away in the fridge, hurt herself in front of the bathroom mirror—her jaw, her knuckles, her anger. But then she went to bed without thinking. She fell fast asleep on the wide, cool mattress where now she didn't have to pretend, where she didn't have to shift, to seek a reprieve or capitulation.

As soon as she wakes up on Saturday morning, she opens Julio's closet. She didn't expect to find it empty, of course, but how had it not occurred to her to look before? Why didn't she check yesterday, when she noticed the missing toothbrush? Because it felt much better to imagine Julio with his bag on his shoulder, walking into the gym. Much kinder, more practical. Less cutting than the image of Julio picking out a few pairs of newish jeans, canvas sneakers, two or three shirts, underwear, jacket. She checks to see if they're in the basket with the dirty clothes, in the stack of clothes to be ironed. They're not, and she already knew they wouldn't be because she remembers putting them away on their hangers, very recently. Her feet are cold on the tile, standing in front of the closet again. Her feet, the feet of a frog or a duck or a gecko, some kind of gelatine oozes from between her toes. Two shirts. Monday. Tuesday.

It's still overcast and the city looks sad even though it isn't a sad city, it never is, even when it rains, even when the hail falls furiously one or two days a year. If the mist descended far enough, perhaps it could be depressing in those peripheral neighborhoods, the ones built with hollow bricks, the cars parked on an angle, the broad avenues. But it isn't a sad city, though its light, its intensity, can be melancholy. And today is Saturday. It's June, the sky is heavy, badly wounded. She and Leo are walking through an enormous park full of burnt geraniums. They pass families that look like they're from another time, little girls in flounced organdy cotton dresses. They've brought rice to feed the pigeons. Sofía doesn't want the pigeons to claw her son's little arm with their sick, mutilated talons or peck directly from his hand. They throw the rice far away, big fistfuls of it, and the birds flock, a great hungry balloon. Later, they have lunch in a vegetarian restaurant. That evening, in the denuded gardens on the other side of the bridge, they sit and watch two couples dancing tango. The small stereo stirs the air with heartbreaking music and the clouds come apart in the sky. Leo is tired but hypnotised by the dancers. When the sun has almost set, he comes alive again and runs about, shyly approaching other children, climbs up on a bench, jumps.

Saturday happens. Her son's companionship, her own calculated silence, the decision to make no plans, their solitude, the two of them alone in the city. If only every day was like that, Saturday repeated in perpetuity: a missing sense of urgency, the oppressive heat at midday, the pleasantness of a walk, of the parks, of not having to do anything. Not having to explain anything, or show fear, or peel off the shell. Not having to open the door to the chain of events that are about to unfold. Just walk, throw rice on the ground as the street birds attempt to kill each other over a bit of food. Let them have it, with their mess of feathers and cartilage. Sofía and Leo, removed from life's violence: it's just empty benches for them, gardens with geraniums, and dissipating clouds.

Nevertheless, there is still the night and its terror. Sofía immobile on the couch, the boy already fed and asleep, the house tidied and ready to be buttoned up, shut down. And then the darkest hour comes and she twists and turns and her chest pounds and she can't get enough air and her phone is in her hand and at last she dials. Damp eyes, tight jaw, tongue mashing against her incisors. He doesn't answer. Like an automaton, she writes: why are you doing this to me? It takes a long time for her to fall asleep. She checks her phone as many times as her eyes will allow, turns off the light, doesn't cry, then it's over.

Sunday is another hue. The sky is empty and blue and it's hot. Leo suggests they go to the beach. Why don't they call his dad so he'll come back with the car and bring them to the beach? That's a wonderful idea, honey. But papa is pretty far away, he has to work all weekend, I don't think he'll get home in time. She tries to speak naturally, behave the way she's seen so many people behave, in the movies, on TV, in the street, in her own family. Is this how it's done? That's a wonderful idea, honey. And she doesn't stop moving: wipes down the counter one more time, and another, then a clean dish towel to dry, moves smoothly as if she were dancing. That's a wonderful idea, honey, but we could also take the bus to the beach. It's not that far. Yes, mama! A weight hangs from every one of Sofía's organs, one of those round, polished fishing weights, and she wishes she could let herself just drop to the floor, right there in the kitchen, disconnect, that simple, as if she were dancing. No bus, no beach, no child. Go back to sleep, not wait to see what happens, not come up with a plan for her life while time passes. She leaves the kitchen, shuts herself in the bedroom. She calls Julio. Once, twice, three times, four, five.

They don't go to the beach. Sunday turns out to be bright, sizzling. A pitiless Sunday that sweeps through the people's bodies, hampers them from moving freely. They've come to a school friend's pool. Sofía is sitting on the side, her shoulders and back burning, her forehead. She didn't put on enough sunscreen. That never happens to her because she is careful. Obsessive. But she senses her skin getting red and isn't capable of getting up to get the bottle of SPF 50. She can just about manage to stay close to Leo, so he doesn't drown, to occasionally shout for him not to go too deep, bend down to adjust his water wings. The boy slips away like fish guts, wet and happy. She manages not to speak. She manages to remain on the side of the pool, feet in the water, shoulders broiling. She looks good, her face hidden by giant sunglasses.

Was she hoping that he would come back at night, perhaps?

That he and his solidness would open the door and plonk down in the middle of the living room with his overnight bag? Two shirts: Monday, Tuesday. She wasn't expecting that. But before Sunday comes to a close, freshly showered, her wet hair combed back violently, and on the couch again, she calls. He doesn't pick up, but it rings. She thinks he won't want to turn off his phone in case there's an urgent message. An urgent message is not "Why are you doing this to me?" but "Our son is in the hospital. He's been hit by a car." She calls again. Her eyes are glued to the television screen, to the bottle of wine she opened on Friday and is drinking little by little. She checks the time, quarter to twelve. She pours herself what is left of the wine and decides to call Rita. She drinks beforehand, breathes deep, as if she were leaping into the unknown. Rita doesn't answer the phone either.

Later, much later, she closes her eyes.

JULIO'S VOICE SOUNDS ELECTRIC on the other side of the phone. She doesn't know where that side is because even though it's Monday and Julio should be at the office, nothing is the same. Is it not? Has that moment come, the point at which nothing is the same, when it isn't enough to just keep going a little longer, clear the plates from dinner, snuggle into the hollow of his shoulder, slide her hand under his shirt and find warmth? I'm at a hotel, I want you to come see me. Sofía's stomach turns, something is wrong with her eyes, she can't quite focus, she rubs them. Do you want me to bring Leo? No, I don't want you to bring him, that's ridiculous. I want you to come so we can talk, don't you want to talk? Sofía wants to speak but her tongue sticks to the roof of her mouth. When do you want me to come? Right now? Aren't you working? She grabs a glass with one hand and fills it with water but doesn't drink, she just brings it to her mouth, cools the skin on her lips. Of course I'm working. Come at five. But Leo. Well, fuck, call and have someone pick him up and watch him for a little while. We can't have this conversation in front of him. Tell me which hotel.

Sofía, you need to listen to me. I'm not going to start apologizing, because I think we have to understand each other another way, make a radical shift. Yes, I did, I disappeared for three days. I'm in a hotel. I left home. But you really need to listen to me. You have to promise me that we aren't going to take even one step backward, no matter what conclusions we come to today. I'm talking about deep down, not anecdotes, precisely so we can avoid staying stuck in our situation, to avoid the drama, the victimhood, the guilt, the tragedy, everything we've been chewing on for so long now. Sofía, listen to me and quit repeating the same sentence over and over. I left because it was the only way. The only way to make any progress. God, our life has been stagnant for years. And fuck, the last couple of days I feel I'm finally doing something, the only thing I could do—the only good thing, actually, that I've dared to do in a long time. Leave. That's it, Sofía, it's done. Yeah, I recognize that, and it's not such a big deal. Now, we just need to get organized. I'm going to help you with that, don't worry, don't be dramatic about the material stuff, you know we've stayed together for the last two years because of money and now I realize that it doesn't matter. I don't want to go to a lawyer, I don't want to make things hard for you, I don't want anything, I'm going to help you, I'll give you everything you need, but we can't live under the same roof for another minute, and god, Sofía, you know it as well as I do, shit, you started all this a long time ago, you can't keep clinging to you and me like a hyena with a damn carcass. I haven't felt any sympathy for months and if I don't even have sympathy for us—for you!—then there really is nothing left, we've had all the conversations in the world, we've hurt each other in all possible ways. Oh, so you don't agree with that, either? You started it, Sofía, but that doesn't matter now, I've spent a whole year, twelve fucking months telling you that I don't love you, not anymore, that it's gone, and now I'm not even talking about love, Sofía, no, love is intangible, it doesn't last, you taught me that, it exists with us for a while and it feeds our memory but it's actually fleeting, arbitrary, escapist. I'm not talking about love, Sofía, I'm talking about something else, compassion, honesty, nostalgia, I don't feel any of that for you anymore and you know it, you know it better than I do, you've known it all this time but you're hard as a rock, you are a fucking concrete wall.

I haven't been able to make you get it because your only defense is to act as if none of this was happening, you think you love me but you don't, I know you don't love me, in fact *you* stopped loving *me* first, but you're closed off, there are things that you are never going to allow, a separation, abandonment, a broken family, economic insecurity, am I right? You're fucking yourself over and you're fucking me over and you're fucking over our kid because you don't want to recognize the crap we've been swallowing for so long. God, if only you could bring yourself to tell someone, if you would give yourself that luxury, I don't know, you keep everything secret, as if you really think that other people are better than us; okay, okay, that's enough, I know, it isn't like that, we're all the same, it went to shit, I can't keep thinking about it, you don't have any money, I don't care, I'll pay for everything, whatever you want. Of course I won't ask for shared custody, be with the boy all the time you want, we'll just see how we manage, but don't turn it into a tragedy or melodrama, it's just a matter of opening your eyes and getting a move on, and I don't give a damn about your arguments, I'm gone, I'm out, think about it carefully, think about everything I'm saying and most of all think about this situation, the past few days, it's happened and it's realer than you and realer than me, fuck, that's it, that's all, I left and now what we have to do is get organized, we're going to do a good job and we are not going to take even one step back, Sofía, stop repeating yourself, please, stop saying that, I'm not with somebody else, I haven't spent the weekend with anyone, regardless, don't be such a cynic, you don't care about that, that's the least of our concerns at this point, anyway, and if I *were* with another woman at least it would be a step forward, don't laugh, don't look like that, seriously, I know you're smart and now you're going to take a walk or go sit somewhere and think about all of this carefully and calmly and we'll see each other again tomorrow, tomorrow we'll see each other with Leo and we'll explain it to him together, or you can bring him to me and I'll explain everything and we'll work out the details over time, but it's over, it's very easy, you say you love me but you don't love me and I don't love you and of course this isn't easy for me either but it's done, it's done.

Sofía is holding a tissue in her hands. The tissue is a small ball, soft and damp, like petals ripped suddenly from a chrysanthemum, from a hortensia. It passes from one hand to the other and sometimes she uses it to blow her nose, the little ball that can no longer absorb anything. There's a buzzing in the room. She eventually realizes that it isn't coming from her brain but from a fly trapped between the window and the mesh curtain. The fly is like a thing possessed; tireless, tenacious, out of control, it's been trying the whole time to escape, pass through the glass, flee. Can you open the window? There's a fly. Julio, standing in the middle of the room, his sturdy body sinking into the thick white carpet, looks at her, stupefied and indifferent. I can't, you can't open the windows in this hotel, I'd have to call someone to come open it. You're a son of a bitch. I do love you. Don't you dare try to convince me that I don't love you.

TUESDAY. THE HOUSE IS A CAGE. She hears new noises everywhere. She inspects the bathroom ceilings. The ceiling down the long hallway. The impassive ceiling of her bedroom. There aren't any leaks but it sounds like there are leaks and it even smells a little damp. She goes from room to room because pacing like a caged tiger in her own home is an effective way to think. Sometimes she stops, grabs her stomach or forehead. She does this when the images are too sharp. A few words dance in her brain, little dolls somersaulting, little scraps of tulle glued to their waists. She goes to the front door, her ears prick up: ghost leaks smack jubilantly on the wood floor, on the bathroom tile. Maybe the whole apartment above is now a giant pool because the upstairs neighbor forgot to turn off the faucets, because now she is swimming down the hallways, floating, ninety kilos of raw meat bathing in tap water. Or maybe the pipes have burst on another floor, the fifth, maybe someone smashed them with a hammer.

She already has it worked out, actually. First thing, the boy's room. The open suitcase on the bed, his summer clothes inside, neatly folded in little squares, nicely organized, with space still available for his bath things, shoes, and books. There is an open suitcase in her bedroom, too, where she expects to find a big puddle flooding a waterlogged mattress, where she expects to slip on water that falls to the floor, from the ceiling, from the bed. She peers inside it anxiously, touches the folded garments, the sandals lined up edge to edge, underwear, miniature balls of cotton in a corner. Everything is ready to go but it's like she can't take another step. Last night, a mostly silent dinner and then explaining a few things to Leo as she sat on his bed. His eyes opened wide and that coveted expression of peace kids have when they rest their heads on a pillow. Misleading and incomprehensible words for a child of five: temporary, distance. And then those other words, soft and covered in fuzz, so hollow: Everything's okay, it's all okay. There's a lot left to explain because there's still a lot to be worked out. She can't think about that right now, she has to think about the house, the hallway, the leaks, the packed suitcases. She makes a couple of phone calls; although she has become unaccustomed to it in recent years, she realizes she's still efficient enough for the simplest of logistics. In a short time, she accomplished several tasks on her to-do list, including one very important item: place an order for several kilos of organic brown rice, pasta, quinoa, wheat. She wrote up a list of things they might need, the most pressing things, and she has just about everything already. She has also checked her savings account. What irony—no normal person without a reliable job has a savings account, but she does, because Julio didn't want to touch the inheritance from her father and so they put it in an account. It isn't much, but it allows her a margin of error. In a large box, she has packed her sewing machine, her patterns, the dresses she's already started on, and several other pieces she's trying out. The box is taped and addressed and soon the courier will be by to pick it up. She looks over the books she has selected one more time and makes room for them in her suitcase.

The beginning of June, the monstrousness of a tiger locked in the house, on the verge of escaping, the bad caged-animal smell. She turns on her phone for the first time that morning: five missed calls from Julio but no message. She has disconnected the landline. She doesn't check her email and turns the phone back off. She made do with every usable item in the fridge to prepare and store a few meals, and she took a second shower and changed her clothes and returned to the kitchen to make sandwiches for the afternoon. She puts the sandwiches and what's left in the fruit bowl in a backpack and checks the weight. There is still an hour before Leo gets out of school and Sofía is sure, a sudden, strangling hand, that she is not going to make it. The two suitcases, her bag, the backpack with food, the child. She is not going to make it.

A sob threatens to sweep it all away but she contains herself one more time and sticks her head under the kitchen faucet, a new faucet that Julio installed with his own hands, a shiny, tall, flexible faucet that turns that kitchen into a place for professionals: the faucet and the knife set and the ceramic frying pans, the pots without a speck of Teflon, the glass jars filled with chickpeas, lentils, pinto beans, loose spices bought in bulk; in her house, a person could grab spices by the fistful, leaving their whole hand smelling of tarragon, thyme, cinnamon stick. The water slowly wetting Sofía's head, its robust hair, her white neck. It's extremely unpleasant that instead of streaming over her crown, the water crisscrosses her face at the ears; her eye sockets are two choppy lakes. She straightens. She knows she looks awful, but she isn't going to cry, and the two suitcases, the backpack with food, and the bag are at the front door. She lowers the blinds. All that's left is to call a cab.

The bus is full and the sun streams in through the window, illuminating Leo's bony knees. There's not much noise because it's time for the siesta, it's almost summer; the air conditioning, always colder than necessary, doesn't seem to cool things down enough today. The passengers doze. Sofía and Leo eat their afternoon snack. They're hot but there's a benevolence in both of them. They aren't fleeing but *going* somewhere, making the short trip to the sea. That, in all its contexts, has a positive connotation and Sofía clings to the sunlit landscape of her son's legs and the avocado sandwiches and the juice and the stories they read together and his insistence they speak very quietly, and out the window the highway and the fields, some sad, some green, the factories. When they are close to arriving, Leo gets nervous and asks again why he isn't going to go to school anymore. Why won't he be able to go to the end of the year party, the school play, the jamboree? He knows his lines by heart, he's one of the rats in *The Pied Piper of Hamelin*. The rats speak to the audience and among themselves and they sing a song before the piper leads them away. Sofía hasn't had time to convince herself that that isn't important and that she will be able to make it up to him in the future, and so on this point she fails; she doesn't know how to respond and she cracks a bit, just enough for Leo to crack too and want to cry and to be angry with his mother. Leo doesn't have tantrums often; his parents have been lucky because they haven't done anything in particular to avoid them, they simply don't tend to happen, that's all. Leo manages his frustration in other ways. He doesn't become furious, but he does have character. A smooth, sharpened character, a sweet but alert personality. Fortunately, he is a calm child and that's what everyone wants, a calm child who doesn't cause a racket, doesn't squirm at the table, controls himself in public places. A child capable of concentrating. Sofía wonders if the dam won't burst, if it all won't go flying out, tossed onto her, to be sunk and crushed beneath a torrent of emotional chaos.

Sofía tries to apologize to Leo, snuggle him, because she senses that his glassy stare is the resentment she will have to get used to in the future and she must learn to combat it, to pass above it and offer warmth, in spite of everything, emanate tenderness, a mother's hand, tepid and impermeable. Of course you're going to go back to school, Leo. You're just going to have a longer summer vacation than the other kids, a couple of weeks, not even . . . In September again . . . September is an eternity or maybe it's absolute nothingness, but it doesn't really matter at the moment because the bus has entered the town, it's crossed the bridge, and the wharf opens before them with its tangle of masts and colorful banners and floating wood. The bus station is around the corner and Leo's glum face transforms into the face of a happy child, impatient to arrive.

It's mid-afternoon and the humidity from the sea fogs the air. Sofía is soaked in sweat again and now that she spots the street she quickens her step, dragging a suitcase in each hand, backpack on her shoulders, bag crossing her chest. Leo carries his school bag and hops along. It has taken them more than half an hour to walk across town from the station and reach the houses on the road to the beach. The towering eucalyptus trees, ancient and creaking, shade the avenue. Sofía and Leo turn onto the third street. A final effort and it's Leo who opens the gate and goes running onto the patio, excited perhaps, confused. It's the first time he has gone to his grandfather's house since he died. But Sofía has explained it all to him. She has tried to define a map of absences and presences that makes some kind of sense. She believes Leo will know how to accept the consequences. She doesn't quite know what those consequences are, but god she hopes, please, that Leo will be able to handle them and that, with time, she will understand them better herself. She unlocks the door to her father's house, again. She didn't think she would be back so soon. She didn't imagine coming here with her son, with two suitcases, with everything.

After three hours they have managed, between the two of them, to turn the house that was half-emptied just days ago into a place where they can spend the night, the morning, the afternoon, the next night. Sofía is relieved she and Rita didn't finish the job, that she left all those boxes stacked next to the front door. Appliances, dishes, sheets, towels. Now the house is ready. She moved some of the furniture around and rearranged her father's room, which is where she will sleep with Leo for now, in the big bed pushed against the wall, on cool white sheets. The kitchen is also put back together, clean and provisioned with the essentials, the fridge rumbling into operation with the sound of an old boat. The handful of things they brought put away on the shelves, resistance.

The sky is finally dark and Sofía allows herself to be wrapped in the breath of her sleeping son. Now is when the sound of the sea enters the house. Sofía tries to isolate this element, to prevent it from mixing with the atmosphere pregnant with bitter nuance. Before it turns ten o'clock, the sea has already seized hold of the walls and she associates its perspicacity with something that seems like peace, something that comes from afar, from her first nights in that house, the first nights she can remember. Her parents, her sister, the country furnishings and brand-new crocheted bedspreads. She switches on her phone and steps outside, to the table on the patio. There are notifications: four more calls from Julio, no message. Nothing else. She has goosebumps from the chill, from guilt. They line up one after another like wobbly dominoes, the reasons why she should have done things differently. She has taken their child without telling him. She wrinkles her nose, a tic that darkens her face, makes her look aggressive, or unhinged. Her eyes are heavy. Better not to think, not to cry. She's too cold to stick her head under the faucet. Looking straight ahead, she calls her sister, Rita. Rita picks up this time, right away.

Rita, it's me. How are you? Yeah, I called you the other day, but it's fine. I don't know if you're busy but I have to tell you something. Okay, I'll wait. Look, we can't sell papa's house yet. No, seriously, we can't. I'm not making a big thing out of this, the thing is, I need it not to be sold. Actually, I've already taken down the sign and deleted the online ad. Yes, without consulting you. Yes, the sign. Wait, Rita, don't hang up, I haven't gone crazy. Yeah, I'm here, with Leo. Julio left me, but it's fine. Yes, Rita, I'm serious . . . Okay, yes, finish up and call me right back.

When Sofía hangs up the phone, it's like a big fish, viscous and cold, is finally out of her throat. The fish gasps for air, dirtying her lap with its thrashing, and then falls at her feet, maybe dead. It's enormous and blind and from the deepest reaches of the seas, and now, in her throat, there is an enormous and blind hollow. A hole has opened in her trachea, her larynx, her esophagus, a tremendous hole through which the air and saliva and the night breeze rush in, and this excess of oxygen stings, blurs her vision. Still gripping the phone in one hand, with the other she strokes her throat, touches to make sure there isn't really a hole through which this unbearable amount of salt air enters her. The phone still hasn't rung and it feels like her heart is stopping in intervals, desperate. Sofía breaks into sobs, spasming, her face burns, her lips are covered with a hot slobber. She knows she's making too much noise and if someone walked by they would see her; if her son woke up he would hear those rasping sounds coming from her stomach, but she can do nothing to stop it. There is neither will, nor intention in her tears and moans, she can't even manage to bring her hands to her face, to touch her forehead in consolation; all her muscles are sleeping lizard flesh—she cries with her chin crammed to her chest, her shoulders sunken, back bent in an arch. The phone rings and, docile, she answers with the hiccuping, dopey voice of a productive cry, and she cries as she speaks, and the fish, now definitely dead at her feet, looks at her with tremulous, filmy white eyes. He left, Rita, he left me for someone else, I have nothing, I'm alone, I don't know what I'm going to do without him.

His mother's sleeping body looks strange to him, like she's not in her usual position. Leo doesn't know *exactly* how his mother sleeps, but if he did, he would know it's always the same way: on her side, stiff, her legs at a slight angle to her torso, knees together, head tilted downward and buried slightly in the pillow, arms folded. This is how his mother has slept every night for many years, sometimes on one side, sometimes on the other. In any case, it's obvious to him that right now his mother is sleeping strangely; she doesn't look like herself, or maybe she is herself but metamorphosed or unmasked or who knows? Something has happened, plain and simple, something isn't right, and that's why his mother is sleeping like this. Leo stays in bed for a little while, chewing on his thumb, observing her. It looks like his mother has been thrown from way up high and has fallen on the mattress in this manner. Leo's breathing is easy beside hers. He watches his mother's deformed face just as he would watch a television screen. He isn't afraid.

It took him a moment to recognize the room, to remember that he isn't in his own home but in his grandfather's, that he left school before the year was through, that his father hasn't come with them, all of that. It's very early. Leo always wakes up early and last night he fell asleep right away, right after dinner, tired from the trip. He knows it's too early and he should let his mother sleep a little longer, but even if he didn't know, even if it weren't a ritual that formed part of his life, he would let her sleep because the truth is, he doesn't want to touch her. Sofía is sleeping on her stomach, her head off the pillow. Her face is turned toward Leo: half her face is flattened against the mattress, half her face squashed, her mouth is opened partway, her lips plump and dry, her shiny tongue peeking out like a mollusc. And her legs separated like a pair of scissors, her arms alongside her body. Leo has never seen his mother sleep in this position, and he isn't wrong to imagine that she has been flung down from on high, from a helicopter or air balloon, that she fell like this and now can't move. He thinks that if he were to touch her, she wouldn't wake up, that's exactly why he doesn't want to touch her; he doesn't want to bury his hand in his mother's hanging cheek nor push at her shoulder and find that she doesn't react. Sofía is snoring, a whistle strums from her nose, congested after a long night of weeping. She's snoring, so she's not dead, Leo doesn't have to worry about that. He decides to get up and climbs over his mother without grazing her, successfully making it over the obstacle—he is an agile child, and brave, after all.

He wanders through the house, not looking for anything in particular. The living room seems bigger to him now. The tile floor in the kitchen, where the first hours of light enter the house, is warm and everything is in its place, like it always is wherever his mother is. Sofía isn't especially demanding with the boy, she hasn't taught him how to organize everything, but she follows him, as if she were harvesting fruit. For Leo, this house is both unknown and familiar, like summer homes are in childhood. He never spent much time there when his grandfather was alive, but it is a reference point, his summer vacation, his beach. The house is different without his grandfather. He enters a different bedroom, closed and dark, the blinds lowered, and leaves it, there's nothing interesting, two beds and a closet. He suddenly feels like he's going to pee his pants and he runs to the bathroom, where a yellow sun has already entered, colliding with the white tile, and he pulls down his pyjama bottoms and lifts the lid. He stands up straight and pees and notices that last night, his mother didn't flush.

It is truly incredible that Sofía isn't awake yet. The morning is already high over the house and cars pass on the avenue outside and there are people heading to the beach, speaking in relaxed voices, foreign voices, going early so as not to fry under the sun. Leo spends some time wandering through different rooms. Because his mother told him when they arrived, TV is only for the afternoon. He's taken out the few books they brought and his colored pencils and is lying in the middle of the living room, on the floor, looking at them, doodling, bored. He's hungry, too. And his mother isn't dead because she's still snoring with that snake's hiss, even if she hasn't moved. Leo goes to the kitchen, opens the fridge, and is very pleased to find milk, and two yogurts as well. He drags a chair over to the counter and gets a cup. He carries it all to the living room and eats his breakfast on the floor, beside his books. When he has finished his glass of milk and eaten a yogurt, without a spoon, sticking his fingers in and stirring until it is liquid, he feels full, satisfied, and dirty, and he goes to wash his hands and face in the bathroom. He brings his chair wherever he goes, in case he can't reach something on his own. In his house, there are little stools for him all over, to encourage his autonomy. He drags the chair back to the living room, making more noise than before, happy to hear it bang against the door jambs. He is really bored, he's starting to get restless, he needs his mother to wake up.

Despite the fact that he feels something akin to repulsion, he climbs back into bed and lies down beside her. This strange animal sleeping so intensely that it disappears. It's no longer in the room, or in the house, so deep is its slumber, this animal that is not his mother. It's as if her eyelids were sewn shut, never to be opened again. Leo senses exhaustion and again the urge to cry, like yesterday on the bus, and before he starts shouting, he puts his hand on Sofía's shoulder at last and pushes at her brusquely, quickly, three, four times. He calls, mama, wake up! Mama, please wake up. He's been out of bed for two hours already, a terribly long time; normally he wouldn't have waited so long to get her, but waiting was easy this morning, he really hadn't wanted to bother her, not until he couldn't wait any more. Just a fraction of a second before he starts to cry, Sofía opens her eyes and rises from the swamp, gasping with a terrified look on her face. She can't speak right away because her tongue is enormous, it doesn't fit in her mouth, and her eyes aren't fully open, or maybe something is coating her pupils. All of this lasts no more than a few seconds. Sofía can't think clearly, and though she senses he wants to pull away, Sofía sits up, her muscles and bones still inert, and hugs her son in an attempt to regain the solidity of his presence. She invents a silly voice, a joke, a kind of falseness; her trembling fingers find their way between her son's ribs, pretend morning tickles, but then she pulls him to her tightly, I'm sorry little guy, it must be really late.

Tidy the house, again. Check the boxes in the small room's closet in case there was something important in them, something useful. Wash her face more than once, every half hour, more or less, never managing to banish the haze completely. Prepare her usual tea but extra strong, eat lots of dried prunes, finish them off and leave the pits clean, drink cold water. With Leo, make a list of plans and things they need. Today: grocery shop. Take a walk into town. Get toys. Eat out for dinner. Walk the perimeter of the house, inspect the patio and the small piece of land, look for a solution to mitigate its sordidness. Speak to Leo as if he were much younger, experience the same regret over and over, every time the boy turns his back, distracted by this or that, every time she senses impatience in his voice, every time he looks at her with expressionless eyes, regret the night before, having lost control, taken a sleeping pill, a strong one, she never does that, she constantly tries to regulate her emotions and achieve a functional balance that allows her to behave with relative fluidity, looseness. Eat, sleep, escape. But wasn't last night inevitable? After the convulsive tears that lasted a couple of hours, instead of exhaustion and surrender, she was stricken with wounding lucidness. Her sister had encouraged her: Take something if you can't sleep, I know you have them with you. You need to be strong tomorrow. And she did take them, but too late, at four, five in the morning, a mess. Things to do. The shopping, for example, a serious challenge.

The wharf is Sofía's favorite place. The town has grown a lot in recent years, but it hasn't grown nicely, just as other towns in the region haven't. It was already fairly big when her parents bought the house, and that was thirty years ago. The long main avenue is now a narrow artery filled with businesses and bulky cars parked along both sides of the street. The sidewalk has turned into a defeated, dry riverbed that runs from the beach to the main plaza where the town hall stands. With the exception of a few giant pharmacies, glass-fronted and very modern, and a tacky florist that sells more artificial centerpieces than fresh-cut flowers, the majority of businesses on this street are Moroccan-owned: bazaars, internet cafés, produce shops, a roast chicken takeaway. Cars are double-parked, people stop on the sidewalk outside the shops to speak to other people out on their balconies, obstacles to avoid. It's getting to be time to bring out the enticements of the season: beach umbrellas, straw mats, inflatable floats, net bundles crammed with sand toys, pails, shovels, rakes, water guns. Sofía walks with Leo, she doesn't let go of his hand, doesn't let him stop to look. Occasionally, the boy pulls at her and she feels weary tugging back. The sun has set and it's time to walk into town and get dinner—that's what they put on today's to-do list—but when it was time to go Leo had dragged his feet, he didn't want to have a bath, didn't want to leave the house, he was on the patio, playing with some little blocks they'd bought at the grocery store. A common enough occurrence, it happens with all kids. But Sofía had insisted, stubborn, aggressive. Something isn't working between her and Leo. Sofía tells herself it's perfectly natural, the most natural thing in this type of situation, and yet she can't stop questioning her own attitude: she's sure that if she could only feel a little better, everything would turn out fine. Leo isn't off because everything is off, but because she is. It's a kind of battle: with herself, with Leo, with the cobwebs coating her eyes, sometimes her mouth as well.

The narrow streets that lead to the wharf originate just beyond the town hall plaza, which was renovated some years back but which has retained the same iron benches, the same fountain, the same generous flower beds. Sofía sits on a bench while Leo approaches a couple of kids kicking a ball. The kids are older and ignore him; Leo gets bored and they resume their walk. Sofía wishes she could lose herself down the old streets. She wants to imagine them, lined with whitewashed walls and paved entirely with round stones, black and uneven. She seeks the darkness and skirts the bustling terraces. Gripping Leo's hand, she leads him down a hushed passageway that ends at the pier. I want to sit here a minute before we eat. The sound of boats rocking. Creaks. Where are we going to eat, mama? Hmm, shall we get some fish? I want a hot dog instead. I'll bet. That's because we passed a burger place before and it sounds good to you now, but wouldn't you like some nice fish, with French fries? You love fish! With mayonnaise? Okay, mayonnaise. That's fine.

During dinner, Sofía pads the conversation with lists of all the things they're going to do together this summer. They won't have to stay in the city all of July, waiting for papa's time off, so it will be a nice long summer. Sofía ad-libs and eats her salad and fried anchovies—Leo's choice, she hasn't had fried fish in a very long time but now she can't help herself. She was careful when they talked about Julio; above all, she tried to be realistic. You're going to see him soon, she told Leo. Then Leo asks why they don't call him right now on her phone, and she pops two more anchovies into her mouth and feels her insides deflate—her stomach, her pancreas melting—because in her circumstances, having a conversation with a five-year-old, even an intelligent five-year-old, is exhausting. She imagines a repeat of last night's insomnia and the panic rises. She pushes away the image of the pills—the strong ones—tucked in the inside pocket of her toiletry bag.

Leo wants an ice cream. Not Sofía though, Sofía thinks that they've both eaten too much junk already. They start to argue as they head the long way home, away from the pier. They're moving away from the restaurants, the lights, and Leo realizes that the possibility of ice cream is growing more distant, that if they keep walking it will be non-existent. Everything is dark, the streetlamps at the edge of the harbor seem to shine too dimly. They're going to turn at the last street and then they'll be in a residential area, with low houses and small gardens, where people will be sitting outside, finishing dinner, getting some air, the sound of televisions, snippets of conversation. Leo pulls at his mother's shirt, Sofía brushes his hand away, and spins around, cross. Leo, I can make you a special dessert at home; we went shopping, remember? I want ice cream, I don't want your special dessert. Leo, please. I want ice cream. A knot lodges in her throat and Sofía resists the idea that all this has started so soon. She takes solace in the fact that it's probably just these first days on their own, even she, the mother, is confused and upset, unsure of what's going on in their family. The truth is she has no idea and she can't let on to Leo because then they'll both be lost. They just need to get home, she needs to be pleasant and sweet and say it's okay, it's okay, and then she can work it out later, examine the situation she has before her, get a handle on what is happening and what is not. She attempts to pick Leo up: he has come to a dead stop in the middle of the street, in front of a small front garden where an enormous couple is eating dinner. The couple look like they've been together a lifetime; they're both immense, bodies stuffed into plastic lawn chairs, armrests dug into their sides, they chew and chew, the man gives an occasional cough. The TV is on in the living room while they eat outside; the window left open so they can hear. Leo is stopped in front of their house and the couple watch him, nonplussed. The man coughs, it's the rattle of bad lungs, the wife bites into a mammoth slice of watermelon. Sofía can't handle Leo, he stiffens his legs and crosses his arms, making it difficult for her to grab him. Sofía would have to haul him like a rolled-up rug, like a block of ice or a statue. The other option is to drag him behind her or turn around and start walking and hope he follows. She gives him a little push. Just a small one. Backward. Leo cries. Sofía frowns, her eyebrows knit together straining to contain her scream, or her wail, or whatever it is that might come out of her. Leo cries and sits on the ground and Sofía looks down at him from above and the fat couple looks on from their porch and the child cries and cries and says I want ice cream and says you never let me eat anything yummy and finally Sofía realizes that she has no choice and, furthermore, it doesn't even matter, and she crouches down and puts her hands in his hair, rubs his scalp, hot and sweaty, his forehead, and tells him that they are going to go and get him an ice cream, and she's going to eat one too, a really big one.

In the end, they go to the ice cream place on the promenade, very close to the house. They sit on the stairs that lead down to the beach. They take off their shoes and bury their feet in the cold sand. They're barefoot but have put on the light sweaters

Sofía tucked in her bag. Leo looks happy with his cup and three scoops; Sofía devours hers too quickly and regrets ordering just one small scoop of lemon. She assumed it was the flavor with the least dairy. The least stuff. Leo stands and moves away from her, holding his cup and a little wooden spoon. Mama, I'm going over there, to the swings. Be careful, it's dark, watch where you step. Then she's alone. She would like to lie back, right on the ground, feel it hard against her skull, and close her eyes, but she turns on her phone instead. A call from Rita. Five from Julio. A message, finally: All right, I got it. I'll give you a couple of days. Don't fuck up anymore.

When they get home, the kitchen counter is a blanket of riotous black. Teeny tiny ants organized in multitudinous ranks cloak the fruit bowl, the open package of cereal, thankfully secured with a clothespin, the small loaf of rye bread wrapped in paper that was so hard for her to get her hands on. Leo shrieks, a shout that lands somewhere between disgust and fascination. Sofía is paralyzed, she doesn't know what to do. She goes to the bathroom to look for some kind of salvation and screams when she turns on the light: the bathroom vanity, her bottle of body lotion, the soap on the edge of the sink, an endless march of little feet, black antennae. An unstoppable battalion covers the glass holding their toothbrushes, climbs greedily through the bristles, eager for any trace of saliva, for any trace of a word.

THERE'S ONE WEEKEND I'VE never forgotten. Hardly a day and a half, really, but it has always proved that—from the perspective of a child—intense, joyful familial bliss leaves dregs as thick as bitterness does. It was winter. Or spring or fall. Not summer, anyway. There was school, the city, weekends short and coarse. That Saturday morning, my parents loaded us into the car and we went to spend the day in the mountains. We didn't go by ourselves—another family followed us in a red car, friends of my parents who also had children, a boy and girl. I had brought along a little doll, which wasn't typical of me. It was a little plastic doll with black hair and a cloth body, it fitted in my pocket, in my cupped hands. I know it was a regular Saturday and a regular day trip, but there was a current that ran through the outing and made it memorable. The smooth mountains, the swollen, dark-green woods, the dirt roads with paths of crushed grass. The still air of the sierra, laden and deep. Villages. Where did we go? A few hamlets, steep and white; I suppose we must have eaten at an inn. We were all happy, the whole time, that's what was special about it. Not just my father or my mother, but both at the same time, and the other couple, too. There was a laxness, a complicity, and I can't remember our route but I know that well into the afternoon we arrived at the magic spot. A big, rambling house in the middle of nowhere, part of some village, and we went to visit. The grown-ups spoke with the man who ran it (Was he a priest? Was it a monastery? A retreat?) and he seemed to join in our high spirits (our parents' spirits, which were contagious and amplified our already good mood, validating and permitting it, magnifying it, in any case). The man had white hair and smiled and spoke smoothly, not with a priest's affable, neat indifference but with an unstudied calm, a buoyant camaraderie. He showed us around and told us kids that we could have the run of the gardens and woods behind the house. We flitted here and there, discovered a river with a bridge—or maybe it was a stream and an old board, I don't know, but I do know that the play of light made the grass shine like glitter and that the stream burbled and that, though we had little practice with nature, our rambling connected us to it, and suddenly we were wrapped in the din of the forest, of the strange trees that grew there, the grass, the sound of lizards under the leaves, the gurgle of water. We often visited the country, of course. But this was different, this place was special. A cultivated forest, wildwood made garden. A singular place, I understood later, after I'd been in others. I don't remember the faces of my parents or the other couple, but I remember our joy, the perfect conjunction of commotion and peace. I know everyone was happy.

Then a shift took place. The original plan, typical back then, was to spend the day away and drive back in the evening in a trance: the car, the curves, the silence, it always depressed me, I always wanted more of almost everything. But we didn't go home that Saturday. The grown-ups decided we would sleep there, in the big old house; they had made arrangements with the white-haired man. This change of plans, this last-minute decision to prolong our bliss, to extend a good thing for nothing but its own sake, this flouting of the established plan, this purposeful turn of good luck, this *why not*, converted me from that day on, and for many years it made me a militant dedicated to draining pleasure down to the last drop, carrying it to its final consequence. My parents' attitude that day—the aura of a happy couple, almost blasé, their real selves absent for a few hours, the lightness they suddenly possessed or that I suddenly

46

saw in them—shocked and thrilled me, marked me, opened a path. I was already a little bit like that, in my childish world, but this was different. This wasn't the result of my dogged insistence on making something last, only to later regret it, this came from upstairs, from superior entities who commanded us to enjoy ourselves, to enjoy ourselves because we were happy and that was reason enough. That was how I understood it, at least. And in the future, it would bring a barrage of pleasure to go along with the attendant frustrations and wounds.

We ran up and down all the hallways in the old house, peeked in the bedrooms, all with very high ceilings. I suppose we children must have all slept in the same room. We went into the village for a few necessary items. A pharmacy, I remember. The mothers asked for paper underwear. To me, that was the stuff of science fiction, but they were dying of laughter and thrilled not to have to forgo their daily hygiene. I was surprised my mother even knew such an artefact existed. It shocked me and she seemed very wise, a woman of the world. I imagine now that maybe there was some special reason for purchasing a box of paper underpants, just to spend one night away from home, because why be so fussy otherwise? But in the moment, it was the appropriate thing to do, and furthermore, it was part of the game, another instrument of merriment. The underpants were huge on me. I suppose they didn't even stay up around my sister's waist, but they were fun to wear. And I remember my mother looking pleased as punch when she bought them. That also made something of an impression. Provisioning for pleasure. Logistics on the fly. Things one does in order to keep up the revelry, to not turn back or break a sweat. Things like picking up paper underpants in a pharmacy. It shaped my life. Even though I later realized that all you had to do was turn a dirty pair inside out.

It's freezing! Leo jumps, driving his feet into the flat sand on the shore, craters that quickly fill with water and disappear. I don't want to go in! He hops parallel to the narrow waves, moving away from his mother. His shouts aren't refusals, but excitement. It is an easy moment, the whole morning before them, the beach empty. Sofía tries to get Leo to go into the water, to splash around, it would be like some kind of prize that neither of them deserves. Leo doesn't want to swim but he's euphoric, he leaps and shouts and runs. Sofía has brought a chair and set it down by the water; she's dressed and wearing a visor that shades the better part of her face from the sun. Leo is smeared with sunscreen, a tiny flea hopping about in the distance, his shoulder blades poking through the white skin of his back, paining his mother's eyes. Only some bones should have permission to show themselves. The water is freezing! Freezing! Mama! Leo is now wet to his calves. His knees and thighs break the flat plane of the surface, he is caressed sporadically by small, curling waves.

Sofía brought a book as if she's planning to read. Marina Tsvetaeva's *Confessions*. She's been wanting to read it for ages but is currently incapable of opening it. The Russian poet's life interests Sofía more than her poetry. The revolution, the exile, the difference in her treatment of her daughters, in her love for them, in each one's fate. The book is heavy in her lap, it's a big book, a hardcover, and she touches it while she looks ahead and to either side, while she hears Leo calling for her; she touches the book because it's the only promise in sight. A bag with a few beach toys and two towels sits in the sand beside her. She realizes she's brought nothing to eat or drink, not even water, but she doesn't punish herself; the morning sun gathers up the implications, postpones them. In a sudden outpouring of initiative, she takes out a yellow ball and tosses it to her son, still far away. The ball soars through the clean air and bounces once, twice, three times in the sand until it lands at last in the water, where Leo scurries to try and reach it. Sofía wants to believe that her son doesn't feel the same way she does, that his boyish mechanisms haven't been affected by the situation the way hers have, but still she concocts their daily plans as if preparing for a battle at sea: Germany against Russia, 1916. After throwing the ball, her arms hang down at her sides, iron hands, mortar. Leo has managed to reach the ball, getting wet to the waist (the tide is very low, the waves mere tickles) and now he runs again back toward his mother, a smile on his face, his fringe damp; he is coming at her like a projectile missile and Sofía can't move because her hands are hanging, useless, from her arms. She sees him coming straight for her, closer and closer, and she wishes she could turn and run even faster, escape between the dunes, or defend herself, at least, from all of this energy, crouch and cover her face and chest with her arms, curl into a ball; she wishes Leo would shoot past her, not see her, leave her alone. Lucky for them both, she doesn't move and the boy manages to hug her with his tense, cold body, wetting her clothes, her thighs. I'm thirsty, mama, I'm thirsty I'm thirsty I'm thirsty.

They decided to go home then. They haven't been at the beach long and it's still early, but any disturbance at all is too much for either of them, the bar has been lowered. Leo dilly-dallies, like always, dragged along, lagging behind his mother, and Sofía hurries to reach her front gate and hide inside; she didn't stop at the fruit-seller on the promenade, as was her intention when they left the house, nor has she gone for bread. She's annoyed and uncomfortable because the insides of her thighs are chafed and burning, and she enters the house quickly, without a glance, barely muttering a Come on, Leo, let's go, hurry up, and doesn't realize the door was unlocked until she's about to cross the threshold. She stops short, throws her hand out behind her forcefully, commanding her son to halt, the tendons in her hand and wrist elastic, live. She hears nothing. Could she have left the door unlocked when they left? Impossible. Burglars? At this time of day? Impossible. But her feet, immobile on the threshold, are stones, anxiety rises in her throat. Julio? Maybe it's Julio, come to find them and bring them home, a gesture of goodwill, but he doesn't have keys, and even if he did, he wouldn't be able to find them because he never showed a shred of interest in this house, but maybe Julio? Leo is behind her and she grips him by his T-shirt and the expectant child doesn't make a sound. Julio? she dares to say very softly, because all her insides are trembling, her stomach, her lungs, she is going to stop breathing in a second if nobody answers, but suddenly, her face through the doorway already, neck craned, the door to the bathroom at the end of the hall opens and she appears, of course, like music; how could she not have guessed, of course, Rita comes out of the bathroom as if she were floating, as if she'd been there for a century in perpetual summer, rosy cheeks, big smile, sturdy teeth sparkling in the middle of the living room, an airiness, the angel comes out of the bathroom; she was finishing getting ready, preening her feathers, was she wearing lipstick? Her lips look plasticized, so soft and unwrinkled, she opens her arms to them, to her sweaty sister shaking in the doorway, to Leo, hidden by his mother, who is pressing him too tightly behind her knees. Rita has come for them, not Julio, and she's wearing a pretty straw hat with a very wide brim, a gauzy shirt over her hard body, Roman sandals. Hey! Say something, you guys! Aren't you happy? I'm here! And Sofía goes limp and Leo steps out from behind her. He leaps about, even higher than their first hour on the beach. He's even more buoyant than his aunt, he runs toward her like an exhalation, toward those delivering-angel open arms; he jumps, hugs her, scales her body, kisses her jubilantly. Auntie you came, you came, you came, everything was full of ants, you know, everything, auntie, the kitchen, the bathroom, it was an army, mama said so, and we killed them and it was all black, but they can come back, mama says they're under the house and that they're going to come back, for sure!

Sofía tries to control herself but in the end she stops resisting and yells or howls or maybe no sound leaves her throat at all because her epiglottis has closed over and she is really, truly, seriously suffocating.

*

It passed quickly. Sofía opened her arms, elbows out, a chicken with wings spread wide, then managed to sit down in one of the porch chairs, breathing through her nose. Four or five open-mouthed spasms, a finger pressed to that hollow at the base of her throat where her epiglottis must be, and suddenly, and a miracle, air pours in again and she coughs, her hair falls over her forehead and she sloshes into the chair and, god, it would be good to cry, but she's already made too much of a scene. Her small son is finally relieved of her presence, anchored securely to his aunt's arm, and they try to look after her, they bring a glass of water, lay their fingers on her trembling knees, their smiles in the sunshine, on the patio, they're not really worried, it hadn't been too bad, thirty seconds is all, meanwhile cars are scrabbling out on the street, a few fat, slow ants at her feet, sniffing at grains of cement, the slightest trace of organic material, desiccated cadavers of mosquitos. These ones aren't dangerous. They do their own thing, even if they do look like spiders.

Are you planning on staying here? You're crazy. No, really. Crazy. Here with us the whole summer . . . I don't know if I'm staying all summer and neither do you, sis. It's painful when you call me sis, I swear. I know, I know, you never liked it, you always said I seemed like I was from a different family. Why are you here, Rita? Come on, Sofía. They have dinner outside at the same plastic table where Sofía suffered the panic attack that morning. Which you probably faked, Rita teases Sofía, who is going increasingly soft on the inside, not soft as in tender, but weaponless, boneless. Leo fell asleep early because his day had been dramatic and exhausting. His aunt had brought him presents, taken him to the beach for the whole afternoon and—unlike his mother—played catch with him, and then they had hamburgers in town, early, while Sofía rested at home. Now he's sleeping in the big bed, where, later on, his mother will lie with her eyes open for a long time. You need to set Leo up in his own room. Or are you going to sleep with him every night? I don't want him to be alone right now. He's not alone, he's with you. If you're having awful nights, I think it's best for him to sleep in his own room. He should have his own space anyway, shouldn't he? He'll feel better. I don't know. Okay, why did you come? Are you planning on staying all summer? Sis, I am not going to respond to your nonsense. Besides, you're the one who owes me some answers, don't you think? I came because I felt like it, I could take a vacation and so I did, and here I am. But the important thing is: are *you* going to stay here all summer? You took the boy without telling anybody. The child has a father. Damn it, Rita—did you just come here to state the obvious?

Rita has caught the sun. Her forehead shines from the bulb overhead, from the heat. She delicately picks the bones from the hake and puts the flesh in her mouth, licks her fingers clean, observing Sofía with condescension. She has assumed her role and seems to be enjoying it, she has something important to do; she'll tire of it soon enough, but for now she's just begun. Sofía stretches her lips and readies herself to face the jury, and win. Julio knows where we are, he sent me a message, so it's fine. Sofía, you haven't returned his calls or replied to his messages, and, actually, I was the one who told him you were here. This is a pretty untenable situation and I think you need to talk to him. Sofía jumps up and moves to go inside. Fucking hell, I knew it, I knew it! On her plate are four spines from four hake. Her wine glass is empty. Rita continues to eat, listening for a slam of the bedroom door. But Sofía comes back out onto the porch, she gives Rita a scathing look, but there is so much misgiving in her eyes that none of her daggers hit their mark, none of her bullets. Do you have tobacco? Don't tell me you're going to fucking smoke. Do you have some or not? I don't know, probably, I probably have some for joints. Give it to me. Rita arches her eyebrows: Go get it yourself, it's in my bag.

The tobacco is dry and Sofía attempts to roll a cigarette; her fingers are fat, disobedient worms, too damp, yet she manages a trumpet-like cigarette. It's weak at the filter, but it lights. All of a sudden she feels better; she is angry with her sister, a feeling she can cling to. She inhales. Surprisingly, she doesn't cough; her throat burns and she swallows the smoke, holds it as if it's a treasure. Rita has cleared the plates and silverware, leaving just two glasses and the bottle of wine. She's rolling a joint. Since we're here, she shrugs. Sofía wants to reproach her, after all they're practically in the middle of the street, anyone walking by would see them, but she holds her tongue and, after the third drag on her own cigarette, realizes it doesn't matter at all. The other thing does, though: Why did you call him? Whose side are you on? Fuck, sis, he called me. Ah, of course. What freaking planet are you on? You take your kid out of the city, don't answer your phone, and you think your husband isn't going to call me? But he always calls you anyway, doesn't he? Rita looks up from the little mound of tobacco where she's crumbling the hash between her fingers and stares at Sofía. She opens her mouth to say something, but shuts it again. She must be patient because Sofía isn't all there, she must stick to her new mission, stay on task. Sofía looks away, smoking, sipping her wine, holding out against the empty silence. Then she picks up right where she left off: What did he say? He left, you know. No warning. He left home. That's conjugal abandonment. Desertion. He left us. I don't want to talk to him, I talked to him before I made my decision. Actually, he was the one who talked, he knows exactly what he wants to do with his life and the mess he's going to leave mine in. What did he tell you? Outraged, is he? Don't tell me . . . Two drags on the spliff and the night has softened; tiny insects flutter around the light bulb, sometimes around Sofía's hair, almost blonde under that light, the halo of a saint, of a madwoman. I think you need to talk to each other. You should go see him. Me? Again? Why doesn't he come here if he knows where he can find me? Look, Sofía, I'm with you. With you and with Leo. This is a mess, but you really need to fix things between the two of you. I mean you need to agree—for Leo's sake—on whatever is going to happen. Maybe it's better for you to know exactly what you're going to tell Leo before he sees his dad. There's still time for you guys to do things the right way. What a shitty fucking sentence, Rita. What a fucking crock of shit.

THEY HAD BEEN REMINISCING: the summer their parents bought the house and they stopped spending the summers with their grandparents, they both came down with chicken pox, right in the middle of August. At first, they didn't know who gave it to whom, who caught it first, and after arguing back and forth, they concluded it had been the little sister. Fifty sores, two or three on each face, several days of high fever. Sofía shows her the scar, between her eyebrows, look, mine's right here. It was an awful summer, wasn't it? They are sitting in the main plaza, at a bar after dinner. Rita does not enjoy eating with her sister. She'll have to reach some sort of agreement with her, or perform an act of contrition; but Sofía's manias aren't Rita's problem, in the end, and who even cares, everyone has their hang-ups. But Sofía's constant intolerance is excessive, what with all the problems she has going on, and the way she's transmitting the phantom threat of food—mass-produced or not—to Leo . . . Rita would like to ridicule her about this, to call her out, she wants to offer Leo sweets, take him for hamburgers, hotdogs, pizza, ice cream, doughnuts, and sandwiches made with white bread, ammonia, refined sugar without thiamine, stroke his head, so soft, while the boy sucks Coke through a fat straw, while he sticks his anxious hands into big bags of ham-flavored potato chips. She wants to watch him swallow without guilt. She drops hints for Sofía, along the lines of, don't you think the poor thing deserves to enjoy eating just a little bit, a treat every once in a while? He is a child, after all! Sofía doesn't rise to the bait, doesn't defend herself. Gloomily, she replies that eating poisonous junk isn't a treat, it's a tomb. But he's just a kid, Sofía, you're going to make him paranoid . . . and since when are you so extreme about food, anyway? Have you gone vegetarian or joined the nutritional grass brigade or something? Rita mocked, a corner of her mouth turned up in the same chilly smile she always wears when poking her finger in a wound. It's weird, though, because Sofía doesn't seem to want to argue. She's watching Leo play with his marbles in the middle of the plaza. A younger girl, two sparkly elastics tying back her exaggeratedly black hair and with still-chubby legs, has approached him. She squats beside Leo and greedily eyes the marbles; she'll make a move for them any minute now, there'll be shrieks. Leo is a peaceful child, and though not always generous, he is docile. However, he isn't often fond of younger kids, even less so if they're girls. Sofía thinks, of course, that this is her fault because he doesn't have siblings. Because he hasn't socialized enough. She even thinks that it isn't simply a natural childish tendency but a congenital defect, the prelude to some future psychopathy, as innate as the shape of his shoulder blades. Paranoid, her sister said. Sofía smiles. Did our grandparents eat that crap, Rita? Oh for fuck's sake, they ate bread and chocolate after school. Well, sometimes Leo gets to have bread and chocolate, too. Okay, whatever.

The summer they had been reminiscing over hadn't been so awful, really. They had chicken pox and scratched themselves when they shouldn't—Rita always more than Sofía, who was a stickler for the rules, terrified when faced with unforeseen pain—they read a lot of stories to each other in bed, first one would read, then the other, it was terribly hot and the smell of fresh bread baking wafted through their bedroom window very early in the morning, practically at daybreak, from the bakery on the corner. Nah, Sofía, you're off, the bakery was by our grandparents', not our house, Rita said when Sofía had started rambling on about the past, with the evening's first beer. Then it had gotten later into the night and there they still were, at the same table outside, drinking slightly bubbly, very cold white wine. Sofía had accepted Rita's correction but still maintained it had been a good summer. A lot of time in bed, a lot of visitors, presents. The two of them the same. No, it wasn't a good summer, Rita responds. Or, maybe it was good for you, but bad for me. Sofía straightens, on guard. Why do you say that? But Rita is quiet. She lines up a few peanuts on the table, never taking her eyes off Sofía. When Rita finally opens her mouth to speak, Sofía feels a chill. Because it was the first summer we didn't stay with our grandparents. Oh, yes, I remember now, Sofía sighs, relieved that Rita has relented. I totally remember, papa insisted on buying a house that year and mama didn't want to leave her family during the summer, she always said we already had a house, why did we need another one in the same town. This house was better, it was right by the beach. It was just for us. But mama didn't want it. That's why it was always papa's house, because they started badly with it, on the wrong foot. Well, like with almost everything. Yeah, okay, Sofía, that's why.

The air is cool. Sofía is wearing a thin cardigan, long and gray, that is too big on her and makes her look like a marionette. The problem is that she hasn't made a good choice with the rest of her outfit, it doesn't go with her loose dress, which has a voluminous neckline. With the cardigan on, she looks like a doll. Sofía couldn't care less. Her sister says she's paranoid, that her son will be paranoid, her sister tells her what she should do, her sister has come to save her and humiliate her a little, just enough—right now her sister is her only reference point in the world. From where she sits at one extreme of the plaza, she can see the wide avenue leading all the way to the breakwater in the distance. Suddenly, her eyes make out the form of an abandoned gray building on an unilluminated corner, obscured in the dark. The drive-in cinema. Remember, Rita? What? Rita observes her sister, who is mumbling something under her breath through dry lips. Her eyes are smoky, and Rita knows it's not just nostalgia, but the effects of the diazepam or alprazolam or whatever Sofía took a little while ago. Sofía polishes off her wine. A little more, a cocktail to sleep, a free fall. Do you remember? We didn't go to the drive-in once that summer. Rita frowns, that isn't something she remembers. The mention of the drive-in fills her with lukewarm but asphyxiating childhood memories and connects her to her sister in a fragile way; Rita pities Sofía and when she focuses on her clothing, that pity grows, she feels responsible, doesn't her face look puffy? Sofía, that cardigan . . . Here, take it off, I'll give you my jacket. Sofía ignores her. It's chilly, but the air coming from the wharf is pleasant. That smell. The people from the town are strolling with a different kind of slowness, one befitting to the vacation months. Occasionally, a motorcycle exhaust pipe rips through the avenue, their ears, their memories. There are so many ugly things. The streetlights don't appear to be fully lit, the washed-out yellow transforms the plaza into a foreign location. Less noticeable are the strident new glazed tiles, the disorderly ensemble of buildings; their beautiful facades, preserved for over one hundred years, are revived under that irregular light. The drive-in, with its gray concrete painted with graffiti, is like a gaping hole.

Sofía, go get Leo. Hurry.

It happened quickly: the little girl with the black pigtails didn't manage to get Leo's attention, much less have the chance to play a game together, so she has decided to stick both chubby, brown hands into the bag of marbles; in spite of her short stature, the girl is agile, in three seconds her two hands are in the bag and grabbing a good fistful of marbles—she turns and starts to run over toward her parents with her haul, her mouth smiling, drooling, her teeth small and spaced—in the fourth second there is a jubilant shriek, in the fifth, Leo turns, his eyes dark, and he extends an arm, an arm that is suddenly the arm of a seven- or eight-year-old, not a child of five, and grabs the bottom of the girl's skirt of cotton muslin, organdy with a fuchsia print, closes his fingers like a claw. But in the sixth second he isn't satisfied with stopping her, with having trapped her, so in the seventh second he yanks her back toward him, really hard, as hard as he can, and nobody is looking at his face but there's a sheen on his cheeks, a hidden desperation. In the eighth second the girl falls flat on her face—with the marbles in her hand she doesn't have time to catch herself—her damp, round face, her suckling lips and chin and button nose smash against the old paving stones, smash with a sharp, unmistakable blow, the marbles skittering in all directions, a mini Big Bang, she might have cracked a tooth, her lips are bloodied, crimson drool, the biggest scream, a howl. Just ten seconds, the speed of innocence.

Swiftly, the girl's parents have come to her aid, they look like an army, but they're just a pair of adolescents. The father is wearing white knee-length shorts and his solid buttocks and thighs strain the fabric when he squats to pick up his child and lift her, like the titan he is, up to the heavens, like a trophy, examining his bounty. His head is shaved and an inked drawing rings his brown neck. The thump of his heart can be heard in the middle of the plaza, a countdown. The mother cries louder than the girl, louder than the father's thundering heart and in a piercing voice she insults Leo, Leo whose eyes are bugging out of their sockets but who doesn't move from his marble-shooting position on the ground, under the deluge of shouts, wails, curses. The mother, in her tight clothes, bosom swollen with love, breasts tumbling out of her neckline, out of her neckline and toward life, full-blooded and quivering, covers the girl's mouth with a cotton handkerchief plucked from her giant handbag with its glittering chain. The hanky quickly turns red; it doesn't soothe the child's screams. And now the parents aren't looking at Leo, aren't shouting at Leo, although the father's shoe, a leather sandal from which protrudes square toes with nails of stone, is too close to Leo's stomach, is too close to Leo's face, but now the pair of them are swivelling, searching for the people responsible for the boy, searching for someone to hate, to fight. By the sixtieth second, the guilty mother of the guilty boy still hasn't moved from her metal chair. She watches the scene as if it were an image on paper, an image on a drive-in screen from another world. The truth is that the boy's eyes, open very wide, are inside her own wide, smoky eyes. They are of the same color, the same earth at this time of night, and the air is cool. Leo has on a short-sleeve T-shirt and maybe his little arms are cold. The titanic father lets out a battle cry, is no one coming to the attacker's defense? But it isn't the mother who responds, the mother is wearing a cardigan bunched at her shoulders and she is a clown in a metal chair, a tired or cold or nauseous and glassy-eyed clown, the mother cannot move but the aunt runs to the middle of the plaza, her legs agile and muscular under her jeans—she is so delicate beside the teenage parents—and when she is actually up close, she sees that despite their histrionics they aren't teenagers at all, their faces are weathered, their teeth considerably blackened from tobacco and love. She's sorry, she apologizes, she tries to stroke the little girl's hair, but of course they don't let her, her hand hangs suspended in air, Rita is so small next to them, the loudmouthed, armored family. She's sorry, she apologizes, she even offers a telephone number in case they can do something for the girl, even though it's nothing, she'll be fine, a tooth-punctured lip, a scrape on the nose, not a trace of it in a week's time. One more shout that the aunt submissively accepts as she takes Leo by the arm and pulls him up, tugging him, pretending she's angry, pretending that what she would really like to do is grab him by the ear or sideburns and lift him off the ground, nephew and aunt not so light now though inside they are nothing but fresh air. The boy is soon on his feet and the aunt manages to remove him from the crime scene, she flies with him to the bar terrace, puts distance between him and the armored family finally moving off in the other direction, either toward their house or to the emergency room. Now Leo and Rita are shaking hands, making a pact, and Sofía watches as they come toward her. She is absolutely incapable of moving, it's that paralysis again, that desire for them to keep walking; she wishes they wouldn't speak to her, she doesn't want to have to be responsible, to scold, to cry, Leo has never hit anyone, Leo is such a good boy, so calm, come on Sofía, get up, I already paid, let's go home. Sofía pulls her cardigan tight over her chest and grabs her bag but she doesn't move quite yet, she is looking Leo square in the eye, he's close, very still: Mama, he says, she took my marbles.

The glass marbles loll in the middle of the plaza, some transparent, others with a burst of color in their interior. Tomorrow, some old guy will step on one and crack his head open.

THE SOUND OF THE SEA. It's a sputtering motor, air colliding with air. The echo of a long word, the last syllable of something difficult to pronounce. The intermittent certainty of moving water envelops the house, the neighboring streets, the eucalyptus path and stone promenade, the stairways penetrating the seemingly white sand that, in actuality, is contaminated with cigarette butts and wrappers. The sand is fine-grained but firm. Sofía labors to wake up. Suddenly, she opens her eyes, her empty stomach heaves. She is still by the sea, like she was in another time, a time in the past when she was just as irresolute, complacent. She clings to the vestiges of the dream she has surfaced from, the darkness of someone else's room, the faceless bodies, the image helps her vomit, purging the cocktail of wine and pills from the night before, and then she shrinks back into the big bed that smells a little like her son. Not too much, because it's been days since he slept with her. Now they each sleep in their own room, Sofía in the largest one and Leo and Rita in narrow beds in the two small rooms. Their father always bought hard, generic mattresses. Finally, she gets up, stumbling over the sandals at the foot of the bed, then the door jamb.

The house seems empty, but the door is open, so they mustn't have gone far. Everything is just as it was last night before she went to bed, though she can't remember which of the two of them turned in last. The whiteness of her face under the radiant sun when she sticks her head outside, how sharp the sound of the sea is in spite of the light. She covers her eyes and receives the warmth on her chest and on her legs, passing through the blue cotton of her pajamas, the stretched-out elastic waist. Nobody outside either. On the table, a glass with a bit of juice left. Had that been Leo's breakfast? Is it breakfast time, or mid-morning? She goes over and collects the glass and then scuttles inside; whatever time it is, she needs to eat, she's starting to feel dizzy. Barefoot, she notes the chill of the living room tile. She moves slowly, observes her toes, the too-long nails yellowing at the ends, the bone of her big toe twisting dangerously toward torture. Upon reaching the kitchen door the surprise causes first anxiety and then tenderness; Leo has his back to her, he's standing on a chair, moving something around on the counter next to the sink. He's in underpants and his skin has started to brown. The tendons at the back of his knees, the curve of his shoulders, and the bone that lines his neck define the boy's growing body. Sofía stands in the kitchen doorway and emerges from sleepiness and stupor while covertly observing her son. Maybe she is ready again. She wants to be ready, wants to go up and hug or tickle him, lift him off the chair and make him hers, the two of them disappearing into that morning with its sound of the sea. Leo doesn't look up from his task, he hasn't heard his mother, who, on the other hand, hardly dares to breathe. But something makes him break his concentration and turn around: Leo sees his mother in the middle of the kitchen, halfway toward him. She hasn't had time to reach him, to pet him. She is there and she is much bigger that morning, she looks enormous to Leo, she looks so straight, so incredibly tall, even though he is up on a chair. His mother in her blue pajamas, barefoot, her breasts bulky and spread under her T-shirt, holding the glass of juice he drank when he woke up and then left on the table outside. Just before Leo turns around, his mother has a sweet expression on her face, the wrinkles by her eyes relaxed, her eyelids puffy and pale, but the moment her visual field widens, the moment Leo turns to find her there, her sweetness becomes confusion, disgust. In his hand, Leo holds another glass like the one in her hand—glasses that at one point were jars of Nutella, hard glasses scratched by years of the scouring pad—but Leo's is a living glass, a glass in motion, in constant flow, a glass in four dimensions, black, a patina of devouring ants that spread over the boy's fingers, the back of his hand; several have separated from the masses and—deranged—rapidly climb upward, upward toward his wrist, his arm just starting to tan, his round elbow. The ants, clearly, do not originate on the glass or Leo's hand, but travel in a perfect line down the two-lane highway of the countertop, over the tiling on the wall, ascending in straight lines along the grout until they disappear behind the refrigerator. Sofía is compelled to react because she is a mother, something courses through her veins and activates that effectual part of her person, she doesn't throw her own glass on the floor but tosses it into the sink without breaking it and from her son's hand she grabs the black glass with a hundred million antennae and feet and this glass too goes into the sink and then so does Leo's hand, both hands, he's no longer standing on the chair but is in Sofía's arms, she holds him from behind, under the armpits, feet dangling, both black hands under the running water, what the fuck Leo what the hell are you doing oh fuck and Leo is just as furious as his mother and that's why he doesn't cry even though he wants to, he watches all those ants die under the faucet, the glass he'd filled with honey a couple of hours ago washed clean, his experiment aborted, the hushed morning, alone at last, in his paradise.

Leo, love, you can't play with ants. You can't provoke them. You can't *invoke* them. The ants live under us and there are so many that we can't even imagine them all, they have a kind of giant city, you know what it's like, we saw it on TV and we've drawn it, they have their tunnels and their caves where they put their eggs and larvae and where the other ants bring food to feed the babies, but there are so many that they could eat us, Leo; if the house and the road and the whole neighborhood weren't here, and this was all just a big expanse of level ground, we'd see how they would make a mountain like a volcano and crawl out of the crater to look for food in the empty lots, in dirt, grass or dead bugs, whatever they can find, but we've built this house and all the other houses and they are smart enough to keep making mini volcanoes everywhere and come inside look-ing for food in houses, food that they should be looking for in empty lots, but they don't come in if you don't leave anything out, Leo, one might come, or a thin, thin thread of scattered ants we can hardly see, and they do an inspection and if they don't find anything they go make their holes somewhere else, yes, they make holes in the cracks in the cement, in wood, in whatever, they're small but relentless and they don't just stroll around for no reason, that's why we can't leave anything out, Leo, I told you already, I've told you many times since we got here, the ants don't do anything, they're not poisonous, not like spiders or wasps or the furry caterpillars that give you a rash, but they do bite, ants bite because they have very strong pincers in their mouths so they can carry stuff that weighs a lot more than they do, we saw it on TV, but you can't call them, you can't make them come, not here, if you want to play with bugs we can go somewhere outdoors. Leo, Leo, who told you they'd come if you put out honey, don't tell me you thought of it yourself, come on, say something, I'm not mad anymore, I'm just explaining to you how things really are, I'm explaining what's dangerous and what's not, it's not dangerous to go to the field out back and move them with a stick like we did the other day, but it *is* dangerous to call them so that they invade our kitchen and crawl over your body, it's dangerous to put honey in a glass so they go crazy and leave their ant hill and enter our house, please Leo, please, it's okay, I'm not mad at you, now you stop being mad, who told you, was it Auntie Rita, well, what nonsense, of course she told you, who else, it's okay, it doesn't matter, I'll talk to her, you can't listen to everything she says, sometimes the two of you don't have very good ideas, I don't like it, I don't like it one bit, what's that? Speak up, Leo, and look at me when you talk, I know they're not spiders, I already said that; they aren't spiders and they aren't monsters, but ants really gross me out, I can't stand them, they eat everything, they'll eat everything if we let them.

They go to the beach. Sofía drags Leo the whole way. The sun is scorching, it's already past noon, groups of teenagers lounge in the sand, shiny, sexual lizards, scandalous, handsy. Elderly couples down by the shoreline, lined torsos, deeply browned. A man on his own, the color of birch bark, reads beneath a beach umbrella. He has a young man's body, but his face is old. Sofía applies more sunscreen to her son's shoulders, pulls the cloth hat down on his head, feels their embarrassment. She leaves the boy alone at the water's edge. She sits on her towel and starts to sweat. She hasn't brought anything to read, or drink. She bites into a sandy apple and wants to spit it out but ultimately chokes it down. Leo grabs his hat and throws it on the ground, a small brown wave wets it, rocks it, carries it off. Leo runs after it, momentarily forgetting his disgrace and his mother. After a half hour, Sofía collects their things and drags her son back home, the wet, sand-filled hat in one hand. In the other, Leo's slippery fingers, stubborn in their attempt to escape.

Why'd you leave him by himself? What? This morning? Ah, that's why you've had that sulky look on your face all day. You're angry. Come on, Rita, tell me. Why'd you leave him on his own? He wasn't alone, he was with you. You were asleep, but you weren't dead, right? Shit, Sofía, you were in the house. I tried to tell you, but you were fast asleep. And he doesn't go anywhere, you know Leo would never leave the house alone. Well, I don't actually know what Leo is capable of, in this situation. Your son is the same as he was a few weeks ago, Sofía. You're the one who isn't.

The sky has turned white with the evening, a single cloud, thin but opaque, has covered everything, lowered the temperature. It's still hot, but it's a fragile heat that augurs a cool night to come. Sofía combats what remains of the day with the vigorous movements of a skivvy. She's confirmed the faucet out on the patio doesn't work but has nevertheless decided to clean the entire flagstone pavement, the whole terrace, out front, out back, along both sides of the house. She enters the house slightly winded from her efforts, hauling a bucket of black water that she pours in the toilet, refills with more water and detergent, grabs the mop she left in the doorway and goes back outside. She hardly squeezes out the mop before sloshing it on the stone and splashing her feet. Everything is dirty. They've been at the house for days and they've hardly used the front part of the terrace; that side corner, the only part with dirt, has not been visited by the women, just Leo, maybe he's found bugs there, although it's so dry, so lifeless. Sofía frantically cleans what will soon become dirty again. Little sprays of grass sprout in the cracks. She crushes them with the mop. She decides to dump the last bucket in the flower bed. She knows the soapy water isn't good for the earth, but it can hardly even be called earth, it's a barren furrow, cracked, whitish brown, gulping it all down before her eyes. That little piece of dry dirt depresses her. It means nothing, because it means everything.

She profoundly despises that little piece of dirt, thirsty and sterile and meaningless.

Well, sis, I think it's about time you turned on your phone. Sofía looks at Rita and attempts to hide how much she wishes she would just disappear, right there, right now. I'm not even talking about Julio—though him, too—mama's been trying to reach you for a week. Sofía examines her hands, red from her early efforts with the mop. Why don't you want to talk to her? Nothing extraordinary is happening to you, Sofía, but you're turning it into a sort of crime. Sofía looks straight ahead at the big shelving unit in the living room, practically empty now, the TV, turned on, a handful of books. Mama is really worried. I don't get why you won't call her. She and Leo talked this afternoon, just so you know. Sofía sighs as deeply as possible and wishes she could inhale in one breath the empty cabinets, the TV, the handful of books, her reproachful little sister. I don't want to talk to her because if I tell her, it means that it has happened. She speaks in a voice that isn't her own. If I tell her then everything will be real. Oh Sofía, but mama . . . mama would be a big help. Yes, she would support me completely, and she wouldn't even ask that many questions because deep down I suppose the truth doesn't matter to her. But she'd take charge, like on other occasions. She would come and put things in order. She would take care of me like I was a little girl and Leo would be clean and well-fed. Mama would save me from this, but she would take everything over. If she comes, mama will make this house hers again. How long has it been since she stepped foot in here? If mama comes there'll be nothing for me to do. She'll take care of everything without ever asking a question and I won't have the luxury of being devastated. Rita's forehead rests against her hand, elbow on the table. She stares at her sister's profile. Rita, too, is all exhaustion and impatience. You're not being fair to her, you're not being fair to her at all. No, I'm not.

The cool night enters through the cracks of the window casing, from under the wooden door. A night for shuddering, the betrayal of a beginning. There is no summer, there is nothing at all.

It was her first day of school. Who took care of my sister in her earliest years, while my parents worked and I was at school? Maybe my mother, who—for a time—only worked sporadically. My grandmother on my mother's side, for sure. And I know there was a period when a girl came to the house, her name was María José and she was the closest thing we ever had to a babysitter. Once, we went to her house, which was behind the stadium, close to where we lived, and she put on an *Hombres G* movie for us to watch. I remember her perfectly, but not so much the heavy lady who wore black—and was incapable of kindness, in my judgement—and was also around for a while, maybe just a few weeks. She sat in the sitting room, and despite the fact that there were plenty of overweight people in my family—my grandparents, several uncles—that woman seemed enormous. Enormous and serious and an effective giver of lentils. Did she look after my sister? Rock her while my mother was working and I was at school? Did she wash her fine hair and later dry it with the hairdryer, or did she simply rub her head with the rough towel? Could my sister stand being with her? When she was little, my sister always wanted to be with my mother. I truly don't know who took care of her in those early years.

It was her first day of school, not mine, but I was very anxious. I felt important and at the same time I had the sense of a kind of stratospheric complicity, not directly focused on my sister, who was at a remove from that feeling, but on the world at large, because now I wasn't alone at school, now there was another member of my family there with me, and this was something solid and conclusive, vital. I don't know why I imagined that the fact my sister was starting school would change my own way of being there. I don't remember how she first stepped foot in the building, if a nun took her hand and led her away from our mother, if we walked through the hallway together to our classrooms. I don't know if she cried; I imagine she didn't, but I can't remember. Nonetheless, I know I realized quickly that my day-to-day experience wasn't going to change just because my sister was now in that gigantic building, with its interior patios and gardens. She was a concept, that's all. My sister was at school, but I didn't see her. Nobody treated me differently because of it. Everything was the same as when she wasn't there.

I was anxious for recess to arrive, ready for our reunion. But that wasn't special either because we were assigned to different playgrounds. My courtyard was for elementary-school kids and hers was for the preschoolers. I plucked up my courage, puffed out my chest, and armed with the responsibility of a big sister I asked the nun on duty if I could go to the little girls' patio to see my sister, since it was her first day. The nun let me go, and I imagine I ran down the colonnades separating our two courtyards, or maybe I walked respectably, head high, straight-backed, determined to do the right thing, a pretend little mother, haughty and stupid, proud of my good deed.

The preschoolers' courtyard unnerved me. I felt like a giant (I wasn't much older) among all those little pipsqueaks running around on the hard court. Were there really that many? Had there actually been so much commotion? They looked scattered to me, lost even, on the first day of their imprisonment, like the mess of flowers left strewn on the ground after the chariot has taken its victory lap. I looked for my sister, a little dismayed, like someone looking for something that isn't really theirs. We didn't have to wear our uniforms yet because it was still too hot. For those two weeks in September, the nuns let us show off our regular clothes, our real lives, our private selves: flowered fabric, thin cotton, sailor stripes, summer's remnants. Those dots of color, which I now remember as tenuous, pastel, ran back and forth across the courtyard and were in no way like one another (thin, lime-white arms, plump, brown legs, hair long and short, some ginger, some curly, some shiny manes with little bows fastened at the crown), but somehow I couldn't manage to pick her out from the bunch and my time was running out; recess didn't last more than half an hour and I couldn't spend the whole time on the preschool playground, I had a specific mission and then I was to return to my own pen. From my height, I spied a bewildering thing: there was a dress dangling from one of the green metal wastebaskets screwed to the side of the building. It was an ugly dress with a white background and colorful shapes or drawings, and it literally hung on the rectangular edge of the wastebasket. Its owner was nearby, a little girl no older than four, but enlarged, with round arms and legs and soft, swollen features. All she had on were a pair of slightly baggy cotton pants and her shoes, she moved in little jerks around the wastebasket, as if dancing, with the fingers of both hands stuck in her red-lipped, slobbery mouth. She was disabled, Down's syndrome maybe, something I could vaguely recognize. It horrified me; my clear awareness of superiority, of belonging to another life stage, was damaged. I got scared, because I couldn't find my sister and because suddenly something that was both completely external and completely my own was exploding before my eyes: those little girls were alone, completely abandoned, there was no other explanation. If not, how could that girl have had time to take off her dress by herself, leave it on a wastebasket, and dance in a daze, practically naked, in the school courtyard? Where were the nuns who were supposed to be watching them? Where was my sister? Would it scare her to witness that scene, the girl with the mollusc lips who may have been her classmate? Would it pain her? All of a sudden, I had grown up and begun to accrue the ordinary, sticky knot of prejudices about the lives of other people, prejudices that are always, in the end, about us. Time was running out. Where was my sister?

She was there in the middle of the courtyard, staring at me. She wasn't naked, she wasn't crying, she was there with her straight, shiny hair and her slender body, a beautiful insect among the stray flowers. She wasn't far away (had she been there the whole time?), but I suppose I lunged toward her with open arms and the expression of affected emotion the nuns had taught us to use for special moments. I really was worried, but I admit that my movements might have struck her as brusque and exaggerated. Or maybe not, maybe I was simply more frightened than she was and that courtyard full of recently imprisoned beings was all violence and desolation in my big-sister eyes, and I wanted to stroke her, protect her, guide her into the world so she wouldn't have to cross that border on her own. But I was the only visitor on that playground, the only intruder. There were the nuns, either overworked or simply chatting among themselves in the sunshine, distracted and unconcerned in their brown habits, and there was me. Among the flowers. Interrupting everything. Because my sister, I saw when I got close enough, was frowning. Her eyes were calm and the stiffness in her arms and legs was pure impatience. She was dying of embarrassment. Are you all right, are you doing okay, do you need something from the upper ranks of jail, something only I can offer? I must have sputtered something. Maybe I was even able to stroke her hair. She didn't give me time to crouch down to her height, condescendingly touch her shoulders, pull her into my savior's lap. My sister, from her very own life, said: Get out of here.

And I went.

VERY EARLY, WHILE SOFÍA is eating breakfast, standing at the kitchen counter, someone knocks on the door. Since today happens to be a day when the blood is running through her veins, she goes to answer, to keep them from ringing the doorbell and waking Leo and Rita. A delivery man with jet-black hair and enormous eyebrows, his face mostly hidden behind the box in his arms, says her name. Yes, that's me. Listen, this is my second time here, no one was home the other day and I didn't know if it was the right address. Oh, yeah, I guess we weren't here. You didn't leave a notice? I did, but I was planning on coming back anyway. We didn't see it. Can you sign here? The box is already at Sofía's feet, which look especially good today; she's trimmed her toenails and painted them maroon, she's wearing her nicest sandals, the ones that make the bones of her feet look acceptable. She signs, thanks him, lets him know there will be more packages, suggests he call if nobody's home when he makes his deliveries. Your phone was off, ma'am.

Her phone is on today, lying resplendent on the living-room table. Battery at 100% and charger in her bag, just in case. The keys, the cash she took out yesterday, a small bottle of water, a plastic bag folded and flattened so many times that it looks like a notebook, a day planner, but which contains a pair of pants, the thinnest trousers she owns, the easiest ones to fold. Everything is ready, and now her shipment of organic carbohydrates is finally here, too. She drags the box into the kitchen and opens it, feels the impulse to put each item away in its place, fill the glass jars she bought expressly for this purpose, line them up correctly

74

in the corresponding cabinets, but she realizes she's going to miss the bus and decides to write her sister a note. Another note, because she's already left several instructions taped to the fridge, as if she's been at her best the past few days and Rita was predisposed to obey her. *Rita, the order came. It's all organic. Use it for Leo, please. Don't bother putting it away, I'll do it later. XX.* Then she rushes to the bathroom to put on her makeup. In spite of the sunny days and lizard-mornings on the beach, she isn't tan. She thinks her eyes look smaller, shrunken by puffy eyelids. She makes herself up a little more than necessary, attempts to define her eyes with black eyeliner, loads her lashes up with mascara. Blush and lip liner, too. She sticks a few brushes in a tiny makeup pouch small enough to fit in her handbag and grabs a book from the shelf, the thinnest one, and into her bag it goes as well. A jacket. She closes the door behind her, then the gate. A white van is parking in front of the house next door, beside her sister's car. It's a big van, Sofía observes with disappointment. Both neighboring houses are empty; one for sale, the other closed up. This has made her feel safe, nice and alone, no witnesses. She knows which neighbors they are, she's known them forever. Typically nice people who try to help so as not to miss anything. She runs toward the station, she has a way to go. Her feet are chilly, it's damp at that time of day, in that place.

The ride goes by so quickly that they arrive before she even had time to close her eyes. The nonstop bus had been full of people who live in town but work in the city or are looking for work in the city or maybe have an appointment with a specialist at the hospital or shopping to do in the downtown stores with their cheap, homogenous clothing; ruddy townspeople, women in tight clothes, a few men wearing flat caps, escapist youths, or tall immigrants with smooth, taciturn skin who might make this trip several times a week, or maybe it's the only time they'll do it, passing from one place to another, from the coast to the river. She couldn't close her eyes, but she looked out on the fields and the warehouses on the ring road and finally at the city, luminous in spite of the clouds. She took the book out of her bag and what a bore, short stories by Katherine Mansfield, her father's copy, an old one from 1982. She read the first story, "At the Bay," years ago, she found it boring and way too long; she looked for a shorter one, the shortest one—"The Garden Party"—and set to reading: *And after all, the weather was ideal. They could not have had a more perfect day for a garden party if they had ordered it. Windless, warm, the sky without a cloud. Only the blue was veiled with a haze of light gold, as it is sometimes in early summer. The gardener had been up since dawn, mowing the lawns and sweeping them, until the grass and the dark flat rosettes where the daisy plants had been seemed to shine...*

She didn't read beyond that paragraph. A shiver, something completely foreign to her but which she desires to possess: delicacy. The image of her flower bed—dead, ridiculous—gnawed at her. Maybe that's all she needed right then, a garden party and someone to trim the roses at dawn. It was impossible to sleep. Instead, she returned to page 155 again and again until the spine cracked and the book's innards came unglued. She felt so awful about ruining the old book, about not actually wanting to read it, and was so afraid that the pages would fall out and get lost that she shut the Mansfield again and by then they'd arrived.

She waits patiently, distilling her insecurity. She dares to do the improbable and orders a beer (she's already made a trip to the restroom, touched up her eyeliner, put on lipstick), organizes the things on the terrace table. She doesn't want to look down the street, she focuses on herself, on her phone, the Mansfield book in one corner, as if anybody would believe she was reading it; the sight of the book pins her to the past, the image of her past, to the time in her life when she read books at bars, and the final touch, the coup de grace, she rolls a cigarette with her newly purchased paraphernalia, loose tobacco, and if she concentrates she can project a Sofía from just five years ago, three even, just three, when her little boy was starting to talk, when she still sat outside on bar terraces and smoked, she didn't read there but she did smoke, and she smoked with pleasure. Now she's very afraid that it's all useless. But that's how things were before; it was enough to simply do them. It's different now because of the alprazolam, recently prescribed by her GP, legally, the tight feeling in her stomach, her trembling hands as she rolls the cigarette, the beer that tastes like cat saliva. She doesn't want to check the time on her phone again, she mustn't show impatience, because he might be arriving, she lights the cigarette and inhales, savoring—for an insignificant instant—freedom, what could turn out to be plain, simple freedom, but her heart is tumbling in her chest and the palpitations frighten her and she knows she can't take another little dose of her tranquillizers yet, she knows she has to wait, so she does, she opens the book, looks for the crack in the spine, page 155, and after all, the weather was perfect . . . garden party, what a shame it was all a lie, what a terrible, terrible shame, if only she hadn't skimped on authenticity and had brought Tsvetaeva's *Confessions*, that hard, fat tome she has resolved to read even though she doesn't understand books anymore, if only she hadn't been so concerned about the weight of her bag, the beer is going down so quickly, the cold is lead in her stomach, suggestive, the cigarette goes out and she lights it again and puffs, puffs as if she would feel some relief, but how fucked is this city, how beautiful, this colorful corner near the city hall, sunny even on gray days, it's the only useful thing for her now, to love the lost city, believe in that love so she can feel like somebody; she checks her phone, only fifteen minutes past when they planned to meet, she knows with certainty that he's about to arrive and here he comes down the street, he's talking on the phone, his hair is shorter, he almost certainly unbuttoned his shirt when he left work, and a bit of hair is visible, she can see it clearly, he's thinner, his thighs more fibrous beneath those nice jeans he sometimes wears to the office, and his face is the same as always, now that he's put the phone in his pocket, the same face it once was, nonchalant, loose, novel, two o'clock in the afternoon, it's cloudy but hot, I'll pick you up and we'll drink beer until our heads spin, the others are probably around El Salvador, we can go now, but wait, you didn't finish telling me your story, the two of us alone here, we have the whole afternoon ahead of us, I don't think I'm going back to the office, order another one, what are you looking for? his unconcerned face, his face at the beginning.

Hello, Sofía. I knew I'd find you smoking.

Sofía starts to cry, a brackish flood come straight from the sea.

What can I say, Rita? I don't know how to start. I got to the city, saw the doctor, told him everything. He prescribed me pills and suggested I see a psychiatrist or psychologist or something; anyway, he was most concerned about the epiglottis episode the other day and I told him I thought that the pills were overkill but I don't know, I suppose if I'm going to self-medicate I might as well follow a plan. Then I went through downtown, there was a protest, yeah, the whole avenue in front of the cathedral, a sea of white. It's wild, I'm so removed from everything. I felt like a hypocrite, smiling as I squeezed between them, like I was giving them my approval, there were a lot of young people, middle-aged people as well, even elderly, I got caught up in their excitement, I still don't even know what they were protesting yet there I was walking among them, feeling so proud of my fellow human beings, but from the sidelines, from my hidey-hole. I'm an idiot. I saw the protesters and I thought, oh, I'll buy a newspaper! then forgot about it as soon as I turned the corner and couldn't hear them blowing their whistles. We'd made plans to meet at the usual place, near his office. I sat at a table outside. He came a little late—he made me wait, but he came.

Everything is all set with Leo. I want to be really clear about this so you can stop reprimanding me. Oh, please, don't make that face, let's not start, all I'm asking is for you to be patient and listen. Yes, I know I didn't go about things the right way, blah, blah, blah, but you know what? He wasn't worried about that, he's got everything under control, it's terrifying, he's been spinning this web for months and it's like he has all my moves figured out . . . No, I know it's not like that. Anyway, we've gone over everything in terms of Leo. Julio said all he wants over the next few weeks is to talk to the boy every day; he said I have to keep my phone on in case he feels like calling him, whenever. And then when Julio has some vacatioin timie, he'll bring him up north, to see his grandparents. A couple of weeks, maybe a little longer. He doesn't know exactly when yet but, shit, it's all so reasonable. The ordinariness of separation has penetrated my life. The divvying up. So that's it, that's how we're going to spend the summer. Then of course he expects me to go back and keep living in our home, he's already looking for a new apartment. I see it so clearly now, he wanted an apartment in the center so badly, a big, light, open one with a terrace, and that is just what he is going to get, after all, he always wanted a place like that, now he is a maker of dreams, a serious and practical changer of lives: here, you have the life you can afford and I'll have the one I always wanted. I don't know, that's not it, that's not actually it. I couldn't counter anything he said, but I can't even think about going back now, I can't imagine my life there again, as if nothing has happened; we didn't talk about shared custody or anything, for the moment this is how it is, he wants to see his kid for a few weeks during his vacation, bring him to his turf, talk to him every day, the usual, I guess. And I have this pause. To see if I accept the future conditions: keep living in the same city, plan how I'll spend my days, how I'll earn money, yeah, I know, I don't need a lot, the asshole repeated that I can keep the house, it's paid off, it's no problem, but I suppose I'll have to get a lawyer to establish some real parameters, rights, responsibilities, make sure he can't just up and take away the house all of a sudden, or if I decide not to go back . . . I'm not being ironic. No, of course, I haven't really thought about it, I don't know anything, I don't know what I want to do. Yes, it's my city now, too. Our city, Leo's city. But I need to know that I'm not obliged to reconstruct the same context, that I can begin again. Or not.

Oh Rita, it was awful. I cried the whole time, and for a long time. For stretches. I cried before and after everything. I cried when he turned up; I had prepared everything so carefully, I had it all thought out, what I'd say, how I'd look, how I'd sit in the bar, but he showed up, he spoke to me, and I just started crying. His voice came to me from the other side, it was a brick. I expected indolence, coldness, the limping figure one gets used to living with after years of cohabiting, but suddenly he spoke to me and there was this new thing and the scratch became a sinkhole, and god what an idiot, what an idiot I was to start like that, that's why I couldn't stop, because nothing mattered anymore, the tableau was already in pieces. After I showed him what a fucking mess I am, what was I supposed to care about? It's childish, Rita, but he looks so good. He's like he was right before he stopped . . . Like at the inflection point, like when in reality, maybe, everything might have been possible.

Ah, you're curious. Give me a hit. Pills and joints, bad, right? Pills, booze, and joints. Really bad. Come on, it's a really low dose. Just give me a drag. I have something I want to tell you. Wow, I can feel this already. I hope Leo doesn't wake up.

Don't generalize like that; I know there was an inflection point. There's one in every relationship. It's different from more mundane damage, the kind of damage that's like mould, when there's been prolonged dankness and suddenly a stain appears, who would have thought, there it is, the damage is as noiseless and efficient as life, but the inflection point, the inflection point is different. I'm talking about the instant you realize everything is chipped and peeling and you decide to do something about it, move in some direction, even if only metaphorically. Usually, you don't actually do anything, you wait until the wall has really and truly crumbled, the whole wall, cracked, stripped. There was a very clear inflection point in our relationship, as clear as an *X* on the calendar. Do you remember, at the very beginning with Leo, when he was just a couple of months old, that crisis I had? We had to talk about it, Leo wasn't nursing anymore, I think it coincided with all that, with my insistence on weaning him. He could have nursed longer, I was giving private lessons and teaching language at that academy, I was free, I could have kept breastfeeding. I was free, I see it so clearly now. But I felt so tied down, so manipulated. Not by him, by my baby, it wasn't that, I have never felt any resentment toward him, although who knows, maybe he's gotten stuck with it all . . . I don't know, I was sure something was over for good. Something inside my body. And outside, too. I think you and I had a couple of conversations about it, I'm sure we did. A long one on the phone, now I remember, first you called me greedy and then you comforted me because maybe I still had postpartum, or the baby blues, or whatever we call it. With Julio, I had the same fear, or worse. He was something outside me now. Something that had escaped. No, he didn't reject me. But there was so much distance, and the truth is, I was terrified we'd never—

We have to move now? You're that cold? Yeah, my feet are freezing too, but I'm in the middle of a story. Only a sister would cut you off like that. Well, I haven't told you anything yet, nothing important anyway, but I need you to really get the context. Fine, come on, let's go in. That couch is a piece of shit, we should have bought another one, it pokes you everywhere. Bring the chair over and we can put the ashtray and glasses down. Now you're going to the bathroom?! Fine, yes, I'll wait. You're not going to tell me you're ready for bed, I hope? Yes, I said yes, go.

Right: inflection point, fear. Yes, I'm telling you I started to think that my life was over and that I was irrevocably not the same person as before.

One night we went out, I convinced him that we should go

to a hotel, just for a couple of hours. The babysitter would stay until three on weekends. We gave her so much work back then. We had gone to a new Italian place, I had gotten dressed up, he had shaved, but I was anxious—I ate anxiously, we shared a bottle of wine, me anxious and him, well, calm, I guess, or bored, whatever's supposed to be normal and even pleasant on a Friday night out with your wife who has just weaned your baby. Still, the hotel would be our salvation. As you know, Julio's up for anything; he doesn't need much provocation. Maybe he still loved me then. Or maybe I desired him like a woman ought to desire a man when she stops breastfeeding their child, the exact natural proportion of desire, but who cares, because it was all a ramshackle wall to me. We went to a hotel, one we had gone to a few years before. We took off our clothes. We fucked. And that's it. It wasn't enough. The hole in my stomach was as black as a dead man's mouth.

I brooded for a few days, and I thought: the secret is in audacity. And I said to him, as we both sat on the couch with the baby asleep beside us: Julio, we could go to one of those couple-swapping places. If there was any contempt in the way he looked at me, the slightest hint of disapproval, I didn't notice. The truth is, Julio likes to be tempted. Did I suggest that because I was scared another woman might tempt him on the street, at work, in the gym, now that his little wife was a mother with a scarred vagina and empty tits? Or, was it me who needed to escape? To believe that I was brave, disruptive, like I used to be, earlier, only a few years earlier, like I was on other occasions for other men? I needed for something to break, for something to happen, but I didn't want to be unfaithful to him and I didn't want him to be unfaithful to me, better to do it all from the inside, destroy it from inside, complicit and cowardly. I'm aware of my guilt, I know I started it, but it doesn't matter. Julio took my hand (which must have smelled like baby wipes) and brought it to his lips. I remember it so clearly, he kissed me; maybe he was trying to placate me, relieve me of my madness. Have you ever been to one? he asked. You know I haven't, I answered. I have no idea, actually, what even happens there. Okay, we'll go find out, he said.

You don't believe me. You see me sitting here and you don't believe me—you, you who have always been much freer than me, though at the same time also more reserved. But remember, I lived my own golden age, as well. I've had a lot of fun in my life, and at that point I was sure I either had to take action or I was never going to enjoy myself again. And anyway, I'd always envied all of that, when I found out about other people's lives, heard stories. That negligence that some couples are able to bring into their love, that negligence that is nothing if not the opposite, a monstrous attempt to make love last, in any of its facets. You would be surprised to know just how normal it is, what I'm telling you. I was really surprised at first, but then, even though we always carried on in utmost secrecy, it became normalized, even official. We weren't doing anything out of the ordinary. The thing is just that nobody knows what normal is. What the fuck is normal? Normal: a fucking skull and cross-bones. The miasma.

At first, I was horribly self-conscious and only went to watch. I hid behind Julio, who tried to hug me, joke about it all. He seemed so calm, as if he possessed some specific gene for new sexual horizons, like he'd been going to places like that for years behind my back. It was always the same club. A sort of dance club in a neighborhood on the outskirts of town, on the way to the airport. Tacky, exotic, clean. Well-organized. You've never been in one, Rita? Of course I'm being serious. Look, you could do whatever you wanted in there, within the bounds of the internal rules. Unpredictable rules. I never managed to learn them entirely because that adventure didn't last long. We mostly watched. On the second or third time, I let Julio have oral sex with other women, let them blow him, yeah, that, because he was hard when he walked in and hard when he left, and I—even though I was still terrified—realized that we were there to do more than simply watch and then go hide in a reserved room for a quick fuck. A fuck with an audience, mind, because someone always wound up finding you. Some couple who'd had their eye on you from the start, or those who couldn't get the attention of the superstars, the most successful fornicators. You're about to come and suddenly you open your eyes and there are all these other people, there's the little man with the fat cock and his sinewy, forty-something girlfriend, lying in wait, close by because they want to join in, that must be it because that's what one does there, but I can't. Julio has a smile on his face and I try to hold back my orgasm but I can't and I explode. The third or fourth time, I let them touch me. Don't look at me like that, Rita. Come on, we've talked about sex hundreds of times. Don't be a prude. It wasn't that hard with the girls. You just had to relax. Just go with it, one told me. She was blonde, a real dye-job, she had blue eyes and a little gap between her front teeth. Younger than me, the youngest girl in the room, I think. She didn't pay any attention to Julio, only me, and Julio loved it. She kissed me and started stroking me, combing her fingers through my hair. And that's how I started to make the whole thing a reality, rather than just a concept. Not just, here I am saving my marriage by fucking in front of strangers and watching strangers fuck beside us, but really participating, outwardly, making a fantasy reality or whatever, leaping into the unknown. I know, I know, it was more like jumping into a void but, you know what? The unknown was comforting. It filled that pit in my stomach, for a while I was happy. It doesn't matter, you don't have to understand. Details? What do you want to know? The orgasms with the beautiful gap-toothed blonde seemed like they'd never end, honestly. Go on, cover your face.

No, it wasn't weird when we got home, it wasn't ugly. We were tired, satiated, it made us laugh, we felt like children with our new toy. Julio was really handsome there, in that torture chamber; he was strong, he could last, he was light and relaxed, a little careless, even, like it didn't really have anything to do with him, but he was also intentional, methodical. I think the best part of being there was showing Julio off. Seeing how much everyone wanted him. It rebuilt my desire for him, and that's the key, isn't it? That's why people go to those places, to rebuild desire. Well, among other reasons. Of course, some go because they've lost everything. Or because nothing is enough to satisfy them. Or because there they have access to bodies they could never watch so up-close in real life. Or because their concept of sex is from a totally different realm (and that you could tell—god, how I envied them). Those with a concept of sex both light and deep, so completely natural, an energy that is neither created nor destroyed. The clean of mind. We didn't belong to any category, we were just beginners without grand aspirations, still young, though mature by then, together for years, on paper a perfect couple, our little boy well taken care of back at home, just a couple of liberal yuppies practicing something exotic on an atavistic honeymoon. Innocent. Stupid. It was good to show Julio off, revive a sense of possession. And I had sex with women on a round bed in a dark room. But not with all the women, a lot of times it was the same one, or this other girl—beautiful as well—and never with anybody older than me. I shared my partner with those women and pretended not to notice when he went off with others I wouldn't have touched. But we were never good customers. We were never all in. We had our biases. What's that? How many times did we go? Seven, eight in a year? No more than that. Then we switched tactics.

I was the one who grew bored. Hard to believe, but all of that never unleashed a storm of confessions, the possibility for us as a couple to share our secrets, discuss the multiple ways of experiencing sex. Julio and I never talked much about it. Julio and I never talked much about anything, now that I think of it. He's not a good conversationalist. He has too many boundaries, is content with so little. There was something that changed forever and that was the notion of privacy. From our very first time, I sensed that Julio had already been somewhere similar. It wasn't all new to him. When I saw him move between the bodies I knew it wasn't his first time with that kind of polygamous free pass. The tacit agreement in our kamikaze project was that we wouldn't talk too much. I stepped into my new life with the same naturalness that one accepts their first crow's feet or stretch marks. There was no need to dig deep, only to communicate. And we were communicating again, the current flowed, not only through our bodies but through our eyes. That was enough to transform my idea of what a couple is. Now I was a mother, a wife, and I was mature enough to experiment sexually with my partner and with myself, to flee what most terrified me: stagnant love, the absence of sex, destruction. I was saving the world. The truth is, Rita, I didn't actually like swingers' clubs.

We decided to contact our bedmates outside of the club. Just occasionally, we told ourselves. Just occasionally, and just for us. In a lovely hotel in the city center. An old house run by a gay pseudo-artist who sometimes organized dinners on the rooftop terrace for his chosen few. A couple of rooms, each decorated differently. It was easy to feel glamorous. We started meeting people there sometimes: people we found online. The gap-toothed blonde came one time. Then came two other women, a Catalan photographer and a study-abroad student. We saw them both again, but twice with each was enough for me. Julio and I hung on to the antiquated married life above all else: our son, our friends, work, the house, our standard weekend plans as a family. And on occasion, the stuff with other people. I don't know if you understand, but it was nice. I think we did the right thing. It prolonged our sex life, made us feel united beyond just us two. We were clean, we were careful; I had fun. Some filthy thing, once in a while, but we quickly covered it over with the smooth running of our daily life. Why are you shaking your head? You can't believe it? You don't believe I would want to do all that? Of course it was consensual! They weren't his rules, they were *ours*! Masculine superiority? Why are you saying that now? No, I don't *think* I enjoyed it, I was enjoying it. Oh Rita, let me finish.

In the end, Julio was generous and agreed that we could call another man, just once. But I pulled a trick. The number one rule, which I had clearly expressed on more than one occasion, was that the others had to be strangers. No ties. If possible, they should have different interests. No encouraging of ties. Just our love and our family. And the occasional smuttiness. Don't laugh, that's all it ever was, seriously. But I pulled a trick. I suppose I had already started blurring the lines. If I could have sex with other people, and beside other people, with my partner's consent, why couldn't I have sex with someone who I really wanted to have sex with? Was there really such a big difference? There was a new guy teaching at my school. He was from Chile. I might have told you about him when I first met him, do you remember? Anyway, he was tall, very tan, super black eyebrows, super dark eyes. We had had a few beers, I liked him, he had kept his eyes on me long enough, and I decided to take the risk and write him and tell him all this shit. And he was up for it. We lied to Julio. I asked the Chilean to pretend, to fake that we didn't know each other. He made a profile on the site we used and everything matched up. Of course, we barely knew each other and it could have gone horribly wrong. The truth is I was doing an awful thing but I didn't realize it at the time. No, it didn't seem that wrong to me. Because, well, you're right about one thing, these situations are never completely balanced. Julio had been having more sex with more women than me that whole time. I had had sex with women, something new for me, of course, but he had always participated. I hadn't had sex with another man, not real sex. But I had been watching Julio fuck other girls for the last year and a half. Sure, Julio was generous, and—as he never failed to remind me—it had been my idea. It doesn't matter. I betrayed him. It wasn't a big betrayal, I wasn't a sociopath. Just selfish.

I think the date with the Chilean changed everything. No, of course they didn't touch each other—so respectful, the two of them. Get that I-told-you-so look off your face. I tried to tease them into going a little further but it didn't work and I wasn't going to make them. I should have brought drugs with me that night. No way, I didn't because we weren't used to doing it like that, that was another one of our rules, can you believe it? Nothing, just alcohol. Leo was little and we always went home, at all hours of the night, sure, but we always went home, and we had to be lucid the next day, so, no, we didn't take drugs to have sex with other people. But when we were with the Chilean I really felt like being high. When he started touching me, when he put it inside me and I felt like we were alone. Going home that night was really intense, really sad for me. I don't know about Julio, but something hadn't worked. I suppose it was the end of the ride, that's all. End of the farce. I wanted to see him again, soon after, maybe too soon, but Julio didn't agree. He didn't say anything in particular. Were we already speaking so little by then? How long ago did Julio stop talking to me? Almost two years? He didn't act jealous, he wasn't upset, he simply wasn't interested. He didn't feel like it. It was probably revenge for my betrayal.

Unconscious revenge or not. The balloon deflated. The rain fell. The earth swallowed him up. I don't know what happened.

We never went back to the hotel. We never did any of that again. I don't know why I didn't tell you before. Months passed, normalcy eating away at our consciences. It started to seem like a dream, somebody else's rebellion. There was one night, at one of the few parties Julio and I both went to during that period, when we shared a moment of complicity and I thought we might make something happen with a girl we'd just met. Julio and I looked at each other, but I didn't dare. Now that I think of it, maybe Julio didn't want to be with both of us, maybe he just wanted to go with her. Maybe his look wasn't of incitement, but of annoyance, discomfort. I don't know. Because we didn't discuss it, we didn't dissect our cadaver. The left lung for you, the liver for me. Each one of us with our rotting entrails, with our role in the murder. And it was over.

I saw the Chilean a few more times. How predictable this must all sound to you, right? I was terrified Julio could be doing the same thing, but it didn't seem like it, at least not then. I was thoughtless. The Chilean drove me crazy and I slept with him (by myself, so free, so like I used to be, like falling in love again) for a couple of months. But he wasn't interested in anything more, much less in a mother with a family. I put out the fire, clung to Julio, tried to forget him. And I did. The Chilean was the least of it all. With each subsequent orgasm—further and further apart in time—I felt all the pain, the melancholy, rise in my throat, the urge to cry, not with pleasure, but with emptiness. We'd broken it. Or it had broken us.

I REMEMBER THE SANDY slope that ran from the pine forest down the cliffside, all the way to the shore. We went there a lot of weekends, picnicked outside. Everyone, grandparents, uncles, cousins, some friends. They were long days. In spite of the fresh air, in spite of the trees, in spite of our imagination, sometimes those days felt long to me. Something separated me from the world. The adults on one side, their familial roles, their jokes, their wine, their thermoses of coffee. And us. The kids. Some who weren't so kidlike by then. Being out there wasn't like being in town in the summer, when our reality revolved around the singular axis of hours on the beach. The sea, the sand—period. There was something wild about those days in the country, something I never did quite believe. We had to engage with nature, and we were daring, determined to take advantage of the opportunity: tree bark, pine needles, underbrush in those sandy woods that ended at a cliff. Should we build forts, dig for hidden treasure, climb a tree? The physical always terrified me, somehow. The display of primal abilities. And besides, they were there, too, the boy cousins: strong, agile, brutish, painful. All that racket. And while those days felt long to me, my sister seemed to live them treacherously, because, as I've said, she was different. She was an animal, and I was not.

But there was the slope. The slope was ecstasy. All children want to fly (I thought I didn't, because of the fear, but of course I wanted to). All children want to lift their feet off the ground and soar, because birds do it, insects do it, because there's something inside our chest that tortures us when we're suspended in air, something different that we humans have, something we house inside, twisted scrap metal, miraculous little spoils of war; what species of creature grows inside our ribcage, makes us unique, thirsty, corruptible, makes us eternal children in pursuit of flight? The slope was the ecstasy of the airborne. From up above the pine forest, it descended in a steep curve down to the beach; through the red dirt of the cliff ran the white sand slope, a little genius of nature, a scream of quartz plummeting from the trees down to the ground, a white wall, smooth and hot. The slope was the best thing about those days in the country, because even I—a coward—could erupt, take a risk, be happy. On those Sundays, happiness—that sharp prick of the skin—consisted of this: running down the slope at full tilt, together yet separate, because that flight was an absolutely individual experience. After a few meters, we were lifted off the ground by the very slope itself it was so steep. Our strides lengthened and then we soared, suddenly our skinny legs in their sun-faded sweatpants, thick cotton sweatpants our mothers bought in big department stores, were the legs of tightrope walkers, our legs were feathers, more and more distance between our bodies and the ground, less and less contact with the sand, as if the slope was a vertical trampoline, as if our feet had springs. I don't believe a picture of those moments exists. But I remember our faces, smiles made of air, the smiles of birds, our arms open, bony fingers splayed, sad simulacra of wings. We flew. The sand whipped into clouds at our feet and when we reached the bottom we were covered in it: our underwear, ears, hair, sneakers. We climbed back up. This was harder, of course, and we got sweaty, but it was worth it. Climb and fly again. And then, after several flights, tired and satiated as only children can be, we would run to the beach. Because there behind the red rock, waiting for us, was the winter sea.

The slope made us fly. It also made it so the others didn't

matter, not their shouts or bravado or demands or violence. In the air, we were equals. In the air, actually, they didn't exist.

ARRANGED ON THE TABLECLOTH, the plates look like playthings. The fact that there's a tablecloth on the plastic table outside can only mean one thing. The tablecloth is new, the plates are also new and that's why they look like toys: pastel hues, ceramic, geometric patterns, and diluted flowers, laid out on the white embroidered cloth, an imbalance between the elegance of the new dishware and the sunburnt legs of the plastic table.

Rita arranges the plates again, folds the napkins with care and places them under the cutlery so the wind won't blow them away. The smell of food in the kitchen, fire, steamed-over tile. She hadn't considered the new tablecloth and the plates necessary, there are plenty of plates in the house, plenty of tablecloths, even if they're old and have stains that are impossible to remove, but now that she sees the table set, Rita feels lighter in spirit, soothed by the comfort of fresh white, the dots of color, round and shiny. When the table is ready, she puts back the jug of flowers she'd left on the floor. That morning she had gone into town to get the ingredients they needed for lunch and decided to buy flowers as well, from the florist on the main street. She hadn't been inside since she was a little girl. The wreath of carnations they brought to the funeral home when their father died had been ordered there, but some family member had taken care of that, there had only been one wreath, *we won't forget you*, it said. It hadn't been signed. We won't forget you, in general. She bought daisies, her mother's favorite. Purple daisies, because she'd grown sick of the white variety years before, when every week their mother made them refresh the vase on the bureau in her bedroom, when she exhorted them to be conscious of whether the water needed to be changed or the stems trimmed so the daisies would last longer. For a long time, their mother had fresh flowers in her room—a new bouquet every fifteen days, always in the same glass vase—and she lectured them both about loving those flowers, as if they represented another life that by rights they should be enjoying but nevertheless didn't exist: a life of flower beds and hortensias, a life of gardens. Rita rarely had flowers in her home. She did keep a lot of cacti.

Sofía and her mother meet on the patio. Sofía is returning, hot, from the beach with Leo and she walks through the gate, wet hair full of salt. Leo is starving, I'm starving, Grandma. He drops the net bag with the sandy beach toys on the ground and nobody scolds him. The mother had come out onto the patio just as they were arriving. She carries a big bowl of diced tomato, green pepper, onion, and cucumber mixed with oil and vinegar. She moves the flowers slightly to make space for the bowl on the table, and as she does she looks over approvingly at her younger daughter: not so much because of the daisies, but because of the suggestion of flower beds and hortensias. Both women smile. Smells great, Sofía says. She sends Leo off to wash his hands before lunch. What are we having, brothy rice or paella? Sofía and Rita's mother is shorter than the sisters, her legs are chubby but strong and she has a few tight rolls at her waist, which she covers with billowy blouses in the summer and long shirts in the winter. These days, she wears her hair very short, dyed an orange that's sometimes red, and her face is filled with tiny wrinkles, as if sketched by a hand in a hurry. Her dark eyes are lively, always alert, highlighted by sparkling shadow, sometimes silver-gray, sometimes dark violet, which she never, ever leaves home without. Her daughters have better builds, they're more beautiful, svelte, proportioned. But she is elegant in her own way, she has presence; in her look, in the way she buttons her shirts and covers them with soft-woven blazers, in her choice of shoes, her smile. In any case, for a few years now, her movements and her emotions emanate a joy that destabilizes her carefully constructed equilibrium. It's the kind of joy that springs from people who have spent too many years unaccustomed to happiness, and when they finally get it, it's like it's too big for them, they can't handle it, it disfigures them. She was a teacher, she retired early and almost immediately met a divorced psychiatrist from the Canary Islands, attractive, childish but very good-natured, and went to live with him on his island. In her words, in her new way of walking, there's an ease, possibly feigned, a consciousness of happiness that her daughters cannot bring themselves to tolerate.

It's a summer day, almost the first since Sofía and Leo arrived in town. Sofía was terrified of seeing her mother, of confronting that moment of familial seriousness whose objective is to acknowledge a failure, a lost battle, to grab the stretcher and lift the cadaver. Of course, her mother threw her hands to her head when Sofía told her the truth on the phone, but what came next was easy, as if she'd been waiting for it, desired it even: I'll be there in two days, don't you girls worry about anything. The daughters can't help but feel strange with their mother in that house again. She behaves as if time hadn't passed, as if their father had simply stepped out for a stroll, to go fishing, as if he were at work in the city or had never existed at all. The mother returns to the house of her past with an excess of authority. The daughters allow her that, not up to challenging her or putting her in her place. In any case, is that not her real place? What other place could they offer their mother? Rita puts daisies on the table, Sofía stops worrying, stops cooking, stops policing the origin of every morsel of food. That is the result of the mother's arrival. A kind of submission that makes them happy for the moment, soothes each one of the three. Only the boy is experiencing real happiness, without a flip side.

The mother didn't know so much about wine before she went off to live on the island. She's supposedly an expert now, or an amateur expert, because the psychiatrist has a wine cellar in his basement, and together they organize tastings for large groups of friends and are always up to date on the new vineyards, the new labels. The mother loves telling her daughters about this, celebrating frivolity. Liberating herself from the sacrifice she was always tied to. In the house, she has worked to show her daughters that she will always be their mother: she has cleaned, reorganized the closets and pantry, moved pieces of furniture here and there, filled the fridge. She has been cooking all morning, a light sheen of sweat on her face, tiny wrinkles shining. She brought presents for her grandson and has hugged him tightly, spoiled him, entertained him with games and songs. She is a mother, but she is also a woman freed from her past. She attempts—generally without success—to drag her daughters toward this new concept of herself, make them complicit. They support her, but they keep a distance from this new figure, from the slight shadow of the eccentric. A mother's metamorphosis is something desired, but hard to accept.

The mother refills her daughters' wine glasses, then her own: this wine isn't bad, don't you think? It's the second bottle, the dessert wine. The mother usually pairs this last wine with cheese, but the day is hot and she's brought out a tray of sliced fruit instead. Rita eats and drinks with joy, submersed in her second-child docility. Sofía is relaxed, too, uninhibited, why not, why not this fraternity, this illusion? Suddenly, they toast, Leo too, with his glass of water, laughing, reaching up from his chair. Then he goes inside to watch TV; everything is allowed. The mother says: Sofía, you would do wonderfully on the island with me, with us. Marvellous place for raising the boy. And I would be so happy. We would do so many things, and I'm sure you'd find a good job, although you would want for nothing there, regardless. Sofía takes a long sip and lets the wine roll in her mouth. She takes a slice of watermelon and lets her mother dream a little longer. The house is enormous, there's room for everyone, but there's also the apartment in the center, it's not rented now and could be good if you wanted some more independence. And that way you could visit us on your vacations, Rita. Sofía determines that that's enough but she conserves her sweetness. Mama, you know I can't go that far, Leo has a father. And well, he has a city, too, a school, everything. And . . . but the mother, removing a sliver of melon seed stuck to her bottom lip, is already nodding, regretting her childish fantasy. Of course, of course, what nonsense, it's way too far, and you have a life, it's a ridiculous idea. But, well, anything you need, you know . . . I know, mama. Rita pours herself more wine but doesn't try any of the fruit. Her eyes close and she stretches out her legs, measuring the moment's perfection. The mother returns to the charge, unsettled by the silence, perhaps, as if something might break, you know what, Sofía? You're going to get back together. It's just temporary, it's natural for couples. Some distance, it'll revitalize things between you. Rita shifts in her chair, the plastic legs scrape on the floor, but she doesn't get up, and continues drinking. Sofía looks at her mother, tries to contain her frustration, cling to her mother's good intentions, allow herself to be given advice. I think you two will get back together, maybe even have another baby . . . It's like she lives in a parallel reality, like she wasn't actually listening when Sofía told her, as if from this point forward her mother was never going to understand anything about her life, but she doesn't get mad, Sofía looks at Rita out of the corner of her eye, and between them, in the silence, they agree it's better to let it go. It's normal, in the end, to speak without thinking, to wish out loud, say nonsense.

This is generally what people's communication consists of. It's fine. No reason to get upset. Cook, clean, play with the grandson, it's all good. Sofía is already drunk. She eats more watermelon, searches through her beach bag hanging on the back of her chair and takes out the lighter and packet of tobacco. She too feels free and renewed, like her mother; she's started smoking again and doesn't care about anything, who is going to dare chide her for it now? Not even she is capable of judging herself. She lights a cigarette and notices how the pleasure softens her knees and cheekbones. Rita is watching her closely but there's no message in her half-closed eyes. She's dead tired. She looks at her phone blinking on the table. Slowly types a message. Then the mother, who they seem to have momentarily forgotten, says: I told you a while ago you should have had another baby, but you make your choices, dear. Sofía turns to her blankly, her mother may as well have said something like *and to top it off you're smoking again*. She mutters a what are you talking about, mama—too softly, cigarette smoke—but it's Rita who is roused, she straightens in her chair and observes their mother sarcastically. Sofía sits up in her chair, sliding it closer to the table, cigarette trembling, imperceptible. Over the whisper and the silence, Rita's voice dominates, I hope you didn't come here to lecture on how to save a marriage, mama. Sofía squirms. She's uncomfortable. Is Rita defending her? Against what? The mother contains her impulse and reaches out to pour herself more wine, though her eyes are damp; she should counter the attack now, shut down the reproach. But instead, she takes a sip of her wine and lowers her eyes. Sofía lightly touches her parted lips as she watches her sister; is her mother making the biggest effort of her life? Enough for today, Sofía moves to stand up and clear the table, but Rita isn't finished yet: And you didn't come here to give a lecture on taking care of a child, of course. The mother opens her mouth, which is broken now: Why . . . ? and Rita cuts her off:

Come on, mama. Sofía wants to yell at her sister but she only manages to push back her chair and stand up and the sound of it breaks up the table-talk at last; hunching slightly, the mother enters the house. The sisters hear the bathroom door close; in any other instance they would have raised their eyebrows and rolled their eyes upon hearing the mother's muffled sobs, but now Sofía tries to meet her sister's eye. She's afraid, she's frowning, but Rita won't look at her. She finishes her wine and heads off to her room.

Sofía had predicted a storm, a storm like the ones that used to happen years ago now, three wild animals in a cage, two against one, always, never the same sides, changeable alignments. She had surrendered to it, even, after the conversation after lunch, but nothing has happened. The long summer siesta has diluted the poison. And Leo's contribution, of course: the child as fix-it glue, the communion created around an only child, a spoiled child. The domestic choreography, a dance of the mops, brief, irrelevant exchanges, the running of a home with its routines. They had been on the edge of the precipice and yet they have avoided it once again, the mother shielded by dissemblance and love. But she won't take an earlier flight; the mother will leave when scheduled.

One evening, Sofía, surging with energy, paces around the porch. The effort of maintaining an atmosphere of well-being edifies her. She wants to turn over a new leaf, start a new phase. She disappears around the corner of the house, approaches another part of the porch, over by the abandoned wall. She looks sceptically at the small piece of dry dirt, smiles, returns inside, and pronounces her judgement: I'm going to turn the patio into a garden. I'm going to take up the tile and put down fertilized earth and plant flowers and a tree. The mother looks at her in an attempt to understand. She opens her mouth to speak but has nothing to say. What are you talking about? Rita spits back as she continues to feed spoonfuls of ice cream to Leo, who is hypnotized by the TV. That's a stupid idea. It's not stupid, the house would be so much nicer with a garden. Rita mutters something, the mother tries to control the situation, laughs nervously, maybe it's a good idea, she winds up saying, but very softly, as if she assumes she doesn't have a vote. Sofía still has her halo of confidence. Rita looks at her, despotic. You will do no such thing. This house is for sale. We are going to sell this house, get that through your head. She says this and gets to her feet and in the heat of midday her slender figure is like a wounding shadow. I don't want . . . Sofía starts to say, her face contorting at last. And the violence comes to an end with the scene, with the twist, I don't care what you want, and once again the battalions dissolve and reform, Rita steps past her sister without looking her in the face, only her bird-words float in the brume. She goes into her room, slams the door, it's over. The mother diligently clears the table, places the tub of ice cream, the spoons, the bowls on a tray. Sofía casts about for a place to hold on to. She doesn't find one.

SOFÍA HAS RENTED A BICYCLE. She hasn't ridden a bike in years, but she promised Leo. In the city, Julio-the-athlete used to take the boy on bike rides along the river. At first, when Leo was a baby, he rode in a little seat mounted on the back of Julio's bike. But now that Leo has his own bike, he and Julio ride together, very slowly. Sofía almost never joins them, she's rather lazy when it comes to physical exertion, but Leo has been insistent the past couple of days: Why don't you buy me a bike, mama? Why can't we go home and get my bike, mama? I told papa on the phone that he should come and bring me my bike. Actually, this is the perfect place for a bike, you're right, she winds up admitting. She is being dragged toward the summer by a kind of chagrin. A bike is a really good idea, Leo. Since papa isn't coming for a few days, I thought maybe we could rent one. What do you think? Leo hugs her hard, mashes his forehead against her belly button. Sometimes it's as if he's headbutting her. When he was smaller, it was her pubic bone he hit, and it hurt. But not now, now the boy's head lodges in a soft, spongy realm and he seems to want to sink in, just for a few seconds. Sofía squeezes him and strokes behind his ears, that skin as soft as the underside of a shell.

Early in the morning, too early, obviously, they went over to the bike rental place. It's close enough to the house, but in town, on the avenue that leads to the center. The first two buildings on that avenue, the ones next to the roundabout with the colorfully painted tree trunks, are ugly, unsettling. The bike shop is just past the second block. It's still closed. Sofía looks among the papers taped to the storefront for something to indicate the opening hours but finds nothing, just notices from women offering to clean, give classes, care for the elderly. Leo is impatient and Sofía's starting to feel impatient, too. She feels almost ridiculous there, holding her son's hand, their shorts and sweatshirts, the backpack packed with provisions, their ball caps. A fat woman walks past them, chewing gum. She's wearing a white T-shirt with a supermarket logo, and fuchsia leggings that hug her inner thighs, which chafe with each step, her ass flat and square. She doesn't bother to look at them, and steps into a café. Sofía sighs and decides to follow her, they can have something while they wait for the shop to open. The TV is on, repeating news and current events. Inside is hushed, as if the café's small number of customers were still asleep, or as if they'd never gone to bed. The espresso machine is deafening. The waiter chews on a toothpick. He doesn't smile. Sofía doesn't smile either. She orders two orange juices. Freshsqueezed, please. When the juice is served, Sofía takes away the sugar packets and spoons from the accompanying plates. If we drink quickly, we'll get all the good vitamins into our bodies lickety-split, let's go! But Leo only wets his lips; to him the juice looks infinite in its tall, tube-shaped glass, there's too much pulp, too many clots, they could have at least put it through a strainer. The orange pulp feels solid against his mouth, like insects are floating in the liquid. When does the bike shop open, mama? When you drink your juice.

The sky is cloudy when they exit back onto the street, the sense of sadness more acute. In the bike shop, a tall, young guy waits on them. Tattoos climb from the neck of his T-shirt, snailshaped whorls on his shorn neck. His thin, muscular arms also have markings. Leo looks at him in fascination. Sofía is unable to speak without being aware of her naked thighs, fuller now than when they arrived at her father's house and marked as well, with spider veins, and white, too white, though less white than a few weeks ago. She takes off her hat but puts it back on when she realizes her hair is sticking to her forehead. The guy smiles and speaks directly to Leo, what's up, dude, you want a bike? The decision turns out to be a difficult one. Leo wants a bike without training wheels because he already knows how to ride, but Sofía is very afraid of him being killed by a car or riding off the sidewalk and cracking his skull and insists on getting one with the training wheels on. Leo argues and says, but papa . . . Sofía has had enough and warns him that they won't get any bike if he starts to complain. The guy attempts to mediate but Sofía is mulish and not only does she rent a bike with training wheels for Leo but it's a double bike with a sort of trailer-hitch bar that will attach the boy's bike to her own, two bikes in one. She'll have to pedal harder to pull them both. Sofía fills out the paperwork and pays a deposit and like a clumsy walrus lets the young guy help her maneuver the bikes out the door, adjust Leo's helmet, get her up on the seat. The guy's sinewy hands test out the brakes, the gears, while she sits on the saddle. Sofía and Leo lurch into motion, wobbling away, making Ss on the sidewalk that leads to the municipal sporting complex. It's a wide sidewalk, at least. Sofía prays for the young guy to go back inside the shop but he's still out front, smoking a cigarette, still smiling with his broad teeth and inmate's gums. At the end of the street, Sofía doesn't turn toward the road to the beach, but instead passes behind the gas station, toward the river. Where are we going, mama? Leo shouts. You don't have to yell, I can hear you fine. We're not going to the beach, I want to show you somewhere else. Where, mama? You'll see.

It takes them a bit to get the hang of the two-headed bicycle. Sofía isn't in shape, her knees, their internal mechanism, miniature shards of glass. For the time being, the way is easy; a kind of lane runs alongside the avenue and they don't need to ride on the road with that heavy traffic to their left, nor the hard shoulder. The avenue serves as the entrance and exit to the town, encircling it from the port to the beach, and leading to the cemetery. The marsh is on their right, the swamp grass flush with water, phosphorescent green, the boats, dead, waiting for something, the floating pieces of trash, a sheen on the surface. Sofía pedals. Look at the boats, Leo. Mama, look, a park! he shouts. She sees a park in front of a giant supermarket. We could go some day! You don't have to yell, honey, I hear you.

Leo! I don't want you to miss this! It's the best part of this area, we're going to cross the bridge! And the miracle is performed. They manage to cross, turn right, and climb the bridge in concert with the stream of cars, and without endangering anybody's life. The dock opens up off one side of the bridge, timber boards opposite the canneries, the brightly colored fishing boats, their bellies swaying, almost on land, almost in unison. At the end of the bridge and past the gas station the little road stretches out to the salt flats, another refreshing scene, quadrangles of still water on either side, a Martian expanse of small mountains of salt. Bands of birds cut out against a now-blue sky. The sun casts a shadow on the asphalt, on Sofía's white legs that pedal forward until she finds an easy turn-off, one she takes handily, making a wide turn so that both bikes stay upright as they change direction, and now they're on the path perpendicular to the road that crosses the salt flats.

After another right turn, the narrow path ends at a small jetty where there's a white shack with a few signs tacked on the door. Sofía decides to continue on to it. She's miscalculated and now it's too hot, not a single shadow breaks up the marshes, divided into squares and marked by resistant walls built of stone and mud and supported by the salicornia, the succulent plants through which the stagnant water moves slowly, forming crystals. Finally, they reach the white shack at the end of the path, where the sign reads: FLOR DE SAL FOR SALE, ARTISANAL HARVEST. Come on, Leo, get down, take a rest. What are we going to do, mama? There's nothing here. Well, it's a special place and I wanted you to see it. But I want to ride bikes some more, we'll just see it and go, okay mama? Come on, Leo, get off the bike. From the shack, which is actually a solid construction with a high roof, a man emerges to greet them. He holds a can of beer in one hand and a cigarette in the other. Sofía notices his square-fingered hands first, but then she sees his dark face, black eyes under gray brows, marks on his burnt skin, and wide lips. His jeans conceal a pair of strong legs and his white T-shirt covers a nascent belly that Sofía imagines is mounded with coarse hair. The T-shirt also says FLOR DE SAL, like the sign. She parks the bikes beside the shack and takes out the water and a container of sliced melon. The man smokes beside them silently, too close, perhaps. The melon juice runs down Leo's hands, even his elbows are sticky. Sofía is paralyzed, she imagines the man has been drinking since morning and now there they are, so close, she expects a growl, a get-out-of-here. But he doesn't move, he doesn't speak. It's Leo who asks the man if he lives there on the salt marsh, mouth full of melon, unafraid. The man tosses the cigarette butt on the ground and drains the can of beer before crushing it between his thick fingers. Instead of answering the boy, he looks at the mother, her sweaty face, bright red, and tells her that his business is flor de sal. They are definitely too close because Sofía can smell the beer on his breath. What's flor de sal? Leo asks, and again the man answers without looking at him, tossing the words toward the mother, who looks at the ground and suddenly can't contain the urge to go to the bathroom. It's the first crystals to form on the water's surface. Like ice, Leo says. Flaky ice, yeah, we also call it salt ice, it's the salt crust above the water, the man says, and yawns. His teeth are white, the only real white thing, untamed teeth of a good animal. Come inside, if you want. Dutiful, Leo enters, unaware of his mother's motionless state. The man doesn't say another word but waits for Sofía to shift into gear, follows her inside. And though he doesn't touch her, it feels like a push.

Mother and son are absorbed by the cool air inside the shop: shelves laden with glass jars and plastic jars of varying sizes, flor de sal, salt flakes, virgin sea salt, spiced salt, salt with rose petals, thyme, lavender; at the back, a small counter with a cash register, brown wrapping paper, scissors. Sofía wants to buy it all, just so they can get out of there, fast; is the man being courteous, or is it an ambush? She roots around in her bag and realizes she hasn't brought much money. But the man from the salt flats mollifies her, don't worry, take what you want, you can bring me the money some other time, he says, still behind her, smelling of beer. Sofía is red, her bladder is about to burst. Mama, I'm still hungry, Leo says, and she's glad she can take a bag of rice crackers out of the backpack and hand them over to keep him quiet. Of course I'm not going to take anything without paying, I'll come back another day. No, the man insists, look, I'll give you this sample set. Come on Leo, finish up, we have to go. We'll come back and shop, but the man insists, take it, really. And take my card. I'm Tomás. The man holds out his hand before she can escape. I'm Sofía, and then her red, sweaty hand, a vibrating little frog, is swallowed up between his blunt fingers.

It's a long ride back. Pedalling is hard with this unexpected need to go to the bathroom, but Sofía doesn't stop, she's determined to get this all over with, return the bikes and drag Leo back home. When they've almost reached the bike shop, she has to stop to pee between two parked cars, in plain daylight, half-hidden behind a tree trunk. Leo can't believe it. Hypnotized, he watches the stream of his mother's urine, a volume of liquid that soaks the pavement, that spreads, and without a thought he pulls down his shorts and empties himself too, knees slightly bent, splattering his mother's feet, his mother who is pissing on the ground in the middle of the street in the middle of the day, her eyes half-closed.

IN THE MIDDLE OF the patio, under the new sun umbrella, Sofía sets the table with her sewing things: trace, measure, cut. Her hands are agile. One of her T-shirts sold in the shop on the promenade, bought, presumably, by a foreign tourist, and the owners have asked her for another one. At her feet, Leo plays with pieces of colorful plastic; he builds a crane, a wall. Neither one of them notices that Rita has come outside, dressed only in a high-waisted black bathing suit that cuts into her groin, and is watching them. Sofía is startled when Rita speaks, but Leo is unfazed. Are we going to go to the beach? Chalk in hand, Sofía smiles, safe inside her hard-won mother-son pairing. We'll go later, when it's not so hot. Don't you have to work? Rita doesn't reply, but turns and goes back inside the house, back inside her darkened room.

They drag themselves toward the beach later, quite late by then, when the sun is starting to go down. Only a few umbrellas remain on the sand. The morning heat has become a damp chill at sunset. Sofía, Leo, and Rita reach the shore in silence, their feet heavy from the long day, and sit down by the water's edge. Three silent figures, sitting on that stretch of semi-dry sand preceding the lapping tongue of the sea, where one can easily find shells, seaweed, crabs, and jellyfish. Leo doesn't feel like swimming, but he's the only one who gets his feet wet, as he builds castles with his plastic tools. Sofía watches the horizon with a sense of wholeness, as if all she needed was to trace a few lines on fabric, cut, thread the needle, take care not to prick herself, wear her thimble. She hasn't yet noticed that, beside her, her sister's eyes look shrunken, her brow furrowed. Want to take a walk? she asks, but Rita doesn't respond. Hey, she insists, and then she turns to look at Rita, laying her hand on her knee. Sofía almost never touches her sister, just like her sister almost never touches her, and suddenly the feeling of her hand on Rita's pointy knee hurts. Rita shifts her leg away slightly, and only two of Sofía's fingers remain on Rita's skin, two fingers with nails painted a pale pink. It's strange that Sofía has painted her nails, strange to have those fingers so close to her. I think I'll stay here, you guys go, Rita says. No, it's okay, I'll stay with you. You don't have to. Leo, sitting a few paces away, watches them but doesn't speak. He was about to ask them for something, offer them a shovel or rake to play with him, but he turns back around and continues his digging in silence. Sofía takes out her tobacco and lights a cigarette. By the way, they're coming to do the patio tomorrow, first thing in the morning. It'll be noisy and I don't know if you'll be able to work. She takes a drag of the cigarette, gripping it between her wet fingers, then offers the packet to Rita. Rita refuses with a lift of her chin and changes her position slightly. What? The patio? You know, they're going to take up the patio slabs, to make the flower beds, get them ready to plant in. Ah, so you're still on about that, are you? What do you mean, I'm still on about it? We agreed about this, Rita. It'll just take a couple of hours and then we'll put down new soil and rake it in and everything. I think it's going to come out really nice and Leo is excited to have a garden. Rita doesn't look at her, but retorts: Leo is going to have less space to play when you pull up the patio. Sofía stubs out the half-smoked cigarette in the sand and places the filter in a plastic bag. Look, Rita, I don't know what's going on with you, but I really can't stand it when you get all negative and reactionary like papa. Reactionary, Rita scoffs. Both sisters have buried their feet in the cold sand. Well, who's coming? A couple of bricklayers I found. How do you know them? Did you ask some of the neighbors? No, a friend gave me their number. A friend? Now Rita looks amused. You have a friend around here? It's a guy I met a few days ago, when I took Leo out to the salt marsh. Rita stretches, reaching her arms up straight and cracking her back. Well, that changes things. Now I get it. What do you get? Sofía has decided to stand up to her sister, look her in the eye; from her position of recently acquired calm, she can make out the black dot of the approaching collision. Rita looks back at her with mocking eyes. Let's see: the painted nails, the patterns, the whole day with Leo and no squabbling, now I get it—there's a guy. God, Rita, when you're like this, you're the worst; I was starting to wonder how you'd been so pleasant so many days in a row. I don't know what's up with you, but we haven't done anything for you to attack us like this. Rita laughs again. Hey, don't bring Leo into this. I'm not attacking Leo. Sofía doesn't know what to say. A cold front strikes her all of a sudden, this is the nature of family conflict: without preamble, one passes from nonsense to suffering, to sadness. But Sofía holds out, as does Rita. Sofía doesn't want her voice to break nor does she want to behave dramatically. It wouldn't be rational to grab Leo by the hand and bring him home, shut herself up in one of the bedrooms. She must sustain this fragility, march it through time, destroy it. Leo has gotten up and doesn't hear them, he's in the water, filling the pail and emptying it out, shattering the dark surface of the sea. Well, I guess I just need to get out of here. I feel like I'm in a cage, I'm not doing anything. Rita's voice, at least, is a capitulation. Sofía sighs; they've released it. You should go home if you want to. The sea is muffled. They can hardly hear it, they're inside it, the sound of the sea. Its healing effect has no power on them. No, that's not it, it's not a big deal, Rita says, jutting her chin, conquering something. They go quiet.

Slowly night falls over the three lonely figures on the beach, shapes barely visible by the water. They are skirted by an occasional, solitary jogger, or a couple of retired expats returning to their hotel where they'll drink cava, drink cava again for breakfast, lounge in wicker sun chairs. The sea pulls away from them, too, retracting, exposing the flat sands of low tide.

THE NOISE IS ATROCIOUS. A sound of buildings crashing down or a dinosaur's giant skull, the hard skull of an old Titanosaurus, starved dead, the infinite neck, infinite backbone of the largest animal on Earth. Leo goes in and out of the house with excitement, covering his ears with his hands and hopping around, as if the noise burned his feet. He's having fun. The disaster of the perforated terrace cement is an excess of life, a glut, a celebration. He shouts and laughs and brings his hands to his ears and removes them again, letting the noise in and out, muffling it and letting it explode. And when the machine isn't in use and there are a few seconds of rest, he observes the man and imitates him: his arms in the same position, holding the jackhammer between his legs. I want this job when I grow up, mama. And his mama rolls her eyes.

Two men knocked on the door very early that morning. One, a local, short in stature, with a square head who didn't know how to pull his lips into a smile, and another man, younger and foreign. The man with the square head was the boss and he didn't come to work but to drop off the young man, responsible for putting holes in the cement floor, destroying it with his jackhammer, a kind of infernal handheld blender, a galactic awl for killing giants. Sofía met them nervously, she had everything prepared, as if they were going to break ground on a palace, as if they were going to demolish the walls and bring the house down. She got up at dawn and made lemonade, a couple of pitchers of it, and a few small canapés with cream cheese, which she will store in the fridge until the end of the workday. She knows the bread will get soggy, but she can't risk the ants getting to them. She waged a battle against them last night, hand-to-hand combat, while the others slept. Anxious about the start of the job, she got up in the middle of the night for a drink of water and to use the bathroom, and in the kitchen found the typical distorted map of black feet and antennae in motion. Rita had left a plate with bits of food on out on the counter. She'd been the last one to go to bed. Sofía cursed her, had to resist the urge to wake her up and tell her off. The result of all this is that Sofía slept poorly; when she got up, she had bags under her eyes and two seam-like creases that ran from her nose to the corner of her mouth. Her face is starting to reveal paths, topographies, betrayals. For the first time since she arrived at the beach, she regrets being so fair. She even considers changing her sunscreen from 50 to 30 SPF. Maybe then her cheeks can claim blood, a pulse.

The foreigner works without rest, without glancing at the sky or hearing his client's offers of a glass of lemonade, some cold water, without concern for the little boy who leaps around him; he only reacts, and even then it's only sometimes, when a fly lands on his face, near his focused green eyes, almost phosphorescent in the middle of that terracotta skin, or on the flared part of his nose doused in crystallized sweat that most likely tastes like the water used to cook shrimp. The foreigner makes hellish noise, torrential noise, and in very little time he destroys the patio's cement foundation with his hammer drill, the rectangle Sofía showed him first thing in the morning, which he subsequently marked with a thick pencil. Around him explode ceramic tiles in ruins, flying, shards of the past, it's so easy to make them disappear, as if it were dinnerware made of fine crystal. Under the tiles, a thin layer of concrete is also vanishing in turn. The foreigner grips the hammer ably, that galactic-style weapon, and gives it to the ground, hard. His arms swell. But there is peace on his face, it seems it doesn't require more effort than the concentration in his eyes and the sweat that gently coats him; a mother's hankie, freshly ironed and imbued with lavender or thyme, would lovingly wipe that prawny water that shines on the foreigner's forehead, on his cleft chin, the tip of his straight nose, his heavy eyelids, fanned lashes.

The foreigner doesn't blink when another woman comes out from the house, frowning and shouldering a backpack. That other woman looks like she slept badly, her eyes are puffy, she looks like she woke up to the sound of the foreigner's arms of destruction, like she jumped out of bed and shouted at somebody. She looks like she's escaping. She leaves the house and walks across the patio without a word to him, clumsily opens the door of a car parked on the street just outside the front gate, gets into it, starts the engine, and leaves. In any case, the foreigner hasn't looked at her because his eyes are trained on the gray dirt that appears at his feet, the cement bloodspray of the tile, which allows itself to be perforated without resistance, to come apart, like an expensive crystal goblet, like a cornea.

By mid-morning, the foreigner has already lifted most of the rectangle. The terrace is now a mess of scraps and waste, like a meteor has crashed next to the house. The torn-up section occupies the area along the side of the house, from the back corner, where there was already a small square of dirt, to almost halfway along the front porch. It stops a few meters before the fence at the entrance; Sofía wants to keep the pavement there and put up a plastic swing for Leo. The table and chairs, with the new sun umbrella, will remain near the front door, where they've always been. Disconcerted, Sofía observes the result. She still can't quite grasp the image of what will come next, a kind of garden she imagines as leafy green, the part in the back dedicated to a vegetable patch where she'll grow lettuce and tomatoes. Chunks of broken tiles and ashy dust are scattered across the entire porch. She has stepped outside with a tray carrying a pitcher of lemonade, three cups, and a plate of soggy canapés. Leo's face is covered in white dust, and although his mother has insisted several times that he go inside to watch a show—but I can't hear the TV, mama—or look at a book or play construction—I'm bored inside, mama—he is determined to supervise the foreigner's labor up-close. At least put on a hat, it's hot out today. The foreigner doesn't wear a hat, or bandana, or anything, his hair, curly and almost blond, shines in the distorted midday light. His neck is dark stone. The foreigner hardly speaks any Spanish. Do you want some lemonade? Please, take a break, you've almost finished; and finally, he accepts. Sofía sets the provisions out on the table, playing lady of the house, quenching the workman's thirst. Do you want to sit down? But of course the foreigner doesn't want to sit down, he just drinks the lemonade down in one gulp, a green mint leaf sticks to lips like an insect, he drags it into his mouth with his teeth, then chews and swallows it. Where are you from? Sofía watches him, a little stupefied, like she's never spoken to a laborer before, like she's never quenched a young man's thirst.

She's nervous because she is suddenly terrified of the nuclear disaster she's going to have to fix up on her own, terrified that the guy, once he's destroyed the last line of tile, will collect his weapons and go back where he came from. She fills his glass again and encourages Leo to drink his as well, but I don't like it, mama, it's spicy, I want juice, or a chocolate milkshake. Where are you from? she repeats, fearing suddenly that the foreigner is mute, that he is never going to speak. The young guy opens his mouth and replies with the voice of a flute, a strange voice for a laborer: Romania. And you don't speak Spanish yet? A little. Sofía hopes that little will be enough for him to understand that he has to help her clean up all this mess—only now does she think about how Leo could cut himself on the sharp corners of the tiles. She picks up the plate of canapés and moves it closer to the foreigner, who refuses at first, and then, perhaps fearing the woman's anxious gaze, takes the plate in his hard, dirty hands as if it were all for him. Can I borrow the tool? Leo asks his hero three times in quick succession, his little head tilted upward, pupils glinting. Can I borrow the tool? The foreigner looks at him uncomprehendingly, holding the plate in his hands, and it's Sofía who has to dissuade the child, scold him. Leo, that's a machine for doing work, it's not a toy to play with. But I won't break it! If he shows me how, I can make that noise! Leo, the machine is as big as you are, honey, Sofía says more gently, impatient to end the situation, the job, the debris, impatient to see the lemon tree and daisies and geraniums growing. The foreigner puts the plate down on the table; he hasn't taken a single canapé. Can I . . . bathroom? he asks. Sofía leads him to the bathroom and watches as he disappears, closes the door, and she stands there, imagining the man lifting the lid, taking his thing out and peeing, but there's no sound, she doesn't hear the sound of the lid hitting the tank, or the stream of urine, just silence, and for too long, and while she's on the verge of putting her hand to the door handle, on the verge of doing something, she doesn't realize that in the meantime Leo has moved close to the hammer, eyeing it with desire, touching it, the hammer boiling from the morning's hard labor, he strokes its motorcycle-like handlebar, yet doesn't dare put his finger on the sharp Titanosaurus-skull-destroying tip. Meanwhile, through the bathroom door, Sofía hears water running from the sink faucet, the foreigner must be washing his hands before he pees, and Sofía relaxes, okay, now, now she hears the lid lifting, now the world is predictable again, a powerful stream falls with an exquisite sound, a benevolent liquid tasting of lemonade, of exhaustion. Leo places a finger on the boiling metal, on the hammer's tip, and burns himself. The hammer is alive and it is fire. He stifles his cry and wraps his singed finger in the fabric of his T-shirt. He hides. When the foreigner comes out of the bathroom, he almost collides with Sofía: she's still standing there, arms limp at her sides, milky flesh of her shoulders. And her face, red with embarrassment, bagless, seamless.

Leo is speaking to his father on the phone. He leans on the railing and looks out toward the street. He grips the phone with two hands while also pressing it with his head tilted to one side, squeezed against his shoulder, holding the phone with pretty much his entire body. He's telling him that he saw a wrecking hammer and would love to have one. Then come the distracted monosyllables, which tend to correspond to a thread of questions about his well-being: Are you okay? How's mama? Are you eating well? Sleeping well? Sleeping alone? Are you getting exercise, swimming at the beach? Do you want to see me? Once they've been speaking for about five minutes, one of them gets bored or sad and they hang up, consciences clean. Leo hands the phone to his mother, who is sitting on the front steps, smoking, and drinking the last cup of lemonade. Can I watch TV now? Okay, for a little while. We'll have dinner soon. Leo runs inside and Sofía shouts after him: You need a bath! Your hair is all dusty! The truth is, though, that she would like it if there was nothing else to do that day, if the boy would fall asleep without dinner, watching TV on the couch, if she could also go to bed like that, toes white with cement dust, sweat stuck to her armpits, her neck. She observes the foreigner's work and feels relieved. When he had finished smashing all the tiles and their corresponding layer of cement, careful not to break anything that didn't need to be broken, the foreigner had taken a shovel and a few sacks out from among his tools and had skilfully gone about picking up the wreckage, removing it from the hard, grayish earth that now receives the light. Afterward, he asked her for a broom, and swept. Just as he was finishing, the boss arrived with the van. They packed up and left. It had all been so fast. The next day, the kid will make a small border to mark the plot and turn the soil in order to be able to start planting. All very simple. Soon, she will have something to keep her busy for real.

She holds the phone Leo handed her when he ran inside to turn on the TV. She looks at it, searching for some sign of life inside. She needs to get dinner started and run the bath, but she lights another cigarette, looks for a number in her contacts, and calls. That voice, dark and inviting, answers immediately. She turns red just hearing it in her ear. I just called to say that everything went really well. To thank you for the recommendation. The man speaks and she smiles, she doesn't really know what else to tell him. He asks when they're going to see each other again and she proves indecisive. They don't make any plans. We'll talk soon, she says by way of goodbye. Talk soon, he repeats. Typically absurd conversation that makes her happy, a typical nothing. Nothing; but she is stirred. Then she calls her sister, who doesn't answer the first time. Out of inertia, she repeats the call, twice more, and, on the third try, Rita finally picks up. Where are you, are you coming for dinner? I'm at home, Sofía. At home? You went home? Rita is quiet. Suddenly, Sofía's ear burns where the phone presses against it. She changes sides. Like magic, the cigarette has gone out. Her throat burns as well. But what's wrong? Why did you leave? You're not coming back? She is raising her voice, the tone somewhere between longing and a plea. Rita speaks as though from very far away: I'm sick of being there. Is it because of the garden? It must be, Sofía says. The garden, her patterns, the salt guy, their father's house, her break up, nothing is in its right place, really, and her feet are swollen, to boot. After a few seconds, Rita laughs, maybe she can hear her sister's volcanic breathing. It's not about the garden. Fuck, it's about everything. When have we ever been good at living together? But it's just that now . . . Leo . . . What about Leo? Leo is your kid and you know perfectly well how to take care of him. It's her little sister's hardened voice, a violent bird swooping in, sharp beak striking rock, rumpled feathers, it whizzes by, grazing her temple. You're leaving us by ourselves. Fucking hell, Sofía. You are so alarmist; I can't stand you. Sofía doesn't want to cry because she knows it will make things worse but she does cry in the end, and while she expects Rita to hang up or shout at her, that doesn't happen. Maybe Rita's stoned and that's why she sounds so far away, why she's speaking so slowly. Maybe she's with somebody and is acting tough. Sofía, I'll call you soon. And Christ, don't cry, it's not a big deal.

Sofía lights another cigarette. She has to make dinner, fill the tub, sing a song, rub her son's back, clean the sand from behind his ears. A pair of dead flies lie at her feet, defeated by the day's long flapping of wings.

IT WAS A SUMMER EVENING, after the siesta. Maybe it was already nighttime? The four of us in our grandparents' living room. Our summer home for all those years. Not ours, exactly, we didn't own it, but it belonged to our grandparents and they were the axis around which our lives turned. Our grandparents radiated a certain something—an amalgam of play and obligation, love and household logistics—that gathered their tribe close, pulled us into their orbit to be projected through them. Maternal grandparents, the most natural and potent symbol of a family's love. The four of us were in the living room, spread out across armchairs and sofas covered in a fake satin that was always slipping off. There were no grown-ups. No grandparents, no aunts or uncles, no mothers or fathers. Just the two boys, and us. That there were no grown-ups is a manner of speaking, because the oldest boy was quite old by then. I don't remember his exact age, but I suppose I could guess. It doesn't matter. He was big, tall, really tall, dark-skinned, with a sort of long, bulbous face. A teenager, all grown up. I don't remember what we were playing, probably nothing. Was it late in the evening? Was it already night? There was a sort of peace among us, a result of the condescension that arose whenever they deigned to share time and space with us by choice. I think the younger brother, also older than us, was sitting on the floor, leaning against the low table like he was leaning on a bar, the same indolence, the same watchful tension. That half-smile on his face with its hard, straight features. He was fairer-skinned, though his hair was darker. I suppose I was hanging around somewhere, excited by the truce, this peacetime. Waiting for action too, waiting for them to carry us away, since they held the reins. The time had come for them to love us, which wasn't always the case. Now we had to let them love us, play with us. The four of us were all there and everything was fine. They're our family, they'll protect us, teach us about life, now that they aren't shouting and teasing. The oldest, almost a man, picked my sister up. My sister, that skinny little animal with straight black hair, hair like a waterfall, like silk. My sister, who must have weighed no more than thirty pounds. What's thirty pounds to a teenager? How old would she have been? Three, four? The oldest picked her up, his little cousin, his toy. I watched from below. My sister was a doll in the arms of a giant, who lifted her affectionately in the air. The little brother watched from his sharpshooter's position. He might as well have had a toothpick in his mouth or been wearing a cowboy hat; he liked destroying toothpicks with his sharp, pointy teeth. My sister's little arms and legs— have I said this before?—were very thin. She had been so small. Was there trust in her eyes? Was she smiling? Of course she was trusting, of course she was smiling, when after a few cuddles the oldest began to toss her in the air. All children like to be tossed, all children laugh when you throw them in the air and catch them, toss them again. And so my sister was flying, propelled by the arms of our oldest cousin, the firstborn, the first grandchild, the first nephew, our big cousin who was in a good mood and laughed, open-mouthed, as my sister flew up and down, the fabric of her clothes waving in the heavy air of the summer house. Was she wearing purple? Aqua? A little dress? Shorts and a bright, '90s T-shirt? My sister was flying like all small children fly in the arms of someone stronger: higher, higher each time, and she was laughing, and maybe at some point she felt like it was time to stop, that it was enough, maybe she was even starting to feel sick, I don't know, I don't remember her face rising and falling in the air, but I do remember her body perfectly, her lithe animality, high up, abandoned by us below, rising rhythmically, the circus strongman didn't tire. I think his brother broke into a fit of laughter, kind of nasty; I suppose we all were laughing, watching the show, my sister flying, flying until her little head rose so high that she hit the ceiling, boom, hard, violent, boom, my sister's three-, four-year-old skull hitting the ceiling, he'd thrown her so high, and then *cut,* end of scene, and she cries, but in shock, not drama, she cries in fear, she doesn't understand, and he scoops her abruptly in his arms, his laughter is a confident, what-did-you-think-would-happen laughter, a this-is-even-more-fun laughter, and suddenly his brother catches on, suddenly what's funny is that my sister has smashed her head against the ceiling, suddenly all that came before was to this end, the playing, the kindness, the hours spent among cousins, none of it made any sense without this prize, the four-year-old's head hitting the ceiling, boom, hurts doesn't it, and the younger brother laughs louder, and the oldest laughs louder, a singsong don't-cry-it-wasn't-that-bad, and he leaves my sister on the floor, a scrap, debris, her little arms and legs, her hands on her head, the tears I imagine were on her cheeks, and still they laugh, and I laugh, too, because that's life, it's not a big deal, I laugh in fear but I laugh with them, anxious, false, and I don't hug my sister, and I don't know now what else happened, only that I laughed too, like an idiot, me, the traitor, me.

JULIO. SORRY, I KNOW it's a little late. No, Leo's fine, he's asleep. Is someone there? No, no, just wanted to know if you can talk. You're tired? What are you watching? Forget it, it's okay. We can talk tomorrow. You sound . . . Well, okay. I don't know. No, I'm not okay. My sister left a few days ago. What do you mean, you already know? Have you talked to her? Did she call you? Oh, you called her . . . Oh, I don't know. She left because we weren't doing well, or she wasn't doing well. I mean, I thought she was okay, but then she started with her weird shit, closed right up, I don't know, I think we were too loud and she couldn't work, but it wasn't such a big deal, just the day they came to take up the tiles outside, that was the day she left, but I thought we were okay, she had been really quiet for a few days and hadn't been taking Leo to the beach or into town . . . No, no that's not why I want her here, I'm just saying that we hadn't been fighting. But what did she tell you? Do you know why she left? Why did you talk with her? No, Julio, I'm not trying to control your life or hers. Yeah, I'm sure she did feel like going home for a bit, I'm not exactly the life and soul of the party right now but . . . the truth is, I don't really want to be alone with Leo. I know I left, what was I going to do, stay there, at home, while you fucked whoever you wanted in that shitty hotel? No, I'm fine for money, that's not why I called you. Julio, I told you, Leo's good. Yeah, I know, my family's never really sat well with me, or with her, either. There's like this fly infestation. Ants, too. I'm not exaggerating, it's fucking awful, there are tons out during the day. I can't be down at the beach all the time either, you know I can't tolerate the sun. Oh, okay, so that's ridiculous, everything I say is ridiculous. You're tired and you don't give a shit about this, right? No, I absolutely don't want you to come and get Leo earlier, I want you to come when we agreed. It's just that my sister left and I'm worried about her, about her and about me and Leo. I am not criticising you! Well, yes, of course I could call her, that's what I should do instead of calling you. No, I haven't tried again, but she hasn't called me either. I don't know, Julio. Maybe you could come and see us. Oh, that doesn't sound like a good idea to you? You're tied up, sure. Busy. Don't you want to see your son? You haven't seen him in weeks. I brought him here because you moved out. Fucking awesome. Oh, it's me you don't want to see? Of course, because now I'm the one who fucked up your life. What did my sister tell you? Why did she call you? Or why did you call her? You don't need to talk to her about Leo, you need to talk to me, or to Leo himself. In this state? What state? I'm not taking too many pills, fuck you, those pills don't do anything. Go to hell, Julio, I don't want you to come, I don't know why I called you. Oh, oh, it's normal that I feel alone, it's what I deserve, I don't even know how to be alone with my kid, yeah, sure, that's what's going on. I don't know how to be alone with my kid. No, I didn't say that. I didn't say that! You're a bastard, Julio. A real asshole.

Leo exits the water trembling, his thin lips a shade of purple, his body slick with sea-film. He runs toward his mother and hugs her, arms around her hips. Sofía holds stoically still and struggles not to push away the cold, wet child, who encircles her and gets her wet and cold, too, when she is warm and dry and slathered with sunscreen, her bikini bunching at the groin. She puts her dry hands on his shoulders as he shivers and rubs against her, then she guides him over to the sun umbrella, wraps him in a towel, forces him to sit on the beach chair so he doesn't get all sandy again, takes a container of cherries out of a bag, offers them to the boy, puts one directly in his mouth, careful with the pit; the cherry flesh dyes her fingers, stains them, so much so it seems permanent, the boy's mouth is still purple, not from cold but cherry juice, the boy spits out the pit and his mother picks it up, its warm and tattered shred of fruit, I want French fries, but the mother feeds him another cherry. French fries, mama. And mauve saliva drips down his chin, and it's the boy who takes his hand out from the towel and wipes it away; look, blood. Beneath the umbrella to their right sits an elderly couple doing the crossword, nestled in their two chairs in the shade. They're the next-door neighbors, brown as coconuts, skin like cracked, dry earth that makes Sofía think of the sun at the dawn of time. The old man looks at them and smiles, the water is nice today, isn't it? His dentures shift a little toward the side of his mouth. He wears a hat, even though he's under the umbrella. The woman maintains her backcombed hair intact, surely she sleeps with a hair net, she never wets her hair in the sea. Leo smiles back because the neighbors have a small pool in their yard, and he would love it if they would let him swim there in the evenings, when it's hot and his mother makes patterns and cooks seeds and steams vegetables and doesn't want to go out, she won't take him to the beach and he doesn't even have a bike or anything and only has that patch of fertilized soil that's replaced the patio to play on, the furrows, the seedlings, everything he mustn't touch, mustn't ruin the plantings. He looks for worms. He makes fly traps, an easy catch, then when they're dead he puts them in a jar. He would love to swim in the neighbors' pool because the neighbors almost never use it, just the old man, who sometimes does a couple of laps then sits dripping on the edge, drying his face and pate vigorously with a towel, his little boob-pouches moving to the rhythm of his arms.

Sofía does not want to socialize with the neighbors. She tells

Leo that she's known them since she was little and they're a couple of gossips. She replies with a monosyllable and instead of smiling, shapes her mouth into a taut straight line and cranes her neck, then zealously busies herself with her son. I don't have French fries, Leo. She says this softly, but very seriously, so the neighbors don't hear that he wants French fries and that she won't give them to him, because then, as soon as the man comes by with the prawn-and-French-fry cart, the old man will get up and buy the boy two paper cones with a single coin. But the old man says nothing about the fries: Are you going to the carnival today, Leo? Are you going to ride some rides? Leo looks at his mother very intensely, eyes opened wide in shock, in please please please mama, and Sofía turns to the old couple now and she smiles with her whole mouth, stretching her lips wide, lips dry from the heat, cherry bloodstains on her teeth, eyes smarting from sunscreen and sweat, disgust with the beach at midday now that the temperature has risen, and the old lady lifts her eyes from the crossword which has to be nothing more than a simple word search and in her shaky, solitary old-lady voice says the fair isn't what it used to be. But the children always enjoy themselves, you have to bring the children to the fair, and now she looks at the sea, perhaps some specific point on the shoreline, blurry from the effort of finding lines of words on the gray, dirty, newsprint. Children are the only ones who enjoy themselves, well, and the drunks, I suppose. The old man nods, his head bobbing like it's elastic, he's been nodding his head the whole time. Mama, Leo says, mama, quietly at first, then a little louder, mama, and old man repeats, eh, tough guy, you gonna go to the fair today?

The festooned streets aren't the same ones from her childhood. These days, the fairground has spread toward a giant, treeless park near the beach, behind the town center. Sofía walks between the stalls, games, and rides as if walking down a hall of distorting mirrors. The strobe lights, the absolute scandal of speakers blaring, the agglomeration, the swarm of people, inconsiderate and proud. When she was a girl, the town's summer fair was held only on a few streets, on the avenue behind the town hall, where, in an old and restrained park, the bumper cars, pirate ship, and small Ferris wheel were set up. Cotton candy, churros, and chocolate, trucks that turned into mobile carnival games, the voice of the barker trumpeting the plush toy prizes, ripe for the winning. Was all that not more accessible? She has changed so much since then. She isn't a fraternal creature, she doesn't have a tolerant social consciousness, she doesn't know how to have fun. She clutches Leo's hand as if clinging to a cross; deep down, it is in fact a kind of penitence she's performing. When did she last take Leo to a fair? Is it possible she never has? What does Julio think of this commotion that repulses her, this arrogant tawdriness, which the town has arranged for the hoi polloi? What could be simpler than celebrating your town's annual festivities, getting all dolled up in your summer finest, spending money hand over fist, worshiping a holy Virgin who arrives by sea, climbing a greased pole and snatching a prize from the jaws of the horde? It's an instinct like any other. The people must be given their fun on occasion, fattened up, gotten drunk, encrusted in their finest clothes. Leo observes it all with the same radical enthusiasm with which he watched the jackhammer. It would seem that her calm child, her easygoing, polite child, is not bothered by the noise. Instead, it generates a kind of hyperactivity in him, an atavistic frenzy. She is saddened, and unable to normalize the sentiment: her son is a normal child who likes a ruckus. Like all children.

She walks among the people, her eyes open wider than need be, her nose stuffed up by the burnt sugar in the air, smoke from glaring light bulbs ready to burst, heat emitted by generators running on gasoline. At what point did a town fair lose its romanticism? She recalls a few teenage dances in the plaza, moving to the beat of a simple orchestra. But this thing right here seems like the hysterical construction of the province's longing. The other families stroll past Sofía and Leo as if in a different dimension, a different time, another gravitational awareness: they are fairground roosters leading their tribes. Heavy jewels sparkle at their throats, giant hoop rings in their ears, the line defining their eyes extends all the way to their temples and white is the predominant color on their brand-new outfits (with studs, lace, fringe), contrasting with skin well-loved by the sun, with hard flesh, soft flesh. And the noise. And the dark faces that guffaw, the men drinking at the stalls, the homogenisation of pleasure, of recreation, plastic plates laden with chunks of marinated meat, white prawns piled on trays, groups of people devouring fried food. Everyone around them laughs. Jeers. They greet each other as if they've never seen one another before. As if they had been living in a cave until that very day, the Feast of Our Patron Saint, the holy festival compulsory for both rich and poor.

Leo points to the lights flashing at the back of the fairground, the zigzagging colors of the carnival rides. Bumper cars! Can I, mama? Can I ride them? Sofía tugs firmly on the boy's hand, pulling him to her side. She's about to scold him, but scold him for what? For being just another hedonist? We're almost there, she says, her private Way of the Cross is nearly over, and as she speaks a couple of heavy-metal teens run past and one of them knocks into her right shoulder and pushes her. She loses her balance and stupidly falls down, and since she's holding Leo's hand too intensely and in an odd position, squeezing not his hand but his whole arm against her lap, the boy falls as well; she scrapes her knee on the curb, she's hurt but Leo is fine, his small bones smack the pavement, but only for an instant, hardly a second, a bounce that causes him to separate from his mother and jump up, and in a flash he's vertical again, but he doesn't say, like he always does when he falls on his own, following some imprudence or other, he doesn't say, I'm okay, mama, I didn't hurt myself, he doesn't say anything, he looks at his mother with mistrust, he seems to take a few steps away from her, as if to observe her with critical distance, with the hint of an emotional rebuke, his mother, red cheeks, puckered lips, a little fatter, a little sturdier, kneeling on one leg and holding her other knee, the injured one, glancing around wide-eyed, either looking for somebody or making sure that no one is watching. People walk past her, women push strollers, men push strollers for this one day, pushing too-big kids, wearing too-big bows, with studs, with lace, with fringe, kids lulled to sleep by the fair, sated by spins and screams and sticky junk. From her position on the ground, Sofía sees so many of them; suddenly it seems to her that it's all strollers, strollers and kids, and among them an odd young couple, the girl in a red dress that accentuates her hips and breasts, that barely covers her groin, the guy with spiked hair, a white T-shirt chiselling his biceps and back muscles, wearing long trousers and sandals with too-thick soles, this young couple slipping through the throng, the smug look of having just fucked. Leo looks at his mother from a prudent distance, and behind her is the shooting gallery, the Shooting Range it's called, he can't read the sign but he can see how a father hugs his son from behind, helping him aim the rifle at the target, a line of florescent stuffed animals hanging strangled above their heads; the booth owner is an extremely fat man in a giant cotton T-shirt washed a million times and his gaze is set on someplace beyond the edge of the world. Leo wishes he was that boy, the boy who shoots and trembles from the kickback, knocking against the body of his father, who protects him. Sofía finally stands up, wobbles, regains control, the abominable reggaeton deafens her, she grabs Leo again, drags him on ignoring his pleas, I want to shoot, mama, in the deepest part of her she feels that he isn't hers. No, we're getting something to eat, I'm dying of thirst, come on, and bravely she directs him toward the esplanade where the food and drink stalls are assembled and a man in a pink shirt and white pants obstinately sings a pasodoble—so apparently they still dance pasodobles at fairs. Four or five old couples hold each other on the dancefloor, a few small children spin in circles. Sofía sits at the first empty table. Beside her, Leo is angry and crying, he doesn't make a sound but his eyes are flooded. Pellejitos de atún, marinated dogfish, cuttlefish meatballs, hamburgers.

Sofía is soothed by the sangria, she manages to calm Leo with an orange soda, serotonin-boosting refined sugar. After her fall, she'd been on the verge of taking an extra anti-anxiety pill, but ultimately she decided to hold off, it's fine, she repeats to herself. Just in case, while Leo fiercely chews a hot dog and she pushes around a few worse-for-wear French fries, she writes a message, *I'm at the fair*, and that's it, nothing more, that should be enough, it could be interpreted as a cry for help or as a simple suggestion, hey, man from the salt marsh, I'm at the fair, I came to have a good time, I'm scared to death, I'm bored to death, come, please, get me out of here. Afterward, it's difficult not to check her phone every five minutes. She agrees to let Leo go on a ride, she knows it will be impossible to get him out of there without something in exchange. She decides on a kind of ball pit, installed, as is almost everything, in a trailer. It doesn't spin and so her son has fewer chances of flying out or getting electrocuted. Inside the attraction, Leo has a whale of a time; he climbs, slides, trips, falls, laughs, forgets all about the shooting gallery. Next to the ball pit is the Witch's Train and Sofía makes a maternal gaffe by getting on it with Leo. When they're moving, she is stiff and alarmed by the feinted blows from the witch's broom and the sudden darkness, embarrassed as they finish the first loop and inch out of the dark, passing the ride's entrance before chugging into the darkness again. In the respite, she'd searched the crowd for the man from the salt marsh, who knows, maybe he was waiting for her, he'd come to find her, he knows they're here without her having told him, on the haunted train. Leo grabs his mother's waist as he shouts with joy, he lets go and raises his arms to defend himself from the witch's broom. He can't stop laughing. For a few seconds, Sofía is able to forget everything, and looking at Leo's smiling face, his wide eyes, his little white teeth gleaming between wet lips, at the wonder of a five-year-old's face when he can't stop laughing, when nothing exists but laughter, that natural gratitude children emanate when they laugh, when they're happy, a kind of surrender to the flammable material of happiness, for a few seconds, she sees him and pulls him close and it seems that the world clicks brusquely back into place, that she's regained normalcy, that everything's fine, she's not alone, she's not going to die, she's not going to suffer a seizure, leaving her son traumatized, her sister hasn't left, and her husband hasn't moved out, or if that is what's happened then it's totally fine, it doesn't matter. For a second she is able to catch her son's simple, palpable joy and gulp it down like an antidote to indifference, like motherhood's only reward.

On their way home, they cross the fairground and take the road that leads from the park to the beach. Right at the end, where the crowds thin out and only a few people remain, Sofía recognizes him. His back is to her, he's walking away, toward the fair. He hasn't seen her. It's him, his broad neck, a dark shirt with the sleeves rolled up, and his strong arms, the dark hair on his strong arms. One of them, the left arm, encircles a woman's waist. A small woman with a simple green flowered dress and dyed-blonde hair. A slender, fragile woman who still has something of a teenage gait. His wife, Sofía supposes, the man from the salt marsh's wife. A woman she knew nothing about, because maybe there was nothing for her to know, because wife or no wife there is no stopping the collision between two people when it happens, especially when that collision is no more significant than sweat, than the tremulous heat of a mouth at sunset, the clumsy thrust of a pelvis, the rest is a fantasy. Sofía's stomach turns. The burn rises in her throat, almost reaches her mouth, and she attempts to swallow it back down, reduce the flame.

They walk where the crowd thins out. They can still hear the carnival, the distant drums. But that sound begins to blend with another, because before them, across the large empty expanse of the concrete park by the dunes, a new reality opens. It's another party, another devastation. The trunks of the cars are open, the doors, the kids inside and out, sitting in the seats, on the hoods, strewn over the sidewalks where ice-filled plastic bags, glass bottles, two-liter sodas are also strewn. Close-shaved heads, eyes swollen with life, with thorns, defiant. The cars are not merely means of transport. They are machines from another galaxy, customized spaceships, powerful speakers, earthquakes of sound, of electronic beats, scratches—a musical dystopia. Sofía is no stranger to EDM, to designer drugs. But this makes her uneasy. Aren't all those kids under twenty? Could those girls be any older than sixteen, fifteen? So many people, so many cars, such an explosion? How much money does it cost to soup up those wheels, those trunks, all of it? Leo is tired but he opens his eyes wide because the spectacle really is a sight to behold. This time, Sofía isn't afraid. She decides to pass through those woods, cross the future with her son. She doesn't know who is more of a zombie, the kids with the pupil-moons or the two of them, dragging their feet toward her father's house.

MY SON IS PLAYING alone on the razed patio since sunup. I'm reading a book or two, but I'm not reading much because my mind is high and blurry, somewhere up above in the high, blurry summer sky. My son asks, do you want to play with me, and I always say wait a minute, wait a minute I'm doing something, wait your whole childhood because I can't just now, I can't. I wish I could but I can't. Suddenly, I'm this mother and it's why I pull myself up off the ground each morning, and then spend the whole day trying to distract myself from the facts: my husband's desertion, my sister, the death of my father, my mother's escape, my own abandonment. What do I have to offer him, Leo, the only person who is always with me, the only one who really needs me? What was I doing all of those years, what tools do I have to build his world? What can I offer him, this bored child, this resourceful child, this child? What path can I forge for him in this life? It wasn't me who left, but now I am the one responsible. In the end, it doesn't matter who planted their flag in which territory, who was the one to twist the knife, that final, brave thrust, or who flipped the card lying on the table for half a lifetime, dark as a promise, an empty treasure: the truth. What does it even matter, when for years you've been dragging your life around with suspicion, devoid of resolve or determination? It isn't enough to open the windows every morning and air out the house in which you suffocate. I watch my son play by himself and my body is heavy. I cook for him, sweep the sandy floor to keep his feet clean, exterminate ants and put fly poison in every corner of this dead man's house, all day I'm busy being his mother and I watch him play, mama, do you want to play with me, and I can't, honey, I have things to do, I have to think, and remember, and accept that it's over, that I've reached this point, living is no longer for me, I don't have enough time left, it's been centuries since I destroyed my freedom with apathy, with the melancholy I learned from books, and with cowardice, above all: the cowardice of a good daughter, a good girl. The cowardice I've been proud of since I was small, the avoidance of conflict, because to do damage is much better. To do damage is dirtier. More lethal. How easy it had been, to think that I would give my son a brother, a brother who could take my place, relieve his loneliness, take up the burden that is mine alone, a brother who would build a castle with him, a castle where they would hide from me, where they could shoot arrows down from the highest tower and strike me, it doesn't matter where. How easy it had been to think that our wheels were set in the track, that someone was pushing our wagon, which was sometimes a wagon made of steel and other times a roofless wooden box, a blanket on the floor. How easy it had been to deny the anguish and rid my mouth of the taste of fury when everything was set in place, in motion, on schedule. This is what it means to make a family: convince yourself that all you have to do is keep pushing the wagon and listen to the grind of the ungreased wheels. You roll on and the world at your back disappears. The past falls into the void, the possibility of action comes apart at the seams, the recollection of what you thought you would be. And how easy it is now, to think it's okay that he plays alone, because today doesn't matter, tomorrow, tomorrow, because I have my hands full keeping house, cleaning house, destroying my own memories. The walls of this familial palace are all I need, and there *will* be a brother, a lifesaving brother, as if that brother wouldn't also need saving, as if apathy and emptiness wouldn't destroy him, too. The living and the unborn child both, tumbling from a wagon that lost its back gate over some rut, their father on the ground already, at the bottom of it all, and me—just me—staring ahead, into the mist, the future, refusing to hear their bodies as they become hollow, the wind brushing their thin figures, hazy now, and I'm staring ahead, refusing to admit that no one's pushing our cart, that there's no track below us, just barren earth, but our wagon keeps rolling because it hasn't rained, the ground is dry and I am the only quicksand in sight. My son plays on a patio from sunup to sundown and I watch him. When he's quiet and doesn't talk to me, doesn't tell me what he's doing, doesn't ask me to pay attention and live life with him, I open the Tsvetaeva book, thinking that maybe, after years, I could get into something, concentrate on something again, and I read with horror the passage where Marina describes how she rid herself of her youngest daughter, the daughter she never loved the way a mother is expected to love her children. She always dressed her in a pink dress and dirty white shirt. Everything durable and pretty went to the eldest daughter, even when she finally left them both at the orphanage where they would be fed something more than she could offer. Marina said: I can't feed them both with this onion soup, but I can feed one. Marina said: That girl wasn't born for me to hold on my lap, that girl. And I read this with revulsion, I'm scandalized that she was brave enough to say this so that years later we *other* mothers could feel better, much better, because we would never do that, we would give half the onion soup to each, it would be better to starve them both, we other mothers would never confess to such indifference, we mothers who don't live in Moscow in 1919. We don't have to write something like: I can't love Irina and Alya at the same time, I need to be alone for love. We won't write this because we are already alone, because we only have one child, a child we feed with pomp, with determination, with organic rice and free-range chicken and steamed non-GMO zucchini, sweet raisins harvested sustainably. We won't have to go to the orphanage and see that the food there is just as scarce, the same malnutrition, the girls eat their lentils one by one to make them last, we won't see their shaved heads and rotting rags, we won't suffer because Alya is freezing and has a fever, we won't see the cold-eyed Irina stalking between the rickety beds, a new animal, solitary and rebellious, an animal we have already abandoned, we won't decide to take Alya out of the orphanage to save her life and leave Irina to be condemned. We won't have to write: for me, Irina's death is as unreal as her life. We won't write, won't leave on record: I think of her little now, I never loved her in reality, only unreality. We will never be our daughters' tormenters, our daughters who sway and bob their little cork heads, we will never abandon them and then after their death confess in a notebook bound for history that we hadn't loved them. We don't have those daughters, just like we don't have the revolution. We don't have orphanages, or onion soup. We are neither as cruel nor as brave as Marina, who wrote: I'm not guilty, I had no choice. Even though it's a lie. That won't happen to us. Not to me, who has only one child to love. Only one child to leave playing alone, one child to dress, feed, raise. I have only one child. There will be no Irina in my life. I won't ever become a mother again and I will focus my energy on this single act of destruction.

SOFÍA IS SITTING ON the toilet. She looks at the latched door, the brown door that's already peeling a bit at the bottom, warped by damp. She focuses on a fixed point on the wood, where she sees nothing, just emptiness, perhaps. Her eyes are clouded over. She has finished peeing and her legs bristle, covered in goosebumps. She gently touches her clitoris, wet from urine. She listens carefully to the sounds outside the bathroom. Leo has the TV on. She rubs herself with two fingers, trying to speed up her arousal, trying to return to the emptiness in the depths of the wood. She thinks about sex. She thinks about the man from the salt marsh's arms, she thinks about his legs covered in hair, his teeth. She thinks about his tongue and how he could be licking her swollen clitoris. For an instant, she thinks she can come quickly, do it fast, go back out to the living room and talk to her son. But it escapes her. She gets up, and under her crotch, her thighs are soaked. She takes her toothbrush and wets the handle under the faucet. She sits back on the toilet. She touches herself again, more softly, stretches, leans her head back, closes her eyes and puts the toothbrush handle in her vagina, she moves it in circles with one hand and touches her clitoris with the other. She can't grasp an image potent enough, a memory powerful enough, just the desire and anger lodged in her throat, her eyes squeezed shut. She moves the toothbrush deeper, looking for the spot on the lower wall where the collapse can happen, and she finds it. Her wrists move frenetically now, she spreads her legs further, she wants to come twice, three times, stay locked in the bathroom for an hour, masturbate nonstop, her breasts under her shirt, braless, burning, her nipples need a mouth, a pinch, the pain that comes before an orgasm, she furrows her brow, a small moan leaves her throat, a lament, she wishes she wasn't alone now but she presses the handle of the toothbrush harder against her vagina and slides it in and out again and again and her fingers swirl over the swollen button of her clitoris and finally the spasms begin, her legs burn, her thighs shake, a warmth slips down her ankles, in her sex everything tightens and releases, no control; she's been masturbating several times a day for over a week and this is the first time that she feels all the pain and regret come down on her, the slight disgust from coming alone when one doesn't seek relief so much as salvation, the brutal nostalgia of a body tossing itself over a cliff when there are other hands down below waiting to catch it, to wring it, pummel it, make it bleed. After the orgasm, the TV sounds louder, maybe Leo has turned up the volume. Sofía wonders if some sound escaped her in the moment. She stands, shaken, defenseless, turns on the faucet and rinses her toothbrush before putting it back in its place. Then, with cupped hands filled with water, she washes herself between the legs, droplets fall on the floor. Her thighs are still sticky when she pulls up her underwear and goes out into the living room.

Hi, mama. Leo smiles from his hypnotic bubble. What are you watching? Haven't you spent enough time in front of the TV? Sofía goes into the kitchen for a glass of water and grabs a few rice cakes for Leo. Come on, let's get dressed, we have to go into town. I don't want to go into town, mama. I want to go to the beach. Sofía eats a rice cake as well, chewing lazily. We can go to the beach later, in the afternoon. I have to bring some shirts to the store.

She schleps Leo toward town, via the eucalyptus road at first, then down the dirty main street. They pass the bicycle shop, when are we going to rent bikes again, mama, they pass an ice cream stand, when are we going to get ice cream, mama, they pass a roast chicken place, when, mama, chicken and French fries, when, when, mama? They enter a clothing and accessories store, the saleswoman praises Sofía's shirts, strokes the fabric as she would a cat, yes, what a nice cut, the details are perfect, but she complains about the price, there aren't many foreign tourists at the moment, now is the time for local summer people and they won't spend that kind of money, not on an unknown brand, why don't they price them like the others? Sofía defends herself, the other things I brought you were simpler, these ones took more work, I spent almost a week on them, and the fabric, of course . . . I understand, says the saleswoman. But you're not going to sell them. The saleswoman wrinkles her nose and smiles at Leo, that manner of ending a discussion, that indolence, do you want a sweet? No, says Sofía, and yes, says Leo, practically at the same time. I'm hungry. Sweets don't fill you up, they just destroy your teeth. The saleswoman looks at Sofía, raising her tweezed or maybe drawn-on eyebrows, maybe she doesn't have a single hair left from all that tweezing, tweezing her eyebrows from the time she was fourteen or fifteen, so that now she just has four or five little hairs left and has to draw the rest on with brown eyeliner; if she got creative she could give herself a different expression every day, sweet today, psycho tomorrow, kids have to eat sweets, they're kids. In a shameless gesture of defeat, Sofía gathers her shirts from the counter and puts them, wrinkled, back in her bag. You're taking them? You don't want me to sell them? No, I'll try somewhere else. The saleswoman's eyebrows shoot up in the air again, her fake eyebrows climbing her forehead in sarcasm. Somewhere else here in town? She almost smiles. Well, I'll see. Sofía takes Leo's hand and directs him toward the door. Leo turns his head toward the saleswoman's hand, which holds out a sweet, mint, or maybe it's lemon, he can't see because his mother yanks him away from the danger, containing the urge to shout at the woman, don't you even think about it, he's my son, I'm raising my son, stick that sweet where the sun don't shine, you old bitch, and she leaves the store at last, without a word, face burning, lips tight, eyes swollen. She could cry right there on the sidewalk, what the fuck am I doing in this piece-of-shit town, every time I come here I realize I don't belong, it doesn't make sense, this place was always close-minded, always hostile, before, when the family was here, before, we lived in a bubble with people who came to spend the summer, life as lived in the heat, we roasted sardines, digging for wedge clams along the shoreline at dusk, the long hours of summer holidaymakers, papa, mama, our grandparents, those girl cousins who came from up north a couple of times, the commotion, the books we devoured in the bunk bed, fishing poles, sandy flip-flops, the hose spraying cold water on our backs. I don't belong here. She would cry if she could, if it wouldn't make her ashamed, if she didn't know that she must be strong in front of her son, always strong, always fine, something she clearly isn't good at, some-thing she gives up on day after day, but at least she won't cry on the street, at least he won't see her surrender in front of strangers. I want a sweet, mama, I don't know why you won't let me have one. Good mothers let their kids have sweets. You got stuck with a bad mother, Leo, what can we do about it? They backtrack toward home, fuming, annoyed with life. They walk very close together. They don't hold hands.

They made up after the siesta. Leo never holds a grudge. He's still a child and, fortunately, for him, there is a measurable distance between one emotional state and another. Sofía took a stab at making snack time fun, using pieces of cereal to make a picture of the beach. Leo had laughed and made two designs of his own before dumping the pawed-over cereal into a bowl with milk and adding some more straight from the box. Sofía took her time arranging the landscape with the little balls of cereal, this is how she experiences the positive side of motherhood, when she can't be reproached because she's spent a short time doing the proper thing. And what's more, she's going to take him to the beach. Maybe even take up a shovel herself and play with him, instead of sitting by the water with her book and watching the boy build sandcastles or swim in the shallow water if the tide is out. And now we'll go to the beach, she tells him, as if it is a prize. A prize for what, she doesn't know.

Once they are back home again, with the sun almost set, their fingers damp and the transparent swarm of mosquitos around them, Sofía confesses to Leo that she's had an idea. She's going to sell the clothes she makes at a stall on the beach promenade. Leo doesn't really understand, so his mother explains: she'll set out a table and a clothes rack with her creations and sell directly to the passers-by. She'll price them lower because there won't be middlemen. She is speaking in a special voice, the same voice she uses to read to him. She's excited. Leo asks, is it the same as the people from Africa who sell sunglasses on the beach? Will you be like a Black woman selling clothes on the beach? Sofía opens the gate firmly, hanging on to her smile. It's not the same, Leo. Why isn't it the same? Because I'm not going to walk around selling my stuff, I'm going to set up in a fixed location and people can stroll by and look at the clothes all hung up. It's like an outdoor shop. Mother and son shake the sand off their feet before entering the house. Sofía helps Leo clean between his toes. I think it's the same, because the Black men carry their store around on a board and move it wherever they want. Their way is better! They don't have to stay in one place, because that's boring. You could sell sunglasses, too, mama. I could help you, I could tell people how much each pair costs. Sofía doesn't respond, she walks into the living room, her smile has unravelled some but she is still prepared to fix a nutritious dinner, to not give up quite yet.

Then night settles over the house and it's asphyxiating, in spite of the cool air blowing in through the open front door, the scent of salt that occasionally fills the living room, the kitchen, Sofía's bedroom, the salt that envelops everything, the atmosphere charged with sea. Leo can't fall asleep and his mother reads him the same story again, one they've read so many times that he almost knows it by heart. Sometimes, he traces his finger over the lines and repeats a few words. Sofía raises her voice a bit with him, threatens to turn out the light. Time to sleep, come on. It's late. You're tired. Leo shakes off the rebuke by ignoring it: I'm not tired, I don't want to sleep. Why can't we go outside and look at the stars like last night? It's late, you're tired, her clipped voice, laden with tension. I'm not tired, mama. You are. Sofía gets up and leaves the room.

She tries to masturbate on the couch, the windows open, Leo's bedroom door closed. It doesn't work out, she can't get aroused. She picks up her phone and is about to send a message to someone. Anyone from the past would do, anyone who would tell her something, a word to open the lock, a word to provide relief. She spits on her fingers and touches herself, sticks her fingers in her vagina, first two, then three. Nothing. Maybe she's already dried up, depleted her orgasms. Boredom weighs heavily on her. On the coffee table, the Tsvetaeva book, a blank notepad, the TV remote. It's still too early. Too early for sleep. What day is it? Is it the weekend? A Thursday? She imagines herself two hundred years younger and in that same house, her parents having a late dinner, mixing wine with carbonated water, occasionally brushing their suntanned hands against each other when they reach across the table to take forkfuls of picadillo, dump the empty clamshells onto the center plate. Her little sister is on the floor, growing like a weed. Sofía imagines she can see how her legs are getting longer, but even though she grows nonstop, she isn't free like Sofía, who can see herself clearly in the bathroom mirror. She's in a blue top that leaves her tummy exposed, a tummy that, unlike her friends' flat stomachs, bunches a bit around the belly button, although in her defense she has stronger shoulders, round like woolly mammoth bones, and they gleam now that she's so tan, the blue top shows them off, her long wet hair brushes them, strokes them. She paints her lips with pink gloss, adjusts the waist of her white jeans, everything as it should be, it's time to go out, the only hour of truth, the rest of the day only has meaning in relation to this moment when she turns off the bathroom light and grabs her little bag from the chair beside the door, and if only she can slip away without any questions, if only that typical family seated around the table, the little sister lying on the floor watching TV, stretching nonstop, if only they were made of cardboard, oh please don't let them speak, what time are you coming home, the disapproving faces, the mother pretending, the father's endurance, her about to flee, about to haul ass down the eucalyptus road about to be somebody, out there everything is perfect and new, everything radiates pain, everything works.

She imagines that Leo isn't asleep in his room and that she could get dressed, lock the front door, go out for the night, perform a dance, find a man. It had been fun and intense, going to bed with the man from the salt marsh. She should be able to go to bed with someone else. Life shouldn't be denied her. The phone rings. She's afraid, but it must not be that late if her phone is ringing. It's her mother. She's about to silence the call but in the end she answers. Hi, mama. What are you up to? Her mother asks her the same question. How are you? she says. Her voice is drab, as if something bad was happening to her. But Sofía knows there's nothing wrong, it's just been a while since they talked. She sits up on the couch so as to not sound depressed. She has to appear happy, amused, but it's absurd, she's a snakeskin abandoned on the couch. Yeah, of course he's asleep, yes, Julio will come to get him soon, I don't know, a couple of days. She stands, her legs crack. There's a faint smell of vaginal fluid, that smell around her face; indeed, she holds the phone with the same hand she had used to touch herself. There's a beer in the fridge. She cracks it open. Mama, I'm fine. No, you don't need to come, Leo's about to leave. No, not right now, in a couple of days, I don't know when exactly. Julio's waiting, something to do with his parents. Aren't you guys going on a trip soon anyway? Why doesn't she drink beer more often? Why doesn't she try getting drunk instead of masturbating multiple times a day? Well, I don't know, mama, when Leo is gone I'll be able to do something. I'll go see my friends, sure, I'll go into the city, or, I don't know, maybe someone will come to visit. No one's come because I haven't invited anybody. Do you think I feel like seeing people? That I need people to come because I can't be alone? What? Do you think I can't be alone with my son? Sofía knows her mother doesn't think this, but she feels the obligation to ask, to say so, to berate someone for something, especially her mother, why not, who better than she? All right, mama, that's enough. Oh, don't bring up Rita right now, not today, please. What do you mean you can't talk to me about anything? Then why did you call? The beer can is empty, as if by magic. She looks for more in the pantry, if they're warm she can wrap them in a wet napkin and put them in the freezer, they'd be cold in a jiffy, but no, there's nothing. She almost never buys alcohol, as if she doesn't like it. As if she never drank. I don't have anything new to tell you, really. You tell me something, instead of getting mad. Okay, I know you're not getting mad, and yes, I am. I'm always mad, mama, you know that. Come on, are you all right? Mama, I'm changing the topic, this isn't going anywhere. I'm not making fun of you, fuck. Okay, mama. We'll talk tomorrow. Sofía tosses the phone on the table and it clatters loudly. The empty beer. The void.

She hears a car outside, a car braking, parking. She thinks she recognizes the engine, but since when does she recognize the sound of an engine? But she'd swear that . . . Now the gate is opening. That sound is in fact real, something happening at this very moment. And furthermore, they're laughing. There are people entering her house and they're speaking and laughing. On the other side of the door, something exists, an occurrence, there are people who park a car, come home laughing, walk across a patio without even noticing the giant, recently watered garden bed, without paying any attention to the night jasmine, which does smell lovely, yes, because she is a grown woman with a night jasmine bought at a greenhouse, already mature, already spilling open white flowers, white flowers vomiting the scent of summer, the scent her son needs to recognize as childhood summer, there it is, the jasmine plant, clinging to its pole, flush against the wall, but those too-real people on the other side of the door haven't even noticed, they insert the key in the lock and push open the door, still laughing, nothing in the world could be so funny and yet it is, there's something funny, something supernatural causing those strangers to enter Sofía's house, Sofía's dead father's house. Rita's dead father's house, as well. Sofía's little sister who shot up like a beanpole, all grown up now, she also became a woman, all bones and fine muscles, all unstable, fickle, messy hair dirty at the temples, eyes open immensely wide, giant pupils greedy for all the living-room light, lips dry from so much laughing, perhaps, or maybe just dehydrated. She is accompanied by an ungainly youth, tall, hair even dirtier than Rita's, beardless and fair-skinned, nothing but a dark smudge below his eyes that are like caves, distracted eyes that glance around, passing over Sofía as if she weren't there, as if she's just another piece of furniture in this place where he's been brought to continue, to carry on with whatever they were doing, his eyes blue and smiling, and from the end of his long, skinny arm, hanging from his long, skinny hand, dangles a six-pack of beer. Sofía doesn't move but Rita hurtles toward her, as if in flight, because she is a bird, after all, it's futile to pretend she doesn't have wings on her back, oh it's great that you're still up, so great, the best, how are you, sis, she says in the midst of their embrace, an embrace that smells of tobacco, of multiple embraces. Sofía sways despite her innate stiffness, she's focused on the absurdness of her reaction, her strange, stiff resolve, she can't take her eyes off the guy's interminable arms, that stranger who closes the door behind him, and with the slack laughter still in his throat, sets down the six-pack, the sole bastion of victory.

THE HALLWAYS IN MY grandparents' summer home were white and narrow. It was a large apartment, with those middle bedrooms that serve no purpose but hang suspended at the center of a dwelling, retaining the cold, the loneliness, perhaps the possibility of putting mattresses on the floor or metal folding beds and lodging an entire family. My grandparents' house was almost never empty in the summer, and yet now, when I think of that day, I remember it with no one there, very still. I don't know where our family had gone together, but we'd been out for a few hours. They, the others, had stayed home, and there's that play of absences again: I know that my sister and I weren't home, I know that they were home while we weren't, I know that when we got back, they were the ones who were gone. And so only the house remains as the scene, as the judge, impartial, of course. The house of love and poison. The house where we were pure childhood and where we always will be, in spite of everything. Deep down, the house was the grown-ups, those oppressive eyes that were our own eyes, that watched over us, almost always without seeing.

My sister and I entered the house (did my mother follow behind us, was she also a first witness to the message?) and, maybe to change clothes or something, went straight to the back part of the apartment, to the bedrooms. We must have had something to do there because if not we would have stayed in the living room or out on the balcony. In childhood, one doesn't come home and go directly to one's room. That's a teenage thing, when returning from outside (the outside, glory, the only real comfort zone), they feel the need to hide away for a bit, for the bit of time they're allowed to. But as children, we didn't have that luxury, and much less in summer, at the grandparents' house, where sometimes you were put in one room and the next year in another, even the next week, on occasion. All of the bedrooms were ours, in some ways. We kept our clothes in one or another, according to where we were assigned, but we rarely had a cave to take refuge in. My sister and I entered the house and went straight to the back, passing through the foyer, encountering the long hallway decorated with moving pictures, those ones that showed different things depending on the angle you looked at them from—a parrot whose beak is open, then closed, for example—we crossed that purposeless middle room, wide and empty, and turned down the second hall leading to the bedrooms. That year, our bedroom was the one with the bunk bed, though the bunk bed had been taken apart, and instead, we slept in two twin beds side by side, with a little nightstand between them—nothing else would fit. The window, which looked out onto the interior patio, was enormous and filled the room with light. The room also had a built-in closet with skinny, hollow doors where you could feel the dried drips of many coats of paint. I suppose the door to the room must have been shut, although in that house nobody ever shut the doors to empty rooms. I suppose that right there, at the closed door to our bedroom for that summer, we got a perfect whiff of the soap my grandmother kept in her dresser drawer, in her bedroom just across the hall; the soap, the lavender, the cool cologne my grandfather generously applied, the perfume my grandmother delicately dabbed behind her ears, in the folds of her soft neck, soaking the gold chain she always wore, that whole unfolding of intimacy on display, the narcotic delights of the patriarchs. If the door wasn't closed, it should have been. There before us, before my sister—because she went first, I am absolutely sure of that—lying on the pillow on one of the beds, was that thing, and that thing looked back at us from its hollow eyes, from the now-black hollows where its eyes had been, rubber-rimmed eyes, eyes missing the light blue marbles with the fake pupils and the combed eyelashes, eyes ripped out.

Today, we would call it a construction, a composition or performance, but the truth is, it was an atrocity. One of my sister's dolls, plastic and chubby and pink, with arms and legs moveable from the joints at the shoulders and groin, was waiting for us at the pillow's edge. Her eyes had been ripped out and her blonde curls cut down to their roots. From what used to be her mouth, a pretend mouth with a baby's half-smile statically prepared to wail, giggle, or suck, a leg emerged (was emerging? entering?), a leg torn from another, smaller doll, the foot pointing upward, thigh square with the widened corners of the rubber mouth, chubby pink cheeks containing the violence of a bodiless leg. Jutting from the tortured moppet's temples were the long, hard legs of a Barbie doll, one of the many Barbies we kept in the closet in that room, the ones we dressed in party outfits, miniskirts sewn from cloth napkins made in Portugal, hankies cut in strips to tie back their long hair. A Barbie's shapely legs and pointed toes now served to puncture the hollow brain of the affronted plastic baby, flesh-tone Frankenstein screws, the doll that could feel no pain and had no eyes, her mouth tolerating the swell of the thigh, her gaze twin black holes, darkness. That wasn't all; another Barbie, this one headless, issued from the gash carved across the baby's round belly, outstretched arms begging for help, Barbie born from plastic entrails, expelled at last from that PVC uterus, the fertilization in vitro and vespertine, secret and unfortunate, a headless Barbie fetus cast out of paradise and encased like an alien in the doll's round belly, a femur stuck through each temple, a leg jammed between her lips until it hits her throat. A doll that can still sit, remain straight-backed in her polypropylene idiosyncrasy, her undefeated backside well-supported by the thin summer coverlet, back stiff against the pillow, a hole where her right arm had been, is that synthetic hair sticking out? Little moppet returned from war, sullied dirty doll, nightmare plaything.

We cried, of course. Of course she cried, my little sister, because they had destroyed our toys. The dolls we loved so much, though they spent the better part of the year heaped in a closet. Our instruments for entertainment. It would have been bad enough if they had ripped off all their heads and arms and legs and left them on the bed, but it wouldn't have been the same. The message wouldn't have left the necessary imprint, its domesticating effect, the turn of cruelty's screw. To break them, cut off their hair, pull on their limbs until they popped out would have been inconsequential naughtiness, the malice of all children. And yet this was much more, although I suppose that nobody besides the two of us understood it as such. Someone had taken delight in building that macabre thing. The representation of another's pain. Synecdoche for hurt. Perversion, joyfully indulged. A simulation video game come to life, the youngest member of the family getting the handoff, rushing to beat game over, never making it out from her private survival horror unscathed.

That blistering symbol had an indisputable author. We never knew how many of them had participated in the butchery, but we never doubted who had been the mastermind, the smile that shone brightest amid the torn limbs, the practical brains of the operation. It could only be one. The younger of the two boys, much older than my sister, quite a bit older than me. The charismatic cousin, the one with the determined jaw. It was him, nobody else, who won the machete at the carnival shooting gallery, a real machete, a big prize, with a wickedly sharp edge that could slice plastic like butter. It was him, and the message was clear; a life stripped of pain isn't worth living. My compassion, my shock and outrage, passed muster that night, but I'm sure I missed the best part—those empty eyes, rims of burnt plastic, were not speaking to me.

There was an uproar in the house, the typical uproar that follows some act of bad behavior, the usual indulgent condescension. An injury isn't grievous when no one is conscious of the mark it leaves, of its silent escalation. What animus most sordid and cruel, docile dolly *sine oculis*, the intention to strip someone of their childhood.

LIKE THE SAD LETTUCES planted in the broad garden bed, growing with the ingenuity of something that believes it's going to
come to fruition, like the strawberry plants lining the edge of
the rectangle, strawberries in a land of imported berries, open-
air strawberries without a greenhouse to protect them, like the
woody bunches of daisies and geraniums, their first flowers
dead, this is how life in the house passes all of a sudden. When
the sun isn't so high and the light turns more hypnotic, the
skimpy vegetation takes on an aspect of forced well-being, the
impression of glass blown too vigorously: fragile and precious,
but unnatural.

The boy who arrived with Rita is named Paul and he's
half-Spanish, half-French. He's a little older than Rita and
a little younger than Sofía, but everything about his body
screams pubescence: the sparse hair on his arms and legs, the
few weak strands sprouting on his flat chest and skinny ster-
num (strands that look like they're about to fall out, like they
don't have roots, like they've come to rest on his skin the way
an eyelash alights on a cheek); the hair on his head dark and
greasy, silky for the first hours after showering, fine, straight,
fuzz covering a round skull; even the intense set of his jaw is
juvenile, the sharp cheekbones under sallow skin; even the
defiant, fleshy mouth, the tempestuous forehead, deep-set
eyes, sky-blue irises abandoned in mauve sockets. He seems
so young and inoffensive, and has a serious voice that doesn't
match his appearance. Where did you meet him? Sofía asks
the next day, while the two sisters tidy the kitchen, an unex-

pected quotidian performance. I've known him for a while, I'm sure I mentioned him at some point. I don't remember, Sofía says, energetically drying a dripping pressure cooker lid, are you sure? Doesn't sound familiar at all. I don't know, Sofía, you didn't talk to me about all the people you slept with in the last couple of years either. Sofía lets that slide because sometimes it isn't worth waging combat. Instead, she gives a spirited laugh as she puts the pots and pans away in the cupboards. But are you guys serious? Rita raises her eyebrows ironically, exaggerating her response, her eyes somewhat askew, the lack of sleep and the wear and tear of love and partying. Serious! she gargles, what does serious even mean at this point? No, what we have can't be serious because we're always laughing our asses off. The big sister snorts. What do I know, Sofía, we see each other once in a while and we have a good time. By now, Sofía has finished putting the dishes away and all that's left is for Rita to sweep the floor, eliminate any trace of food that could bring the ants. Sofía doesn't know how to respond, silenced by her own awkwardness. How many times has she tried to initiate conversations with Rita, sisterly chats, trivial inquiries that are always meant to go further because one would assume an innate closeness, obligatory intimacy, a Siamese umbilical cord? So many times, and always unsuccessfully because Rita never says anything unless the questions are direct. Sofía hasn't been very forthcoming the last few years either. When did they stop telling each other everything? Have they ever?

That first morning of the new summer phase, the first morning after her sister's return, Sofía leaves a hungover Rita sweeping the kitchen and goes out to the porch, shuffling her sandals on a floor covered in a fine layer of sand, to look outside, through the brightness, and she sees her son playing with the stranger, there in the middle of the yard, the table and chairs pushed aside to make more space, Leo sweating because it's hot and he's running back and forth, kicking the ball hard, an expression of unbroken joy on his face. She should have played ball with him at some point these past weeks, Sofía laments for an instant, how did I not realize, and turns her attention to her son's adversary, that stranger who must be excreting the night before under his thin cotton T-shirt and long, dirty jeans, the scarecrow, the chimney sweep, who offers Leo the ball with a barefoot kick, who moves in the light with an unbalanced rhythm, and there is something in the two figures playing, in that image of normalcy. Leo's shouts every time the ball escapes toward the street, bounces over the fence, and though it is Paul who, against all odds, goes after it, using his bony hands with the chewed fingernails to move Leo aside so he doesn't run into the street and into danger, and yet something about the situation frightens Sofía, bothers her viscerally, a sense she tries to overcome because, at this point, she feels like she's been terrified since she was born, though she knows that isn't true. More than anything, she intuits she shouldn't be like that, so frightened all the time, she must be clean of fear if she wants Leo to grow up healthy and strong, unhindered, and so instead of getting flustered or pulling the red card on their game, she goes over to the table and, taking advantage of the fact that her son is sufficiently far away at the other end of the yard, picks up the marijuana joint in the ashtray, the joint Paul meticulously rolled and only had three puffs of before he started playing with the boy, and now she, the mother, joint in hand, watches the stranger teach her son to touch the ball with his feet, many taps in a row, one two three four five six seven eight, come on, now you try, first three, then four, and she lights up (the smoke is dense and white), and inhales, two quick drags because it's still the morning and her son is there. She regrets it immediately, even before the weed takes effect, because even though

155

they're outside, the smell is really strong and her son is playing with a stranger high on drugs and she herself is smoking in front of him, and he is so young—and that's precisely why he won't even notice—but what if her sister comes outside now and smokes as well, or rolls another one, because maybe she's smoked already? Maybe before she came out of her room for breakfast? What would happen if they sat out in the sunshine and smoked that loaded joint between the three of them, and only one person was left lucid, one fully functioning brain, and that one person was Leo, the very person she must protect, all the time, tirelessly, even if it's only because he is a defenseless child, because he's weak, or is she the one who is defenseless and weak, and not her son? If that were to happen . . . but it can't, so Sofía returns the joint to the ashtray and goes back inside the house, her head thick and melancholy, a little disoriented because really it would be so easy to let herself go, to finally relax, pretend nothing was wrong because it's possible nothing *would* go wrong, because nothing *has* to go wrong, not necessarily, and because a mother who indulges doesn't necessarily have to be punished, then she too could ride the narcotic wave Paul and Rita seem to have brought with them, real vacation vibes. What if the stranger really has come to entertain Leo and her sister really has come to sweep the kitchen, even when hungover? What if she, Sofía, doesn't have to be so paranoid, so controlling? Still, she can't help but feel guilty about the weed, can't resist giving herself a silent tongue-lashing in front of the bathroom mirror, her eyes look high, why did she smoke, and so early in the day, with Leo awake, Leo right there, why did she do that, what is she after? She will have to watch herself, and watch them. She turns on the tap and wets her face, attempting to wipe the litany of self-recrimination from her eyes. Then she wets her neck and throat, as well, and when the cold drops run down her back and collarbone, when one slips past the neckline of her wide-cut tank top and traces the line between her breasts, she feels pleasure, cheap pleasure, the kind of pleasure that is little more than simple relief.

Apparently, it's true that Rita and Paul laugh a lot because from behind the bedroom door comes a pair of loud, synchronized voices, conversing plainly, not bothering to whisper. All of a sudden, though as far as Sofía can tell no one has put on an intentionally funny tone, the voices twist into laughter and flood everything, not just the room they're in, where the air is probably unbreathable already, but also the living room where Sofía stands like a sourpuss sentinel; laughter in unison seeps out from under the bedroom door, through the door joints, dense and expansible as Little Boy, a kind of Hiroshimic devastation is taking place in the living room, within Sofía, who is dressed in an intentionally large nightdress, her breasts in their softness moving to the beat of her heart. Apparently it's true that they make each other laugh, and so what? It's fine.

The day has passed easily, Paul smoking from the morning on and Rita behaving like she's from another dimension, dispatching the daily maneuvers with a premeditated lightness, though maybe it's that suddenly she really does weigh less, maybe there's a little bit of room between her feet and the ground, because if not, then how could one explain all this heaviness Sofía is dragging around. But so what, it's fine. Leo's face is shining as if he'd been smeared with oil. He won't stop saying it's okay all the time, it's okay, mama, every time a crust of bread falls on the floor or a fork slips into the bin when he scrapes the food left on his plate into the garbage, or when he's in the bath and Sofía mistakenly turns the hot water on too high while trying to regulate the temperature and burns the boy's back for two seconds, or once he's already in bed and he asks for a glass of milk, milk and cocoa, and she brings him a glass of peach juice from the kitchen because she hasn't realized, but it's okay, mama, pour that one out and bring me milk, I'll drink it if you don't want it, Leo, instead of throwing it out, and the boy repeats it's okay, mama. And so it must be okay, because Rita, moreover, strokes the boy's head so tenderly; she could spend whole minutes running her hand over her nephew, sometimes she buries her fingers deep into his hair and the boy stays very still because it tickles and he loves when his auntie tickles him, even though he can't really see the TV when she does.

Paul, at times, manages to be an interesting conversationalist, a little loony, sure, when he talks about UFOs and espionage, but it's entertaining. It seems as if the conversation is happening among all those present when in reality it's just Paul speaking, and he does a good job, holds their attention, and Sofía realizes that she really needs to hear people talk, and for a moment she sits down wherever Paul happens to be smoking and, clutching a mug of cold green tea, she feigns unconcern, peace, and nods along. It can't be bad, whatever this is that's happening. She suddenly can't tell whether her sister has taken drugs after lunch—maybe she *is* a little high, there's a lovely tell-tale shadow under her eyes, as if a dirty fingertip had just touched there, tracing a path, and her laugh is a whistle—but Sofía isn't sure. Does she have to admit that she knows her so little, that she doesn't know her own sister, or is it just that she can no longer tell when a person's on drugs?

Rita is chatty when the boy is asleep in bed after dinner, and Sofía returns to the living room, breaking the unbreakable unit that Rita and Paul appear to be. She imposes her presence on them, momentarily emptying their air bubble by virtue of sitting back down where she sat during dinner, at the table where the two of them are locked in an interminable after-dinner discussion, taking sips of the vodka they brought back from town today. When she sits and restricts herself to watching them and rolling a cigarette with fingers damp as if from cold, Rita returns her gaze—could it be with tenderness?—and asks, when is Julio coming to get Leo? It's a slippery question with many possible outs, and Sofía isn't sure which one to take, unsure of whether or not she's too distrustful, too unkind; maybe Rita isn't fishing for information and quite simply just wants to know—news-flash—when Julio is coming for the boy; maybe she's counting the days they have left to spend together because she's grown used to Leo's presence, his pure fragility, his open, generous nature; maybe that's why she's asking. Sofía lets it pass and says, a week, I think. Oh, another week. Paul nods with his penetrating eyes, another week, as if that meant something to him. Is a week a long time? Sofía says, lighting a cigarette, smiling without showing her teeth. It's not a lot of time to enjoy being with him, but it's been too long since you had a break, Sofía. Ah, okay, Rita's concerned about her, apparently. Well, yeah, that's true, but I'm used to it. Sofía's voice is false, there is no getting used to the need for a break from responsibility, for absolute freedom of action and thought, but she says what she should say, because Rita has given her a lucid, empathetic reply, she has the face of an angel right now, so why shouldn't Sofía hang up her armor? Wouldn't it be nice to have a couple of nights to yourself, sis, to go somewhere? Sofía fully surrenders to the charade, she notes a subtle twinge on the balls of her feet, isn't she lucky to have a nice, normal, sympathetic family, even the strange kid with red eyes who seems to bob his head all the time, constant music in his brain, even this skinny Frenchie is her family now, a handsome boy with a learned, modern junkie air, isn't she the luckiest? Yeah, it would be nice but what can I do, hey, I'm going to pour myself some of that vodka, okay? Paul gets up to fetch a clean glass from the kitchen and pours her a shot, then sits back down beside his other half and lays his big translucent hand on Rita's knee. Rita her Zen sister, her whole knee tucked inside in the hollow of that man's hand, Sofía can sense the softness of their skin merging over that articulated knob of flesh and bone. Rita's questions have Sofía on her guard, but why should they, aren't they just shooting the shit? Well, maybe you could take a couple of days for yourself and we could stay with Leo? Rita lets the words drop from her airy cotton mouth and Sofía takes a shot of vodka. So this is where the conversation has been leading, this generous offer, Sofía hits the jackpot, free babysitters, but she feels a prickle on the roof of her mouth, the worry again, the alarm, but no, she won't give in to paranoia, she knows shutting down this conversation would be a mistake, so instead, she smiles the winning smile she sometimes uses when she wants to change the subject: I called mama this morning and told her you were here. Oh, yeah? How is she? Fine, I think, like she always is when she's fine, you know, she didn't want to talk much because they were heading out on some day trip somewhere. Well, that's nice, she should have fun, anyway I'd already told her Paul and I were coming. Paul stands and asks if he can put on some music and then puts his phone in the middle of the table, leaning it against the cap to the vodka bottle so the speakers sound better and from there looks for a song and puts on something electronic, discreet, and dances with his neck and jaw, where Sofía can now discern a faint shadow of stubble, and she struggles to just let herself flow with the music instead of wondering why her mother pretended not to know anything when they spoke this morning, why is Sofía left out, what is she doing wrong? But then Paul starts in on one of his monologues, this time he mixes an anecdote about a festival with the last movie by some director where a similar story takes place and she doesn't know why but his discourse makes sense, the two sisters watch him, one sister so close she's almost breathing his air and the other with precarious attention, and this scene that could have gone on until daybreak, because what does Sofía actually have to do other than be there with her sister and a stranger, drinking vodka and talking about nothing, this scene that could have gone on until daybreak suddenly sees itself cut short by a devil's spark, a spark that like a spring lifts Rita and Paul out of their seats, almost simultaneously, so much so they must be on the same wavelength, their hearts must beat in unison, and they say goodnight just like that, with a kind of affection, and without bothering to pick up anything from the table, not even their phones. They close themselves in Rita's room, and they hardly make any noise but they murmur, and Sofía is left paralyzed in her chair, interrupted, and still Rita comes out one time, to take a few things back to the room, the ashtray, the tobacco, a little glass of rum, and she smiles at Sofía as she passes, and before Rita goes back into the bedroom, Sofía summons up the last of her reserves, and without thinking too much says, hey, about what you said before: two nights seems like too much, but I guess maybe I could think about one, I'll let you know, and Rita smiles again, her hands filled with instruments to keep the party going, and she says okay and shuts the door. From inside comes a *Goodnight!* that Sofía doesn't return because she can't move from her chair, bewitched by the table that was alive five minutes ago and is now phantasmal, and the voices in unison, full-throated, no whispering, and the laughter that floods everything and the bomb falling on Hiroshima.

Mama! The eclipse is tomorrow! Leo jumps around Sofía and then climbs up on the couch and jumps into the middle of the living room, be careful, Leo, I told you not to jump off the couch, I won't get hurt, mama, watch! and he jumps again, he's a frog, and Sofía, who is sitting at the table with a few patterns spread before her, pretending to measure some floral fabric, tracing lines with light pink chalk, observes the child with disapproval, but patience, too. The day dawned cloudy again and a cool layer covered the sky, so there's no obligation to go to the beach and get wet in the sea that is petrol gray on cloudy days. Later, they'll go into town to do the shopping, to stroll. Mama, Paul told me yesterday that the eclipse is tomorrow, that means we had to sleep two times before the eclipse and we've already slept once, right? The eclipse. Sofía imagines that if she were living a normal life, with her normal connections to the world—her social networks, her online newspaper, the daily news playing in the background while she fixes lunch, while she eats dinner—if she were properly in the world, maybe she would have bothered to find out something about the eclipse. Although, on second thought, maybe she wouldn't give a shit, like now, except that, if she really were living her normal life, Julio would have been talking about the eclipse for days, and he would have told Leo absolutely everything related to the phenomenon, and he would have drawn pictures that Leo would have taped to his headboard, and he would have found a special spot in the city, one worthy of such an event, for the three of them to go watch. Maybe he would have left work early, organized everything, and she would only be responsible for feigning enthusiasm and leaving the rest in his hands; at the moment the actual marvel occurred, Julio would be capable of authentically enjoying it, not for the fact that for a few seconds the moon blocked the sun, but for his son's bliss, that substance both ephemeral and real, pure, nourishing. But none of this is as it should be. Can I call papa and tell him about it? Sofía gets up from the chair and reaches for her phone, which is sleeping on the nearly empty bookshelf. She hands it to Leo, here, it's ringing. Leo runs outside with the phone, he's formed a habit of watching the street while he talks to his father, hanging on to the railing, as if the service were better out there or as if he could see Julio driving down the street, turning off the avenue with the eucalyptus and approaching the house. Sofía doesn't return to the table once the boy is gone, she actually has no interest in sewing, she can't be bothered with the flat fabric, the pincushion stuck with needles. She looks at the books. She can't understand why she doesn't read. If she doesn't do anything else, why doesn't she at least read? For a few days, she tried to submerge herself in Tsvetaeva's *Confessions*, then nothing. She reaches out and touches the spines. She pulls out *Decreation* by Anne Carson, the fat white book she bought on a friend's recommendation, another former teacher at the language academy where she used to work. When she bought that book, as happened with so many others, she started reading it right away. She had even picked up a pencil to underline those passages that interested her. She abandoned it, however, after a few pages. Now she opens the book and looks for her pencil markings. She doesn't have to go very far, the first poem is underlined, *here we go mother on the shipless ocean*, she runs her finger over the lines, bloodcurdling, the rereading. *Pity us, pity the ocean, here we go.* The book in her hand, Sofía takes a few steps backward and manages to sit in the chair again, she sets the book on top of the patterns and keeps searching, *what knife skinned off that hour*, she reads, *sank the buoys. Blows on what was our house. Nothing for it just row.*

Rita comes out of her room, where Paul can still be heard snoring. In the kitchen, Sofía is making a sofrito for lunch while outside Leo practices with the ball. Are you cooking? Weren't we going to eat in town? Well, I don't know, it's getting late, Leo's probably hungry already and I am too. The oil starts to sputter in the frying pan and Sofía adds the contents of the plate she has beside her on the counter: finely chopped peppers, large chunks of tomato, rings of onion. When she goes to lower the flame on the stove, she feels her sister's cold fingers on hers and she quickly pulls her hand away. Her sister's touch had been gentle. She turns the knob and shuts off the stove. Come on, we'll shower and get out of here fast, we can give Leo something to tide him over and you can wait a little longer, right? And so it is. At what point did they take command? At what point did they wrest control of the house, in spite of their innocent, almost desperate, appearance, in spite of the indolence with which they seem to pass the time? Without knowing why, Sofía lets them take charge. She doesn't do it happily, per se, but there is a certain measure of relief, not altogether lacking in vertigo.

Having walked along the wharf and observed the boats tied to their moorings, the activity of the fishermen and net menders, salt water pooling on the stone surface, flakes of mineral shining like neon, they sit in a corner of the plaza, where the sun umbrellas remain closed because it's a cloudy day. Sofía imagines they must look like summer vacationers, a little family enjoying their holidays. They've been served cold beers and some pineapple juice for Leo. Paul orders a plate of coquinas on a whim and Rita claps. She also wants wedge sole, marinated dogfish, and fried cuttlefish. Sofía would prefer a large fish, baked in the oven, one that hadn't sizzled in oil heated a thousand times already. When the cuttlefish are brought, she discreetly removes the fried breading with her fork before putting them in her mouth. Leo chews with his mouth open and she reprimands him. That's right, compadre, don't be a piggy, Paul says after Sofía's warning. Sofía looks up in alarm, made wary by the sharpness of the intrusion. But she sees Paul is laughing and Leo is laughing, too, open-mouthed, showing off the chewed fish on his tongue. It needles her, the suspicion that she's lost control.

Over lunch, they discuss their mother again, and then Rita starts to tell Paul about their father, what he did for work, when he bought the house, her voice breaks more than once, and Sofía is saddened, remembering him; since Paul appears interested, they travel further back in time and Rita gives him a summary of the summers in their grandparents' house. Sofía chimes in every now and then, contradicting her on some fuzzy details, I'm the oldest, I remember it perfectly, that's not how it was. Rita lets Sofía interrupt her, never straying far from Paul's eyes. Leo is up from the table and in the center of the plaza, he's made a couple of friends and it looks like they're playing cops and robbers. They hide behind the iron benches, always in plain view: the three boys know they're forbidden from leaving the pedestrian area. Paul orders a liqueur to aid his digestion and Rita joins him, a pacharán, please. You don't want anything, Sofía? No, I'm all set, I'll just have a sip of yours. They're the ones on vacation, not her. Rita must have taken vacation time now, for sure, because she hasn't said a word about work and Sofía hasn't seen her so much as open her laptop, but she refrains from asking. It's not like Rita has asked how the clothes-selling is going or the state of her own bank account. Nevertheless, Sofía decides she will ask Paul what he does. And what do you do, Paul? To make money, you mean? he answers with an offhand smile, taking his first sip of pacharán and lighting a cigarette. Yeah, are you studying, do you work? Sofía smiles back. Rita gets up to use the bathroom, suspicious, Sofía thinks, didn't she just go? Well, I'm unemployed at the moment. A laugh escapes Sofía, as if to say, oh, aren't you lucky, and she asks, but you're getting a check? Yeah, I get a check, I was an exemplary citizen and now, you see, the State takes responsibility for my poverty. And before that? Rita still isn't back, Sofía asks herself if she isn't taking an awfully long time and keeps glancing at the bar entrance. I used to work in a consulting office, my dad's company, actually. Sofía is truly surprised. She imagined him dealing drugs from the time he was fifteen, or living off unstable gigs, like DJing in neighborhood clubs, for example. As unstable as her own work. She's impressed. A consultancy, wow. She drinks a little liquor from her sister's glass.

So what happened, did the company close? No, I left because I was bored. Rita arrives just then and, after a brief grazing of skin, it's Paul who gets up to go to the bathroom. What were you guys talking about? Sofía is suddenly on edge. She looks for Leo, hidden behind the fountain at the moment, about to be discovered by his new pals. Hey, are you guys taking something? Then Rita's smile expands in an incredible way, is her sister's mouth actually that big? A swig of pacharán rolls over her tongue; she swallows and the fit of laughter continues, laughter that is, in spite of everything, frivolous, light-filled, you're so silly, sis, she responds. Sometimes you're so stupid.

According to news reports, the partial solar eclipse will begin at 9:25 in the morning. The night before, Leo insisted his mother set an alarm for eight so she could please wake him up. Although he didn't choose the time, he did ask his mother how long they needed for everyone to get up and have breakfast and arrive punctually for the eclipse. So when the alarm goes off at eight, Sofía's already in the kitchen, dressed in a pair of cream-colored shorts that make her hips look wide, and a black tank top. She rushes to turn off the alarm and pauses a moment to watch her son sleep, his features, perfectly sketched, that miraculous face of a child in slumber. They'd slept in the same bed, very close together in spite of the heat. During the night, Sofía trapped the boy, wrapping her arm full around him, tucking her hand in under his ribs, she thinks they must have slept like that for hours, unmoving, in perfect symphony. She doesn't wake him yet, returning to the kitchen to finish making breakfast for everyone. Even so, the boy appears suddenly, shuffling, scolding her, mama, I told you to wake me up, why didn't you wake me up, I told you, you promised, what if I'd stayed asleep and we got there late? Sofía doesn't reply but puts a mug of milk with a fine film of cocoa powder in his hands. I'll bring you your biscuits in a second, put this on the table and go wake up Rita, but don't go in her room, okay? Just knock. Two seconds later it seems as if Leo's already been up for a while because he raps hard on the wooden door to his aunt's bedroom and his voice is an absolute scandal of joy: Let's go! Let's go! Time to get up! It's the eclipse, come on Auntie! Paul, get up!

They haven't walked very far, there wasn't really time. They took the eucalyptus path and turned left upon reaching the beach, entering the pine forest clustered before the first dunes. Where the marked trail ends, they start up the dunes until reaching the shore. Just as they'd thought, it's early and the beach is practically empty; there are barely any other people, not even to watch the eclipse. The closest snack bar, some five hundred meters away, isn't open yet. Just a few foreign tourists have taken up positions along the shoreline. The four of them do their own thing, sufficiently removed from the other groups; they want to be alone, as if, like Paul has said on various occasions, they were watching the eclipse from the very moon that will block the sun. They haven't brought sun umbrellas but they do have hats with visors for all, and they spread their towels on the dry sand close to the water. Leo sits between his mother and aunt. Sofía makes him put on sunglasses and, moreover, insists, for the thousandth time, that he not look at the sun too long, even with the glasses on, and under no circumstances is he to take them off before the eclipse has ended. The boy nods gravely. It's nine-twenty! It's time! Five minutes! And Rita applauds with a few weak claps, something she does often lately.

The almost two hours the moon took to pass in front of the sun, in its same orbit, the time it took to pose before the sizzling spherical face and cover more than half of it, revealing two moons, one black and the other incandescent, sun cut on the bias, morning relegated for once to shadow, passed almost imperceptibly, wrapped in good-natured rawness. There was something between the four of them as they contemplated the eclipses behind the special glasses like something out of a 1960s science-fiction movie. If any of them had thought that Leo would get too antsy, abandoning his towel and upsetting their whole repertoire of admiration, they were wrong. The boy maintained his stillness, his serious willingness to observe the marvel, for the entire duration of the eclipse. Only his little mouth opened and closed in a smile or circle, nodding obediently at the comments made by the grown-ups, loathe to break the fascination of the heavens, perhaps, who knows, loathe to break something singular to him: that the three adults in his company had nothing better to do than put all of their attention at the exact same spot as he put his. That they were all consensually, obstinately, in the same place, the same space, the same circle of time. Leo was even quiet when the grown-ups talked about things that didn't interest him in the slightest, like when Paul interrupted the silence to say that the word *eclipse* came from the ancient Greek *ekleipsis*, and meant abandonment, neglect, distancing. Rita seconded the information with an astonished whisper and lay her cheek on Paul's naked arm. Abandonment? Sofía had said, somewhat reticently, I had no idea. Sure, abandoned of light, Paul affirmed. Sofía didn't give in, and how do you know? Rita kept her eyes on the sky, letting them speak, stroking her nephew's head as if in a trance, her cosmic cloud. She was splayed out on her towel. She looked happy. Oh, I read it in a book you have on your living-room table. I was glancing through it and it just appeared. I don't remember the guy's name. *Decreation*, I think was the title. Sofía had lowered her gaze, had almost buried her face in her knees, and removed her glasses to wipe the sweat from her cheeks and eyelids, the sweat of shame and the open sky. The two went quiet at last and went back to watching the eclipse. After a few seconds, Sofía said, *the guy* is a woman, Anne Carson. I haven't finished it yet—and her son, anxious because the moon was advancing, hurtling, tells her to shush.

Abandonment, neglect, distancing. That is what hides behind the wonder, behind the superimposition of two heavenly bodies suspended in the collective imagination, heavenly bodies that fuel us, the only ones that allow for life. One light and the other beauty. And the four motionless figures, as if belonging to one another, watch the sky from down in the sand, but what they don't know, perhaps, is that when the world is restored, that twinkling light, already weakened, will not recover its original brilliance, even if it might now seem so: something is stolen by the eclipse, something is left behind.

MY SISTER WOULD HAVE been four or five years old. I actually know now, from experience, what a child of four or five is like, I know their inner workings, their startling weakness, their brilliance. I know it from a distance and I know it from motherhood. A four-year-old child, their still-round face, their smooth belly, slight knees. But I, too, was a child at that time, a little older than my sister, maybe, but still a child. And immediacy is no ally of perspective. I don't know where she told me, but I remember a big empty room in my grandparents' summer house. Or maybe that's not where it was, but that's where I reconstruct the events in my memory because what she said happened, happened in that house.

Nobody else was there, just me and her, no witnesses, no threats, no surveillance. To reproduce her words is impossible. A four- or five-year-old's words. Ephemeral treasures, clean language, free of cracks. Moreover, even in memory I flee, I am unable to embellish it. She talked to me about the oldest of them, the first of the cousins, the first grandchild, the one who came first. He was already a teenager by then. Not only was he the oldest, but he was very tall. The head of any hierarchy. He didn't have the same character as his brother, he wasn't as clever, as visceral; but he had a special charm, more than a sticky agreeableness on occasion. Of course, the two boys shared the same violent, despotic worldview.

My sister told me that sometimes, when everyone else was asleep, when we weren't around, when for some reason nobody was paying attention, he took her to a room and closed the door.

I'm sure he set the latch. He sat her down on his lap, long tan older-boy legs, and kissed her on the mouth. What do you mean on the mouth? I think I asked. And she said he gave her kisses on the mouth and told her to open her lips so he could put his tongue in. I know I tried to decipher it, I know that, from my stunned childhood, from my grim watchtower, I tried, I hope with sufficient tact, to get my sister to give me details, to tell me exactly what was happening. Among the details I remember is one particular image that, in spite of living as if it didn't exist, I reproduced and recorded: the image of our oldest cousin, at least fifteen by then, with my four-year-old sister on his lap, on the edge of the bed in one of the back bedrooms, moving his legs in a stealthy and terrible rhythm, favoring the adequate friction. I can't, however, see their mouths together, I suppose because the image, in its inconceivableness, annuls itself. The final piece of information I could gather was that he had warned her that what they were doing wasn't okay, not so explicitly, perhaps, but he'd at least convinced her that she mustn't tell anybody and that they had to close the door so no one would see them, because if someone saw, they were both going to get in trouble. Both. How smoothly the executioner makes an accomplice of his victim.

I did what I had to, the only thing in my power, maybe the only thing she hoped I would do: I told my mother. I can't recall the horror that I imagine devastated her face as she listened to me. I know that my mother acted serenely, I suppose she spoke to my sister to tell her not to worry, it wouldn't happen again, or something to that effect. I dropped that pretty kettle of fish in someone else's hands and could breathe easy. The job was done. Why does it seem normal to me that, to this day, I remember being afraid my father would find out? What Rita told me was within the bounds of the absolutely forbidden, a territory that didn't belong to us, territory fenced in by condemnation. The genesis of the monstrous act was the very center of unspeakable subjects. My father couldn't find out for many reasons, and among them—what a cruel construct of mine, what a false prism through which I viewed reality—was the fear that he would go crazy and visit upon my cousin some kind of damage, irreparable damage. But that didn't happen. I don't know if my mother told my father, or when, or how; my understanding is that she did, but the truth is, the subject was never discussed again. I know that my mother undertook the task of making the accusation and that the issue was solved between the mothers, and not directly with the boy. She had a conversation with her sister, our cousins' mother, and told her what was going on. Was I there for that? Unlikely, but in my mind I see my mother, so young back then, talking on the phone in the little front room in our house. The telephone hung in a corner of that small square room, beside the china cabinet that housed the special tableware and coffee sets my parents got for their wedding and never used. She spoke to her sister and told her what her oldest son was doing and told her to take care of it. And so it was. My aunt took her boys aside, one because he was guilty and the other just in case, and told them, for example, something like *that is wrong.* Something like *don't ever do that again.* Maybe she yelled at him. Who knows? I'm sure it was uncomfortable, a strained moment between parent and child. But now I'm conscious of the fact that the punishment was really nothing, a dirty feather floating down from the parapet, barely a flying grain of sand, today I am aware that it was nothing more than washing a white sheet in tar. Was there a punishment, enforcement, reprisal, a natural execution of justice? There was nothing. A dressing-down delivered on schedule, a game of telephone in which the message, with each transmission, is diluted furthermore. There was nothing, but I know peace followed the initial sting of revelation. I don't remember the horror on my mother's face, or the shadow in her heart, never to be brightened; during that period, all I remember coming from her was security, love, and calm. She covered up the hole. She did what was expected of her; they are children, in the end. And that boy was the older son of her older sister, a nephew she couldn't stop loving. And we were a normal family. And she covered up the hole. But someone peeked in to look at the wound. Peace arrived and, satisfied in our bewilderment, we kept on living. Nothing happened, nothing changed in our routines or habits. I was a little girl, I know, but I was bigger than she was. I pushed her out of my games, I escaped on my own when I could, gratified to shake off that little shadow that trailed me everywhere. Abandonment, neglect, distancing. I was a little girl, I know, but the day of that confession, I should have taken her in my arms and never let her go.

SOFÍA PREPARES A SMALL suitcase for two days. She packs a pair of tight jeans and a sleeveless white top she made herself, one of the shirts rejected by the shop in town. She tried it on before folding and putting it in the bag, and her cleanly bronzed shoulders contrasted nicely with the material. The shirt doesn't have buttons, it closes in a wide boatneck that reveals some of her collarbone while keeping her cleavage concealed. She felt attractive when she saw herself in the mirror, sensual even. Her little toiletry bag is already nestled in one corner of the orderly suitcase. She takes a turn around the room, looking for anything else that might be useful for her getaway, and ends up grabbing the small bottle of perfume on her bureau and the Tsvetaeva book, again. She holds Carson in her hand for a moment before returning it to the nightstand. Everything's ready. Upon zipping the suitcase shut, she feels regret, that slimy guilt that creeps up her neck to her eyes, the guilt of the mother who voluntarily leaves her child.

But her son is happy, and it appears as if he won't be missing her. Seated at the table in the living room, beside a messy-haired Paul with swollen eyelids, Leo does a puzzle. Paul helps him now and again, finds the missing piece just when the boy is getting desperate. Leo chats away animatedly, he's retelling the eclipse episode again. And if we hadn't brought the glasses, our eyes would've been fried, wouldn't they? We would be blind, wouldn't we? And then we would have to use those walking sticks out on the street. Or dogs, Paul adds, seeing-eye dogs they're called. Can you imagine if our eyes got fried? And got all bubbly! Like volcanoes! But since we had the glasses . . . Paul nods: Sure, so nothing happened to us. Look, here's the piece you need; you put it in. Sofía observes the scene with relief and envy. But she's about to leave, one step from liberation, so she collects herself and goes over to her son and sticks her nose in his fine little boy hair, in his head bent over the puzzle. She inhales and hopes to retain his scent in her nostrils for forty-eight hours so that it can also serve as punishment. Mama! he complains, I'm doing a puzzle! But he doesn't move his head away, doesn't shift a centimeter from his mother's nose, from her heat.

Sofía grabs his ribs, squeezing between the bones, knowing that this will make him extremely nervous; it will make him squirm like a little lizard, but he'll let out that laugh, that singular laugh, the forever laugh, a child's laugh, a whole sun cackle, healing waters, celebration, stars, birdsong, smashing nuts, new air never before inhaled, the only truth, regeneration of the world, a swinging door to pleasure, a child's laugh, its cackle, hysteria, open mouth, eyes shut in fake grimace of pain, a perfect face, smooth without a nuance of malaise, without a trace of rot, a whole face exposed to laughter, benign rattle of happiness, contracted abdomen Pandora's box, low flight over an infinite prairie, so green that prairie, so bright, the conquering of the meaning of life, the justification for motherhood, a child's cackle, and what's more, the ability to provoke it, that a mother's hands can produce that howl, that purity. Paul observes the mother tickling her son with respect and indifference, though more indifference than respect, of course, from his eternal spot at the table, the chair where he always sits, settled in the same place, as if the house were somehow his. He waits for her to finish so they can continue with the puzzle. Leo is still laughing a little when he bows his head back over the pieces. Come on, mama, just go already, I'm going to do my puzzle. Sofía gives him a last kiss on the forehead: Are you going to be good? You'll call me if you miss me? But Leo is no longer responding. Even so, she has to finish the farewell ritual, the overacted flurry. I'm leaving, but it's like I haven't left. I'm leaving, but behave as if I were here watching. I'm leaving, but don't forget me, don't forget that you need me. I'm leaving, I'm leaving, but I'll be back. Three more kisses, this time on his neck. One more, gentler, near his ear. Ay, mama.

Rita is drinking coffee in the kitchen, her second or third cup of the morning. Not surprising, Sofía supposes. They go to bed extremely late every night, even though they just hang around in their bedroom for hours; Sofía falls asleep to their whispers and giggles, sometimes their music, played low, a few moans, or the screeching of the narrow bed. They've made an effort today, getting up so early, but it was her sister's idea that she get away, after all. Rita is in charge, it's not like she was going to sleep in. Sofía can't criticise her, obviously can't allude to Rita's disorganized daily routine, can't launch a flurry of warning and advice because she, Sofía, is the one who's leaving, fleeing, she's going to make use of the free pass her sister gifted her with so much love, so much generosity. It would be stupid to ruin this moment with too much caution.

Rita clutches her coffee cup and looks out the kitchen window into the measureless distance. Okay, well, I'm going, Sofía says, fearful of something. What is her sister looking at, where has she focused her pupils? In a fit of spontaneity, Sofía goes to the fridge and takes out a carton of oat milk and a small bunch of grapes. She pours the milk into a glass and runs the grapes under the faucet; she starts to eat the grapes but she doesn't pull them off with her fingers, she bites them directly from the vine. Rita continues in silence, her breathing is deep. Rita? Sofía says, frightened, mouth full of grape, of seed. Rita slides her gaze from the window at last and rests it on her sister. There is a shimmering track on her cheek, maybe she's been crying, but her tight, dry mouth and glossy eyelashes dissuade Sofía from saying more. She's beautiful, her sister, in this remoteness. Defined muscles under cotton shorts, perky breasts under the men's T-shirt she's wearing, everything looks good on her sister, everything makes her soar. Although this morning, Rita clutches the coffee cup like it's a rope that will save her from the abyss. Sofía shakes off the feeling that there's nobody behind that gaze, deems her concern a figment of her imagination, the distortions of a guilty mother. Are you sure you don't want to take my car? Oh no, I'm taking the bus, I told you. That way I can read. Anyway, trying to park . . . But it's summer, it'll be a ghost town—plenty of parking. Sofía throws the empty grapevine in the garbage, drinks what's left of the oat milk, and wipes her hands on a damp dishcloth. But maybe you guys will need the car, right? If anything happens . . . Rita seems to warm up just then. What's going to happen, Sofía? Come on, don't be a killjoy. Just go. Her words aren't just indulgent, there's unease, slackness. Something rigid grows between them then, turns unfriendly. They retreat to their respective positions there in the kitchen, until Rita breaks rank and moves toward Sofía. She lays an ice-cold hand on Sofía's elbow, wet feather fingers, come on, go, and have fun, we'll talk tonight, don't worry, sis.

So Sofía leaves, dragging her small wheeled suitcase down the dirt road, then down the eucalyptus road, to the roundabout, where she turns left onto the long street dotted with commercial businesses, the main street, dirty and replete with sad ordinariness, nothing summery about that street, and she remembers that she was going to ask her sister to drive her to the bus station so she could be spared this ridiculous journey with the noisy suitcase packed for two days and the sweat and siege under her armpits.

And just what did that southern city have to offer her, what would justify her presence there, her well-deserved break? The city could have opened like a mechanical flower, with its neon lights, cocks crowing from the farthest reaches, car horns, the squeal of metal locks, the crunch of concrete against brick—the summer city could have fallen silent at her arrival, or gotten dressed up for the occasion, given itself refined, northern airs, pretended to be a city that maintained its elegance, even in summer, but it did not. What did she need to happen there, where she used to live? Or rather, where she still lives, since she is still listed on the register of inhabitants. Her family records, letters from the tax authorities, her son's school. If she does nothing about it (and she would have had to do something about it already), her son will return to the same school in September, the same neighborhood, and that will be the end of it, the joke's over, jig is up, her little field trip; education is compulsory at Leo's age, and if she doesn't bring him back, the authorities could come after her, arrest her, take away custody. But does she have custody? If Julio left first, she has custody, right? She doesn't actually know, and moreover, it's she, not him, who clearly isn't in the family home, and, well, she hasn't stopped to think about anything. Therefore, since this is the city to which she must legally return, it is her city. Her doctors are there, her son's pediatrician, the surgeon who will open her from stem to stern to stir the metastasis with a giant soup spoon—if the time comes—the nurse who will check the now-invisible veins in her arms before administering her next regularly scheduled shot, the orderly who will transport her body down the hospital hallways, elevator, basement, the same orderly who will eventually wrap her in a shroud, wrap all of them. That city wakes up in the evening with the midsummer heat and what does it offer her? Does it reproach her for leaving, for having made do without it, for having stolen one of its children? Or, on the contrary, does it show her brusque indifference, with its terraces unfolded on the sidewalks, its whispering couples, sweaty gatherings of friends just out of the office, pitchers of beer, the colder the better, worker bees that shine like inky-black cicadas? What does this city, which is hers, have now, in the middle of summer, when everyone has fled, what does it have that is good or appealing?

Sofía strolls with a friend along what used to be a boulevard and is now an enormous pedestrian stretch, sometimes she grabs her by the arm and lets herself fall into her as she walks, simulating complicity, simulating, for example, that time hasn't passed or that she's a little drunk. They are on their way to meet a group that used to be something solid and effervescent and is now just dull remains, without hair, with soft bellies, bags under their eyes, some character or other cut off from this life who now returns to the fold, a few of those couples that feed off keeping the friend-group flame alive, the social space where conversations die out soon after they start, better to withdraw, sit in a corner and pick at whatever the barman brings. Sofía's only hope is that her friend has said that an ex of hers, not even an ex, just a guy she slept with two thousand lives ago, only occasionally, only when they were really drunk, only if nobody else from the group was around, that ex, who is now someone's else's ex, various women's ex, just happens to be in the city like her and replied to the group text somebody sent. Hey, let's all get together, it's been years, Sofía's coming. Sofía as decoy, that made her feel good, that she can still be used as a decoy, something people want to see because she doesn't let herself often be seen, or something people want to see because they want to know how much dirt she's had to eat, how much dirt is on her mask-face and how much youth she has left, whatever, Sofía's coming, it's a decoy and apparently that guy has taken the bait, her friend says he never replies to any of the group messages and this time he wrote *On my way!* and that's a good sign, a sign that maybe she'll wind up having some fun tonight. But the guy isn't what he used to be, he used to be a handsome rogue, and now what? Now he's just a perv. The two women laugh so as not to cry.

The most tiresome part of their afternoon was spent in a mall. Sofía made the effort to walk through the stores and touch the clothes as if something interested her, she accompanied her friend to the dressing room and fetched her the different sizes, you have to take advantage of the sales, but she knows already that she has no intention of buying anything, absolutely no intention of trying on clothes in front of somebody else; however, she succumbed in the end and bought herself a silver necklace with a charm in the shape of a boat, the long chain dances on her white shirt, the truth is that she wishes it would dance on her cleavage, directly on her skin, but for that she'd have to be wearing a different top, and she also bought a bathing suit for Leo, it's his summer uniform after all, she's always rinsing the two he has in soapy water and hanging them out to dry. The new one has an orange-palm-tree print on a blue background, it's so small, size 5, she spent very little on both but the necklace cost three times the price of the bathing suit. She decides to put the suit straight into her bag, all balled up like a crumpled tissue, and when they get back to her friend's house to shower and change before heading out again for dinner, for drinks, to meet up with the gang, she forgets to take it out, so she carries it around at the bottom of her bag, next to her wallet and phone, and sometimes when she sticks in her hand to get her lighter or tobacco she grazes it with her fingers, and the jagged edge of a fingernail, an unscrupulous hangnail, catches on the Lycra and she yanks her hand away with displeasure.

The night had been nothing, the city offered her nothing,

or nothing she desired, anyway. It's so difficult to dig into this point: what does one desire, really desire, now, in this moment, honestly, without the additional burden of one's circumstances? If she could evict insecurity, habit, the itchy passage of time, if she could evict all of that from her desire and let desire float like a buoy at sea—a little ratty and with barnacles but gleaming anyway because pure, because alone, because floating—but it can't be done. And what one desires always carries a mix of unease and perversion, or naivete. The night had been nothing, as soon as it began she saw it was going to be terribly boring, she wanted to pluck her friend out of there and take her to some flophouse, so they could at least get drunk by themselves, tell each other how life has really passed them by, take refuge in the corner of a bar and engage in the oratory of survival, that booming song, show their scars, not even scars, their open wounds, but no, she didn't, because she was the one who needed that, not the other way around, she needed someone to grab her by the wrist and take her to a flophouse, someone to push or carry her flying through the air down the boulevard, through the closed summer night, through that city so up to its neck in itself. So Sofía was docile, half-explained that she'd gotten separated, half-explained that she hadn't worked in years, half-explained that her son was five and that on occasion, for almost nothing, she made clothes nobody bought. She didn't really explain anything, just drank a couple of whiskies on the rocks and watched the door in the hope of some miracle, that guy from the Stone Age wasn't anybody to her now, and she wasn't anybody to him, maybe in his mind she used to be a rogue, as well, and now what is she? Sheer boredom, a few gray hairs and a jelly ass and thank god her varicose veins didn't show through her jeans.

And now, lying on her friend's couch, on the clean sheets her friend spread and smoothed with care, cream applied under her eyes and gums cleaned and flossed, she thinks that it's fine to go to bed so early (it's not even two in the morning) because she still has a night, a whole day, and perhaps she should be a little braver and dive in, search her contacts for those people she might not have known well but with whom she shared an important part of herself, a more radical part, volatile maybe, but, oh well, maybe tomorrow she'd get her chance to go home with a story to tell, and so, with the thoughts of a little girl who hasn't gotten everything she wanted out of her holidays, a little girl who feels that life, in general, isn't enough, or that she's ill-equipped, that something is missing, some critical piece of gear she needs to splash down, and so she probably shouldn't try to take the plunge just yet after all, and with that last, freeing thought, she closes her eyes and breathes, and then she hears her phone, not a message alert but someone calling her at two o'clock in the morning. For a second, Sofía thinks here we go, it's the guy who used to be a rogue and is now a scumbag, he's changed his mind and gotten her number and wants to invite her to do something, something clearly more amusing than her current activity, and for the two seconds that follow the one it took her to think this, she gathers her indifference and modifies it in an athletic attempt to take advantage of the situation, things happen when they happen, that's all, it's fine, she could even leave without her friend realizing it, get herself back in her jeans and put on her shirt and bring her toothbrush and she'd be fine. She sits up so the sound of the ringer won't wake her friend, with whom, no matter how well they know each other, and for how long, she has nothing in common anymore, and moreover, there always was something disapproving in her look, in her politely chosen bits of advice, and with a shaking hand Sofía reaches for the phone, vibrating and ringing on the low table beside the pullout couch, and the screen reads: *Rita*. There is only one Rita in her contacts, which means that her sister Rita, her little sister who is far away now, at the beach

183

house, taking care of her son, her little son, is calling her at two in the morning, the phone trembles in her trembling hand and her heart already hurts when she picks up and almost screams: Yes, what's happening, and it isn't her sister on the other end of the line but that greasy-haired stranger, the one who lazes around her father's house when her father would never have let him inside, not in a million years, the one who plays with her son as if he gives a damn about him, and in a voice pierced by something, a perforated voice, he says, Sofía don't worry, everything's okay, your sister is really wigged out, she can't talk right now, and please don't worry but we're in Portugal and Leo is lost.

The highway is deserted, the moon shines on one side of the car, the wide black fields cutting a silhouette against the dark horizon. The car travels faster than the legal speed limit, chasing the road markings, unbroken line, broken line; every once in a while they pass another set of headlights and Sofía thinks how, if it was daytime, they would be flying past eighteen-wheelers and her heart couldn't handle the heavy traffic on this highway linking the city to the beach town, although the truth is her heart can't handle this swift darkness either because there is nothing her heart can handle in this moment except its own beating and need for oxygen. In spite of his nerves, Julio drives carefully. His legs don't shake like hers do, he hardly changes gears because he doesn't slow down, not even on the curves, his eyes fixed on the distance ahead of them. They've only just left the city, but if everything depends on the determination of that straight nose, that set jaw, in no time they will have crossed the border. Sofía's cheeks are covered in a patina of tears, her lips swollen, tongue lapping the drips of clear mucus. In her hands, on her lap, a damp, wrinkled wad of tissues. And her phone. They don't talk, she cries with varying intensity, pulls the hairs at her temples, pounds at her head between sobs. Then she sighs, as if merely suspending her panic could fix everything, could make this situation cease to exist, could make herself cease to exist, none of this is happening, this is not happening, if denial could mean nullification, if she hadn't gone, negligent mother. Julio's voice is grave and floods the interior of the car: Why don't you try your sister again? Maybe she'll answer. It's Sofía who won't answer, Sofía who shakes her head and loudly sniffs back more snot, more tears, she looks at her phone in any case and checks to make sure there are no new messages, Julio keeps at it, call her, please, and his voice now bears the impatient stamp of a command. I don't want to call her! I can't! You call! She won't pick up for me! I'm driving, Sofía, calm down. The headlights on another vehicle blink in the distance, reminding them to turn off their high beams, but Julio ignores them, in three seconds they will have passed this vehicle and no one will be bothered. Sofía hits her forehead with her phone, clumsy taps, as if she's testing the hardness of her skull. A sort of moan hangs in her throat, precursor to a scream, has she ever had this kind of vertigo? Is this what tragedy consists of? Things happen, they happen to others, until one day they happen to you and pow! we're no longer spectators to the dramas of others but protagonists in our own, our own poverty, the most profound weakness, and it turns out to be just like that, just like other people's, exactly as horrible.

Sofía appears to be on the edge of madness, unsure if it's guilt or the compulsory certainty that nothing bad can be happening to her child keeping her calm, deep deep down, in the deepest depths, calm enough not to fling open the car door and throw herself out at 170 km/h, bust open her head on the asphalt, burn her entire body as speed drags her down the road. The thin whine in her throat coalesces into words: I shouldn't have gone, I shouldn't have gone, I knew it, my little boy, my boy, why did I leave him alone, why did I let myself be convinced, my god, my god, where is my boy, he must be so scared, tell me nothing bad is happening to him, Julio, tell me no one has done anything bad to him, I'm going to die, I'm going to die, it's my fault, all my fault, I shouldn't have left him alone, I'll kill her, I swear to you I will kill her if anything . . . But her sentences lack fury, they are born in the pit of desperation, they mean nothing, are nothing but a wail. Shut up, Sofía, you're making me nervous, I'm trying to drive, be practical, something bad hasn't necessarily happened. Julio continues to exercise balance, achieves it, in fact, it's what is expected of him in these situations, that he can drive in spite of everything and get there in time to do who knows what, all the strength concentrated in his jaw, clenched molars, teeth all lined up, fists closed around the steering wheel and his eyes dry, the night is dense on the road, a road he thankfully knows by heart; he just wants to get there so he can finally evaluate the situation. Children don't get lost so easily, in fact it's very difficult to lose a child, even if he's lost for a couple of hours it doesn't have to mean horror, it doesn't mean someone has kidnapped him, or raped him; their son's intact body must be somewhere that the incompetence of others won't now let them see, but as soon as he arrives, everything will get worked out, it can be no other way, and right now his wife must be hysterical, it's her obligation as a mother to grieve a non-existent death, a fictional loss, flagellate herself because everything that happens to a child must be the mother's fault, there is no other way, no other way to face love, any misstep, the mistakes he will make throughout his life, the irrelevance of his existence, all of it must fall on her shoulders, she must bear it, nothing doing, and her sister, that brat . . . Though, mightn't he be the guilty one, ultimately, maybe if he hadn't left . . . But those are not Julio's thoughts, Julio is able to remain lucid and he confronts life with measured, rational optimism, and only in an extreme case of darkness would he moronically assume responsibility for what is no one's. Sofía, why don't we try to look at this with a little bit of calm, it's really very unlikely that something bad has happened, you're not going to kill anybody, although we really should have predicted that your sister wasn't doing well again . . . that's really the only point, I'm sure the boy . . . We should have predicted? Where are you pulling that plural from? What were you going to predict from your five-minute-a-day phone call? Or do you know something I don't? *I* should have predicted it, *I* should have seen it coming, my sister brought a guy to the house and I think they were doing drugs all day but I don't know, I let it go, I don't know why I let this happen, Leo will never forgive me, you'll never forgive me either, what the fuck were they doing in Portugal, where the fuck did they lose my son, I want to die, I want to die right now. And as she says this, her body stops shaking for an instant, it can no longer take the beating, or maybe she's regaining consciousness, she looks for a clean tissue in the bag at her feet because the one she's holding is a mess of fluid, a hole, and when she puts her hand in the bag, she fingers the bathing suit she bought for Leo that afternoon and everything inside of her spills again, the immense tenderness, sorrow for the life that was going to continue normally but is now over, broken, all the quotidian moments she didn't treasure, passing through them with the weight of routine sacrifice, all of it now radiating a light of simple, elusive happiness, everything stinks of the past, it's unbearable, it was so easy, so simple to live, she thinks about her son putting on that bathing suit, running along the shoreline, getting her wet, the inscrutable mother, Sphinx-like in her reading chair, don't splash me, I'm coming, be careful, I can't right now, I don't feel like swimming, we'll make a sandcastle later, it's time for bed, time to eat, time to wash your hair, hold still, just a minute, be quiet I'm talking, be quiet, and now she really is on the verge of screaming, her wail returns like a revolution, an explosion of disease, she convulses in the passenger seat, face buried in her hands, fingers buried in her temples, her diaphragm an act of violence, she wails, wailing is easier than opening the car door and jumping out and dying right there, brains splattered on the side of the road, Julio would have to keep going, he couldn't stop to take care of the lesser evil of a mother's death when his son is lost in a foreign country, lost on a summer night, lost without a hand to hold him, guide him, he must be hungry, tired, a mother's lifeless body on the highway is insignificant, all that matters is that other body weighing twenty kilos and measuring a little over a meter tall, those frank, round eyes, that pointed little nose, the red lips, always wet, the perfect collarbone, spine submerged in flexible flesh, Julio couldn't stop to confirm that she was in fact dead, he wouldn't stop to close her eyelids, lay a blanket over her broken limbs, because deep down he is very angry with her, he has been angry for a long time, even his indifference is the result of his anger, even his distance the consequence of his contempt, who is to blame for everything if not her, to blame for the frustration, the dissatisfaction, the non-acceptance of life, the foulness always present in the passing of time, that negligence, clumsy nostalgia, insistence on being bitter, like putting on an accessory, donning a personality, melancholy as a means of building an identity, as if it was in any way useful, as if it were anything other than a guise for the cowardly and mediocre, a justification for indolence. Of course he's angry, she left their child with a pair of misfits, a pair of deadbeats, and surely when this is over, when there is nothing left to be done, then he will come down on her, with his hollow eyes and big hands and all the authority granted by being a father and by having loved her, and without raising his voice he will reproach her for her mistakes one by one, you took the boy in a fit of spite, you took him out of school, you've had him in that empty house all summer, you shielded yourself behind him, you used him, you knew in your heart that something would happen if you went away, but you needed for something to happen, you needed to build something even if it started with grime, with error, he will say all these things to her, one by one, every day of her life starting with tomorrow, until there is nothing left inside him and he can really abandon her, all the torture she deserves will come, but not now, now she convulses amid screams and calls out for her son and beats her face with her fists while drool drips onto her lap from her open mouth, and Julio won't berate her yet, not while she is shattered, and he puts his cold hand on his wife's knee, with an impossible gentleness that gets her to be still, he offers her a rest and, what's more, he appears to be saying something to her, although she can't hear because her brain is an inferno of sound, but surely he is saying her name in that way he's said it many times throughout the course of his life, pausing on each letter, the consonants, the vowels, as if he were spelling it out, there is still love in that whisper, she is able to receive it, suddenly in the midst of the surge she is unfit for consolation but not for empathy, in the end nobody but him can understand where she is, understand it down to the most trivial detail, nobody better than him to understand the journey, and the hand on her knee is now on her still-shivering neck, and then his two hands gather her up, Julio's two hands ready for her, his arm seems enormous to her, infinite, and it suddenly encircles her shoulders and converts her into a capsule, and that's when she realizes that Julio has pulled off the highway into a service station, he's even turned off the lights, the engine, taken a rest, he's made it possible for a brief lull in the midst of all that, or maybe she'd been screaming too much, twisting in her seat like a worm, maybe she wasn't letting him drive, because who can drive at 170 km/h in the middle of the night while trying to ignore such a spectacle, maybe he saw clearly that they would have an accident if he didn't stop the car. The point is that he has unfastened his seat belt and is hugging her, don't worry, he says, really, don't worry, trust me, nothing is going to happen to him, and she stops writhing, manages to contain her howls, just like that, only tears now, lets him rub her back. He doesn't say anything else, because he has nothing else to say, he just holds her, her body boiling in his arms, perhaps a minute, two, three minutes of breath, a pause, fill the lungs with murky affection, continue the race, step on the gas, cross the border, save the night.

WHAT A CLEAN, WARM DAY; morning raised in the air like a white hanky. On abandoning the shoreline, the seagulls left markings like brushstrokes in the cold sand and now the indentations gleamed. The summer vacationers will get to the beach early today, take advantage of the glorious weather, set up camp along those kilometers of fine crushed shell, the stretch of ocean as boundary, burnt hides, scraps, and trash piled beside full dumpsters, muck sloshing in the showers. But that will be later, because right now the day is still frozen in the beauty of what hasn't happened. The bakery on the eucalyptus road smells like bread dough, the fruit truck drives away, the owner of the stationery shop selling newspapers and sundries drags a rack out onto the sidewalk: inflated floats, little net bags with plastic pails and shovels, Styrofoam boogie boards. All is being readied on this white-hanky morning. In the meantime, the houses near the beach rouse far from the bustle of town, the turning over of engines, the boats resting in the black water of the wharf. Time is paused for the houses near the beach and they stir lazily, with dogged endurance.

Julio's car drives away down the dirt road and Sofía lifts her hand in farewell, though she is no longer visible, standing beside the gate, the same white shirt as yesterday, wrinkled and sour-smelling; in place of jeans, a black cotton skirt hugging her hips and buttocks. She leaves her hand that way, in the air, taking up the space the farewell deserved, she waits until the car turns at the end of the road and disappears, she waits not because she is resisting but because she can't move, because she's in another space, that place she stays when everything else has gone. Maybe Julio saw her in the rearview mirror, a phantom at the gate, made tiny by the growing distance, despite her gravitas: Sofía down the end of the road with her hand in the air, her face uncongested. Julio's window was rolled down, but he didn't poke his arm out to say goodbye, or even honk the horn; silently, the car turned to head toward the way out of town. Leo couldn't see her either, because he was riding firmly buckled in his special car seat, and it's his father's faintly blood-shot eyes and tense brow he sees in the rearview mirror. Sofía had said as short and happy a farewell as she was able.

During the exceedingly short summer night, an exhausted Leo briefly slumbered in his bed, after Sofía had tucked him in numerous times, stroked his forehead, around his ears, his hot neck, that sweaty hollow under his chin; while her son slept deeply in bed, just as deeply as he had slept during the car ride back from Portugal, she packed his suitcase. His father would take him the next day; if nothing had happened, he would have taken him a week later, when it was their turn to spend the second half of summer vacation together; if everything had been normal, Julio would have come next week to pick him up and, amid childish capering and imaginary confetti, they would have gotten in the car together, noisily, the commotion of change, a new phase, his grandparents up north, up at the top of the country, near the green forests, near the freezing sea, to fish, cast the line from the flat river rock, sardine sandwiches, canteen of water, peanuts. Sofía had packed Leo's suitcase, added a couple of sweaters and a raincoat, a new puzzle, two books, some coloring books, hiking shoes, water shoes, his yellow hat, and lastly, the bathing suit she had bought for him in the city the day before, out of her bag at last, folded and with the tag still on, each item given a loving caress, just like the boy's forehead as he slept, his toasted cheek, the hollow of sweat between chin and throat.

They had barely talked about anything since they got back from Portugal, already late in the night. When the sun began rising, Sofía sat down on the couch beside Julio, dozing with his head on a cushion, and offered him a muffin and hot tea. What do you think really happened? Julio had said, opening his eyes at Sofía's touch. Sofía was still wearing the pair of tight jeans, and the waistband bothered her stomach. Her ankles were swollen. It wasn't a sense of calm that had come over her, but emptiness. Not relief, but confusion. Well, I think what happened is what they told us. Do you really think someone could lie during a panic attack like that? What they told us doesn't make any sense, Julio replied, sitting up on the couch and slowly sipping his tea. Oh fuck, it's boiling. Sofía reacted obediently and brought it back to the kitchen, where she poured the liquid back and forth between two mugs until it cooled. It was what she did for Leo when she made his milk too hot, or his soup or his cocoa. Back in the living room, as Julio labored over the dry muffin, she lit a cigarette. Julio smiled condescendingly. What they told us is what happened, Julio. Don't *you* go getting paranoid. They went to a shopping center and there were concerts in the plaza and a lot of people outside the bars and Leo got lost. That's all. Julio let out a squawk, a chirp of annoyance. Yeah, and it took them two hours to find him. In a shopping center. In a fucking village. A village full of people, Julio, they waited to call the police, and I don't want to think about that. I'll take care of it, I'll get more details. All that matters is that Leo was with that German family the whole time, he even had fun. God, the face on him when we got there, the face of someone on a real adventure—I don't think he suffered. Sofía, your sister and that fucking idiot waited two hours to go to the police station after he went missing. And the kid was already there. They didn't even have to search for him! He was there with those fucking Germans! Sofía stubbed out the cigarette in the ashtray and rubbed her face, dry, finally, her impenetrable face at dawn. That's not true, they did look for him, that's why they didn't go to the police right away, they were looking for him. What's up, now you want to make excuses for them? God knows what they were doing. Sofía managed to meet Julio's eye for several seconds. In that time, twice he opened his mouth to say something but closed it again, never breaking his gaze. Sofía was the one to put an end to what was left of the night: I don't know, Julio. I just don't care.

And there she was left standing at the gate, hand raised to the morning, hand hanging from the sky. She wants to cry when she thinks about her son, about how he'd already be back asleep, and how he would sleep the whole way, chin buried in his chest and his mouth open, or his head hanging completely limp to one side, elastic children who can sleep that way and not wake up, total cramp, and she wants to cry when she thinks about how no one will be there to support his forehead while he's sleeping, hold his head up, position it correctly, because it's just Julio in the car and he's driving. And she wants to cry because she remembers that just a few weeks ago they were a whole family inside a car, driving somewhere, and when the boy fell asleep, she reached back from the passenger seat and held his forehead, and maybe she changed the music with her other hand, and inside the car one breathed that conventional air families have, that quotidian greatness, the cohesion of being together, being a bloc, a construction built from love and quarrels, and shit, too, and inevitability, and how that memory tears at her now, in her genuine solitude, how that memory grabs her, the brief words they would speak to one another while the boy slept, the desire to turn up the music, and the silence, then the surprise when after who knows how many kilometers Leo woke up with burning cheeks, and the joy they felt, the two of them, because it's always a joy when a child wakes up, always a surprise that they open their eyes, confirmation that they do in fact exist, that they have been brought into this world, that they are yours, they live, and the two of them changing their tone of voice upon Leo's return, welcoming him, and in that moment, just after waking, the child returning to the parents' world, things adopting their given meaning, the hand of time closing over them, like a glasshouse in which to withstand the elements, and face the future, all warmth and harmony, the noise of a family traveling by car. Sofía has been left standing there digesting her dispossession, and after a while she lowers her hand, goes inside in the gate, closes up, and crosses the patio, where the vegetable garden suffers from lack of water, where the flowers wither, and finally enters the house.

The room is half-closed and Sofía doesn't hesitate to open the door. Because she doesn't open the door to see what's inside, only to enter. An air of sour drool fills the room and in the one bed, not big enough for two people, sleep Paul and Rita. Paul is lying face-up, dirty hair falling across one side of his forehead, one of his skinny arms hanging off the bed. They've kicked off the blankets, and the sight of his white torso turns Sofía completely against him. She observes his legs, stronger and more toned than they appear when clothed, his soft underwear that hides his sex. At least she hasn't seen him naked. Beside him, her sister sleeps facing the wall, all curled up, a hairless cat; she doesn't look like a bird, not now. She is a lump asleep inside herself, hidden from all, remorseful, veiled. Her hair covers her face; one might think she wasn't breathing. She's not naked, either, she wears a big black T-shirt, the same one as yesterday, and a pair of small, blue lace panties. The sheet is on the floor and Sofía picks it up and quickly tosses it onto the only chair in the room. Then she goes over to the bed and gives Paul a shake. She didn't think, didn't hesitate to reach out her arm and shake him, grab him by his skinny shoulder and give him a good shake. Hey, Paul, wake up. Come on. She isn't whispering, it's her normal voice. The man opens his eyes, he's startled, the red orbs questioning from their sockets, mouth sputtering. Get up. Sofía? Paul is still resting in his confusion; it takes him a moment to really wake up. He looks over to the side for Rita but she's still sleeping against the wall. Sofía, what's going on? Paul sits up. He even makes a gesture as if he's about to fix the pillow behind his back, but Sofía grabs him by one of his arms and pulls. I told you to get up. Get out of that bed, pick up your things, and get out of here. Don't you even think about waking her. Come on, get out. Sofía is improvising, she hadn't imagined she would stand in the middle of the room while the guy collected his clothes, while he got dressed, she only thought she would tell him to leave, but now that she's here, in the gloom, she decides she's not going anywhere. She even crosses her arms; it's befitting. She waits.

Against all odds, Paul has gotten up and isn't asking questions. On second thought, she's doing him a favor, maybe he would have left that same day of his own accord, but who knows? Hurry. Fuck, Sofía, fuck. That's what Paul says as he puts on his jeans—has he been wearing the same ones since he showed up?—and his T-shirt, and stuffs a couple of things into a bag, along with his phone charger and tobacco. Once he has everything, he looks at Rita but Sofía won't let him touch her, I don't want you to wake her up, come on, go. The guy, so tall, so young in the tender morning, huffs out of the room. In the living room, he looks at her questioningly, asks permission to use the bathroom, and Sofía concedes. Her arms are still crossed. She stands outside the bathroom door as well, and even has to step aside once the man has finished and comes out. She doesn't need to open the front door, push him out on the street, she doesn't need to do much, now. Paul mutters something to the effect of *tell your sister that* and Sofía dispatches him with a sad but determined smile. Let's go. Out. The man leaves. No noise, no pride, barely leaving behind the crankiness of someone who's been shaken awake. The house is sealed behind him. Sofía waits to hear the sound of the gate and then uncrosses her arms, releases them into the void.

Her sister's room is closed again, Rita is still asleep, and could be for hours. Sofía sits down on the couch. No cigarette, nothing in her hands. The bustle of the development reaches her from outside, the cars dragging their wheels through the dirt, women animating their children. Before her, the house is empty, bar the two of them. Three flies already battering around the living room, and in the kitchen, the refrigerator hums. Maybe Sofía will sit there a long time. She has no intention to move. She'd stop breathing if she could. With titanic effort, she crosses her legs and sighs.

It isn't the end of summer yet. New travelers on the highway from the city arrive and take the spots the others leave, their trashy camp between the dunes, the plastic chair at the beach bar, the sardine on white bread before lunch. If the waves are strong, they'll watch the ocean from their lookout positions, if at sunset the water is like a plate, they'll take backlit photos of their kids in hats and arm floats. At night they'll go out to look for a jam-packed bar where they can spend their savings on cooked white prawns and clams in wine. It isn't the end of summer yet, but there are days when then town dawns deserted and hushed.

Sofía returns bag-laden from the market. She went out very early, prepared to fill the refrigerator with products she would never buy for herself. She has marks on her hands from the heavy bags and she knows she'll be sore later. She's even sweating beneath her dress, because between one thing and another it's already midday. The house is still cool and dark because she left the windows closed and the blinds down. On the table in the living room, her cup of coffee from breakfast and the two books she's been fobbing off all summer, Tsvetaeva and Carson. The pencil for underlining famous lines has fallen on the floor. Sofía drops the bags on the kitchen counter and returns to pick up the pencil and tuck it inside *Confessions*. Leo's absence is the open wound in the house. Of course, she feels some relief, enjoys the silence, sleeps through the night and is even able to relax in the sun. But it's conceptual: the boy's absence is unnatural, somehow, a symbol imposed by modernity; like a mass-produced, factory-baked cake, bright and orderly on the outside, poison within. She looks at her sister's closed bedroom door and hesitates. Finally, she decides to fix Rita breakfast, clean and store the fish in the refrigerator, wash the fruit. Even when she has everything ready on the patio table, under the sun umbrella, she hesitates again. She observes her abandoned plot, after all the effort she put into working it. What if she set to deadheading the dry flowers and pulling up weeds right now? How did they grow so quickly in the new soil? And the vegetable garden is laughable. Only the lemon tree survives, a stranger to adversity. But she can't put it off any longer, soon it will be one o'clock, it's time to wake up Rita. She is saved by the ringing of her phone, which she practically jogs over to pick up, light on her toes, anything to avoid opening Rita's door. It's their mother. She decides to eat a fig on the porch and roll a cigarette as they talk. She's still asleep, mama. Well obviously I know I'm not her maid. Okay, try to understand for once . . . you know what I'm talking about. No, mama, I'm not in a bad mood. Leo is great, fishing all day, like always up there, I'll talk to him later, tonight. Of course I miss him, how couldn't I? Anyway, how are you? Worried? Don't start worrying more than you need to, please. Everything's fine. Nothing happened to Leo, I've told you twenty times, it was only for a little bit, a scare, these things happen. Yeah, bad luck, terrible, but what can you do . . . ? Mama, come on, go for a swim or do something relaxing, did you already make lunch? Yeah? What did you make today?

When she hangs up, she sees that the coffee she made Rita has gone cold and the orange pulp has settled on the bottom of the glass, it will need to be stirred. She goes inside, into the silence and semi-darkness. She pauses before her sister's door, touches the knob, comes close enough to rest her forehead against the wood: she hears nothing in the room, it's almost one o'clock, time to get up. She makes a movement of her wrist but stops herself in time. She turns around, grabs the Tsvetaeva book, and heads back outside. Under the sun umbrella, she chews a few cubes of fresh cheese then starts on the bread. She stirs the juice using the fork handle and drinks it down in one go. It's bitter. She opens her book and begins to read.

That night, when there's nothing to do, the house clean and the kitchen tidied, not a single grain of rice to draw the ants, the flies asleep, Sofía plays around on her phone in bed. She taps the keys as if she were going to type a message, goes through her contacts, pausing a few times on the man from the salt marsh. She hasn't seen him again. For a few seconds, she imagines inviting him for dinner. Preparing a fish stew and buying a couple of bottles of white wine. Sitting on the porch, the three of them, her sister, the man from the salt marsh, and her, gulping down chunks of white flesh and drinking wine with greasy mouths, leaving a film of oil and saliva on each rim. Her sister doesn't know the man from the salt marsh and the truth is that Sofía would like her to see him. If her sister gave her consent, Sofía could allow herself to go with it, seek contact with his hands again, run into him by accident when they brought the dirty plates to the kitchen, brazenly sink her gaze into his clear eyes; she would take pleasure in his teeth and not feel desperate. Of course, the way things are right now, her sister wouldn't look up from her plate, maybe she'd be pecking at her fish like a half-dead bird, a bored and nasty little-girl look on her face. If she deigned to speak, she would surely ruin the meal. It's not a good idea. And anyway, who's to say if the man from the salt marsh would even accept her invitation? He hasn't called her again, texted her, has he? He knows she's here, she hasn't gone anywhere. She wrinkles her face and shakes off the feeling of rejection, dropping her phone on the bed and picking up the heavy Tsvetaeva. She tries to concentrate and reads *if I were* taken beyond the sea into paradise, and forbidden to write, I would refuse the sea and paradise. I don't need life as a thing in itself; Sofía arches her brow contemptuously, Marina's determination, her tenacity in the presence of her passions, the deep awareness of the essence of her being makes Sofía feel stripped bare and mediocre. Although she still has a lot left to read, she flips back to find the passages that interest her, the part about the orphanage, her relationship with her two daughters, how she cared for one and abandoned the other, and she relishes this: *Do you understand, Alya? It's only a game. You are going to play that you are a little girl in an orphanage. You will wear your hair shaved, a dirty pink dress down to your ankles, and a number around your neck. You should have lived in a palace and you are going to live in an almshouse. Do you realize how extraordinary that is?* A strange satisfaction moves through Sofía upon reading. It isn't pleasure, it's the throb of something dark, the controllable pain, self-inflicted, of scratching a cut, pulling a scab off before it's ready, and starting over with the blood, the clotting. She keeps looking, finds the passage in which Marina narrates what they tell her about her youngest daughter in the Kuntsevo orphanage: *Ah, Irina! She is without a doubt an abnormal child. She eats a tremendous amount and is always hungry, she spends the day rocking and singing to herself. Whenever someone says a word, she takes the opportunity to apply herself to repeating it meaninglessly. We have her on a special diet.* Et cetera, et cetera. Again, Sofía dissolves in compassion. She struggles between the immense tenderness she feels for the younger daughter and her efforts to understand the mother's feelings, to analyze them from a certain distance. But deep down, this isn't what interests her. It's something much more personal, something swimming in her unconscious. That distinction between two beings born from the same bosom, that predisposition for fatality: how much is on a mother's hands? Marina Tsvetaeva ran to the orphanage when she learned that Alya, so beloved, was ill. Fevers, whooping cough. She brought her two lumps of sugar and two biscuits. Alya, in spite of the fever, ate greedily. Someone asked Marina, and your younger daughter, won't you give her something? Marina writes: *I pretend not to hear. God! To deprive Alya! Why is Alya sick and not Irina?* Of Irina, she says: *Irina wanders between the cots. Irina! Get down from there, you're going to fall! Her pink dress, ankle-length, unspeakably filthy, the shaved head, the slender, elongated neck. Shakes her head from side to side. She wanders between the cots. Her face is a little different. Immense eyes, dark greenish-gray. She doesn't smile. Bristling hair. Irina,* Marina shouts, *get down from there, you're going to fall!* Sofía reads with a furrowed brow, marks the paragraphs again, draws asterisks in the margins. If she only knew what she was looking for, what she's so set on finding. Alya was rescued from the orphanage, Irina stayed. When the little girl died a short time later, Marina didn't attend the funeral because Alya was sick with malaria and she *couldn't* leave her on her own. Sofía clenches her jaw when she reads that part from Marina's notebook, and the strange satisfaction returns, the sense of superiority before Marina's justification, implacable and sordid, the vast difference between two hearts. Marina, who writes: *her stupidity was irritating, her gluttony, I didn't think she was going to grow up, somehow, although I didn't think of her death, she was simply a futureless creature;* who writes, *but now I remember her shy smile, so bewildered, so uncommon;* who writes, *Irina's death is as unreal to me as was her life, I know nothing about her illness, I didn't see her sick, I was not there for her death, I didn't see her dead, I don't know where her grave is, what did they dress her in for burial? Her little coat was left there too.* Sofía is inflamed when she reaches the bottom of the page, where it says that twelve years later, in August 1932, Marina wrote in her notebook: *When one has had a child who starved to death, one never believes the other has eaten enough.* Sofía pants, suspended in her discovery, and to wrap it up, she flips to the middle pages of the book, to the printed photographs: in one, Irina and Alya in Moscow, 1919. Every time she rereads those sections she finishes the same way, spellbound by the photograph of the two girls. Alya's eyes, incredibly clear and deep despite the black and white of the photo; Irina's eyes, round and darker, her perfect cleft chin, the sketch of her mouth, her frizzy hair. Why? she wonders again, thinking it's safe to ask. Who holds the weak, who protects them? Poor, thin link pulled off the chain. Does life really push so forcibly, with so much violence?

Through the bedroom wall, Sofía hears the sound of a bang and sits up, startled. Rita? she calls. What happened? No one answers and Sofía leaps out of bed and into the hallway and then enters her sister's room; the door pushes right open. That smell again, the darkness, Sofía recognizes her own aversion. The bulge on the bed that is her sister moves, maybe she's turned her head or raised her hands. At the foot of the bed, Sofía makes out a dim light, light from Rita's closed laptop, which despite being shut, still glows and purrs. She goes to the bed. What happened? Are you okay? Rita speaks and in her voice there is depth similar to contempt: my computer fell. It fell? That's what I said. Or you threw it? Rita sighs, lifts her head to look straight at Sofía, standing in front of her, bigger, more robust in the darkness. Were you watching a movie? A movie, Rita repeats, her neck stiff, hair falling straight onto the pillow. She says it as if she doesn't comprehend. The silence smells the same as the room, same as the sheets. Finally, Rita lays her head back in place, her whole body parallel to the mattress, pulls the covers up to her shoulders and hides her hands. What do you care about what I was doing?

The two sisters walk along the eucalyptus road, toward town. The sun will soon set and Sofía suggested they go to the beach to watch but Rita doesn't feel like it, she prefers the park, the wharf, the main street. That terrace in the church plaza, she says. Let's see if we get lucky with a table, Sofía accedes. It hadn't taken much to convince Rita to go out. She spends most of the time in her room on the computer or watching TV on the couch. Sometimes she steps out on the patio and sits in a plastic chair and watches Sofía pretend she knows how to fix the garden, bring it back to life. In those moments, Rita pulls her feet up onto the edge of the seat and rests her chin on her knees and a smile appears on her face, but if Sofía encourages her to participate, she recoups her sarcasm and says something like, this isn't a detox center. She also tends to focus on cleaning the kitchen, which is the only spotless part of the house. Their yogic routine, repetition of what they learned through so many hours of maternal instruction. That afternoon, when Sofía said you should shower, your hair is gross, Rita went docilely into the bathroom and came out shiny and new in a pair of white shorts and a blue camisole that Sofía had finished sewing the day before. Maybe that's why Sofía had been so encouraging, let's take a walk, let's watch the sunset, because it suddenly seemed her own recovery was beginning—not Rita's, what exactly did Rita have to recover from? Was she being consumed by some evil?—but Sofía's recovery of her sister's presence, Sofía regaining her sister. Had she lost her, then? Who had lost whom?

They walk side by side but Sofía has to keep slowing down, make-believe her feet are heavy, in order to adjust to Rita's idle pace. Though Rita doesn't speak of her own accord, Sofía knows there is a breach open in their communication, that if she set out to, she could converse with her. She knows this by Rita's face, her sister's lips don't sting and when she blinks, the movement is relaxed, a flutter of dry falling leaves. Moreover, she left her phone at the house, undoubtedly an act of rapprochement. Sofía has the idea to suggest they go to Portugal one of these days, have a cocktail in that pool that's on the edge of a cliff. Rita's laugh is a snarl and Sofía realizes the mention of Portugal was a clumsy step. It should be the opposite, it should be Rita who has to watch what she says, but it's never been that way. Either her little sister doesn't speak or she says whatever she wants, she doesn't need to measure her words. She hasn't even apologized for all that, not that Sofía expected her to. She knows the little information they exchanged on the subject the first days following Paul's departure is sufficient absolution. The proper space for performing reconciliation doesn't exist between them, it must be produced without preamble, as implacable as a prison sentence. Since she was little, Rita has been uncomfortable with apologies, she doesn't need them: she pivots from estrangement and hostility to everyday familial naturalness, a territory swollen with insults and affection. I don't know, we could go to another town, we don't have to cross the border. Yeah, we'll see, Rita finally responds. Then: I think I'm going to take a trip. With that, Rita quickens her pace a little, rhythmically, imperceptibly, and Sofía has to speed up to walk beside her. She thinks about taking her arm, girlfriends on an evening stroll, but she knows Rita would get spooked and make a fool of her. This is another of Rita's peculiarities: on normal days, she is much more comfortable with physical contact than Sofía, she knows how to wield her fingers and encroach on the distance between herself and the bodies around her; Rita has a whole repertoire of caresses and comradery that makes her life easier. Like with their father, for example, she used to put her skinny arms around his neck and hang from him, even when she grew taller than he was. That was how Rita got what she wanted. And yet, if she's having one of those other days, as she is right now, no one can touch a hair on her head, just like no one can expect an apology from her, nor—and this is the strangest part—offer her an apology. Rita doesn't have to say it: she radiates barbed-wire fence, broken glass set in cement.

A trip? Sofía is wary. But why must she be? Can't her sister take a trip right this very minute if she wants to? Is she not better equipped than Sofía herself? Isn't Rita the one taking care of Sofía, keeping an eye on her? But Sofía can't help it, she's anxious now. She takes out the packet of tobacco from the small backpack hanging from her shoulder. They're near the new park, the one with wand-like trees that'll take years to grow and turn the park into something more than a concrete track for skate-boards and scooters. Gangs of teenagers hang out around the benches, families escorting children on tricycles stroll where the trail is widest, a few old men simulate jogging, alone or in pairs, in their fluorescent-white running shoes. So, where are you going to go? To see mama? As she poses the question, it dawns on Sofía that it's a marvellous idea and she doesn't know why they don't do it, now that the two sisters are alone in the beach house, why don't they hop on a plane and go visit their mother on the island, beaches with reliquary waters, palm trees, rice dishes, and king prawns; she can't understand how it didn't occur to any of them earlier, or why it's an absurd idea. No, I'm not going to see mama now, maybe later, I still have vacation time. Sofía smokes, glances around to see if there's a familiar face, a man she likes, a distant relative. And then? Then what? Then where will you go? Well, I don't know, I'm thinking about it. But alone? Rita turns to look at her sister; she hesitates. Are you asking if you can come with me? Rita's face softens in the moment, Sofía sees her break away from her severity, but only for a second, a joke. No, I just wanted to know who you were going with. Are you telling me that I need your permission, that you're going to evaluate if the company I keep is appropriate? Is that what Sofía is saying? Is she thinking of Paul? Of herself? Is it that something's wrong with her sister, that she's sick, handicapped in her competence for living? Is Rita competent at life? Is she scared for her to travel, or of being left alone? Well, no, actually: I was asking if you planned to go with friends, for example. I don't know anything yet, all I've said is that I want to go on a trip. But international? Fuck, Sofía, you're so annoying. They drop the subject. This isn't the place that will bring them together, Sofía sees that clearly. Deep down she knows it would be much easier to talk to her about herself, as if nothing was wrong. If she told Rita her own plans—what plans?—or if she told her how she was feeling—would Rita have any interest in talking about feelings right now, in listening? She should chat plainly, play the parrot, aren't they just two sisters strolling through a park in a fisherman's village on summer vacation? Is there anything more pleasant than this? There's no orphanage, no whooping cough, no malaria, no dirty pink dresses dragging on the ground.

Are you hungry? The red sky on their left, behind the dunes on the other side of the park, is clouding over. We're going to eat again? We just had a snack. Well, let's get a glass of wine then. Sofía tries to be light and cordial but it doesn't come out right, her voice sounds more forceful than is necessary; she's in a hurry to do something. She stops and looks around, there are a couple of kiosks filled with people, they're already at the end of the park and will soon reach one of the town's main avenues, bound for the wharf. Why are you stopping? What are you looking for? Aren't we going to the terrace by the church? Rita asks, walking backward, observing Sofía. You're right, I forgot; come on. And when Rita turns around and walks a little ahead of her sister, Sofía sees that there's a red stain on Rita's white shorts, starting where her thighs meet and spreading upward. How long has it been there? Did it just happen? Did that hot fluid, so thick to the touch, just spill out of her vagina and leak through her pants, her shorts, or is it a dry stain, the product of another time, twenty-eight days ago, and her sister simply didn't notice when she got dressed? But the shorts are white, that's impossible. Oh, Rita! Wait. What? Rita turns and automatically brings her hands to her hair, as if there were something off about the way she looks or as if she were about to be attacked by a flying insect. The two sisters stand facing each other, and Sofía grabs Rita's hip and turns her a bit so she can get a better look at her backside. You have a stain. What? Your period. There's blood. What! Rita raises her hip to one side and cranes to look, twisting her neck, as she touches between her legs, and yes, it's fresh blood, her fingertips are red, sullied. Her whole face trembles, and for an instant, she looks Sofía in the eye. Sofía would say Rita's glare is hot, boiling, there is anger there, something more than frustration; Rita is blaming her. Sofía is guilty of everything, no doubt about that. She tries to calm her because she knows Rita is going to start crying, not with embarrassment but rage, that's the end of the glass of wine in the church plaza and it's the end of intimacy, as well, the end of trying to make conversation that doesn't hurt. Don't worry, I'm sure nobody has noticed, hold on, I have a cardigan, here, tie it around your waist, I bet we can buy you some underwear and a pair of shorts at one of the hippie stands in the plaza. You can change. But Rita doesn't want any cardigan to cover her ass and she doesn't want comfort either and now her mouth is a wicked dragon and her eyes a puddle: Don't say stupid things! And she sets off running toward home. She runs with childlike intensity. She's a little ungainly, also like children, and despite her knees pumping gazelle-like, despite her elbows cinched aerodynami-cally to her sides, it seems that she'll trip and fall at any moment, out there, too far away for Sofía, who hasn't moved a muscle, to pick her up. Sofía is spared, spared her sister's terror, her sister who flees this clash of realities and falls apart. Rita sinks down,

down to the bottom of it all, she precludes a return to normalcy, resists the very existence of what's real, life's small and ordinary rough patches, she's always been like this, absolutely overcome by the tiniest situation, by the what-will-they-say, by her violent self-consciousness, the hyperawareness of what she should be and perhaps is not. Rita disappears in the distance, Rita and her shorts stained with uterine blood, and night falls completely. Sofía knows there's nothing to be done, at this point everything will be dead for many hours, her sister seething, a tear-soaked girl hiding in her room, maybe under the bed. Any little thing capable of breaking her delicate sphere. Sofía won't be able to laugh at her, don't worry, it's not important, or console her, bring her a lemon ice cream and a few almonds. She can't do anything and she sighs: it's a great relief. Maybe it's a step back from the crossfire; everything partisan wanes. When she can longer see Rita or her stained shorts or legs or hair rending the air, she turns and walks away with peace of mind, even pride. She takes her phone out of the little backpack and dials the man from the salt marsh's number. It rings. He picks up. Hey, how are you?

When Sofía gets home, her body still smarting from the clumsy skirmish, heart sullied by the meager comfort, her sister is, in effect, shut inside her room. Sofía doesn't dare check whether she's in the bed or under it. In the trash can, the bloodstained white shorts that no one will ever wear again. Sofía considers rescuing them, sticking them in the washing machine, but she knows the situation is more serious than that, that such a gesture would barely shine with the intensity of a firefly's tail, and she surrenders because she can't be bothered. Her sister's crisis, repeated every so often over the years, has conquered Sofía, taken possession of her. She knows this isn't strictly true; fundamentally Rita's plight has nothing to do with her, that Sofía isn't even welcome. But she also knows that until it passes, she won't be able to attempt any other endeavor: all her energy must be focused on Rita, the black hole. She could have slept at the man from the salt marsh's house, it turns out he doesn't have a wife, *just me, myself, and I,* is a free and sought-after man is all, a man with a plain, cool house, pilled sheets, a seasoned, friendly body. She could have slept there, he suggested it after sex, while he held her as though he didn't want them to move apart, do you want to spend the night? he said, and she knows spending the night means another helping of sex in the morning, and even if that's all it was . . . but no, I prefer to go home, my sister's there. The man didn't ask anything else and she got dressed, after washing herself in the bidet, after rinsing her face and hands. She left feeling like the emptiness was already starting again, like some kind of magnetic force was drawing her toward the eucalyptus, like now really wasn't the time to be constructing her own life.

Now, at home, she doesn't want to open the bedroom door. She realizes that, ever since Paul left, she never wants to open the door to her sister's room. That when Paul was there, she had gone in almost angrily, to be a bother, and now that the sisters are alone, there's something about the room that frightens her. Something in the distance growing between them with the passage of time; something containing more than one way to acknowledge that abyss. Her sister is in crisis, again, and Sofía doesn't know how to face her. How many times in her life has she had to deal with this? Several. Maybe three. It isn't the same this time; in the past, it was never really Sofía's responsibility, their parents were always there. In some ways, Sofía had always been a complicit spectator, she was on both sides, depending on the moment, the condescending big sister looking after the common good. When Rita cracked up those other times, Sofía's own life seemed to shine, and they were so young that, to be honest, none of it had seemed so significant. It was good to play-act big drama on occasion. Observe it close up. Her parents, of course, had always suffered, yet they never considered Rita's crises to be real tragedies; rather, they were the distressing problems of a young woman, problems that had to be solved so she could move on and everyday life could resume. With the image of the white shorts in the trash bin, trash she diligently tied up and brought out to the dumpster on the street, still in her mind, Sofía admits that now she's on her own. The ball has come to land on her roof, a rooftop littered with rubble and chipped paint. She taps softly with her knuckles. Rita? Are you asleep? Rita must be asleep because she doesn't reply, and instead of knocking again or just opening the door, Sofía decides to go outside and walk around the house to see if, by chance, but, oh, the shades are drawn, just little cracks and no light. She must be asleep, it's very late. And Sofía also gets into bed, without realizing that she didn't call her son that day, without realizing that she never ate dinner, of course her sister wouldn't have eaten, either, without realizing that she's no longer thinking about anything serious or concerning but is falling asleep to the pulse of her memories of the night, tussling in the man from the salt marsh's house, the long-awaited shouts and cries, spreading her legs extravagantly, unthinkingly, to let herself be eaten. All the rest, such a bore, so much effort, so strange it all is.

Why don't you finish your toast? Drink a little more juice. I'll heat up your coffee if you want. It's just her imagination but Sofía believes she is watching her sister grow thinner by the minute, each day there's a little less of her sister sitting at the table, a little less flesh shut up in her room. Why don't you put a little more rice on your plate? If you don't like it, I can make you something else. Or put tomato sauce on it. I'm not your son, Rita says then, looking up from the shadows. Sofía thinks she can see her sister threatening her from under her lashes, it's like she's shooting arrows, accusing her of monitoring her, of being insincere, of not knowing how to reach Rita where she is. Why don't you try these cookies I bought? Do you want some milk to dunk them in? Or maybe I should make you a bowl of cereal? God, Sofía, leave me alone, seriously, I just want to chill here. But you haven't eaten a thing. I *have* eaten. Sofía believes she can tell that her sister lies to her constantly, even when she tells her to go away, to leave her, she knows she's lying, her sister doesn't want her to go, doesn't want to be left alone, it's a defense mechanism, a cry for attention, the way she behaves when she isn't well. I made fish with potato and onion. Will you come and eat out on the porch? What's wrong, do you have diarrhea? That's sick-people food. You've always loved that sick-people food, Rita. Yeah, when I'm sick. But I'm not sick now. And anyway, I already ate. What did you eat? Rita is sitting on the bed with her laptop and she turns her back to Sofía, but she briefly turns back and looks at her again, pulling her deep eyes up from the darkness, fluttering in her pupils is a glimmer of fight, of desperation, of stop-acting-like-you're-our-mother. Holy fuck, you're worse than a cop. And Sofía, even though she can see her sister getting thinner by the minute, a little less of her sister in the room each day, even though she knows Rita is lying, telling her the exact opposite of what is true, even though she knows that what her sister needs is for Sofía to feed her, to bring sustenance right to her mouth, part her lips with hardy fingers, introduce the balls of rice, the soft, boiled potato, the boneless white fish, even though she knows all this, she slams her sister's door hard, as hard as she can, she wants it to make a lot of noise, and tells her to go to hell, just go to hell! and doesn't stop there. She goes straight out to the porch, what a nice night, how peaceful it would be, the little plates set across from each other on the table, a cucumber salad in the middle, the open bottle of chilled wine, two short, stem-less glasses, how stupid she is, how idiotic sometimes, she can't tell if it's because of her sister or her loneliness or boredom, or because she's sick and tired of not understanding or not wanting to understand, and she inhales the still-warm night air and removes her sister's dish, takes it in her shaky hands to bring it to the kitchen, she'll clear away the silverware and wine glass too, Sofía will eat alone on the porch, with a book, she might even put on loud music, she doesn't need anybody, and when she passes Rita's room on her way to the kitchen with the shallow bowl of succulent oily broth, cooked potato, hake stew, she suddenly has a better idea and whips open the door again and, with all her might, throws the plate inside, there's Rita at the back of the room, looking at her in shock, eyelids open, round mouth, the dish flies, the liquid, the potato, the fish, the dish shatters on the floor, no one's suffered an injury, it's only the mess now, the fright, the shards of glass, the green glass of the beach dishware, she should have hit her in the head, the face, she should have smashed it against the wall, made it all the more ridiculous, all the more real. Sofía doesn't wait for Rita's reaction and shuts the door again, she's crying because she can't do that kind of thing without tears, not because she feels bad, what she feels is more like bewilderment, fear of what's to come, tentatively she continues on to the kitchen but there's nothing for her there, so she returns to the porch where her dinner awaits, still warm, and she sits down to eat, picks up her spoon with an unsteady hand and with the other serves herself a glass of wine that she downs at once in the absence of something stronger, aguardiente or poison, and she pounces on her plate like her father would when he got home from work, elbows bent on the table, head down, until she hears a door open inside the house, and shortly she comes out, her sister, the injured bird, the nasty piece of work, how razor-sharp her face becomes at times like this, her hair looks harder, stiffer, her mouth fenced in wire, her sister is a nasty piece of work when the time comes, when neither can take it anymore, and she's standing in front of her, Sofía has seen her out of the corner of her eye but now she must look up, her sister's body, elastic, vanished, or is she the same as always? Her beautiful bones under the tank top, those singular, narrow, vibrating hips under the cotton pants. What the fuck did you do? That's it, here it comes, the wave, Sofía continues eating, she knows Rita is right but she says, nothing, nothing happened, I'm talking to you, look at me, and Sofía looks at her even though she's embarrassed to have her mouth full, to chew in this situation, so she fills her wine glass again and washes it all down, wine potato lumpfish, at least leave her mouth empty so some sort of reaction can fit inside, some mad raving befitting the circumstances, what the fuck did you do? And then she is able to say, you saw what I did, but she won't meet Rita's eye because the truth is she's scared, not of Rita, of course she isn't scared of her little sister, but she's scared of all of this, the same shit as always, the new shit of now, the two of them there, incapable of taking care of each other, charging at each other, standing in for the figures that should be there but aren't, or not even that, she's scared of that old millstone where they're sticking their tender hooves, when the wolf comes no one will be able to recognize him, lamb's clothing, shout, plate on the floor, I don't know who the fuck you think you are, Sofía, I swear I don't know, a few weeks ago you were here all fucked up, you couldn't even feed your son, who the fuck are you pretending to be, a battle nurse? What the fuck do you think, that I'm not eating, I'm puking, I'm a teenager again, what the hell do you think is wrong with me? You're the one whose life has gone to shit, you just got separated and you have a kid and you don't even have a job, leave me alone, leave me alone for once, just because you've grown up a little after the Portugal thing doesn't mean you're in any condition to play the mother and much less to play the cop and I don't know where you get off with these reactions, do you have any idea what you did? You threw a fucking plate of food into my room! Are you fucking crazy? What would happen if I did the same thing? Sofía has no idea what would happen because she has limited herself to watching how her sister speaks, how she spits all of this and how it leaves her mouth at greater speed than her lips can form it, Sofía only had time to take one bite, and she watches Rita calmly, thinking that maybe it won't be so bad, that maybe this is it, her sister came out to say what she had to say because she's probably right, but that's when Rita comes closer, and in two steps she's very close, on the other side of the table, and her wing-arm cuts through the air and her fine hand, so thin now, grabs the plate Sofía is eating from and dumps it on her, no, there's no intention to hurt anyone, although maybe there was when Sofía threw the dish, but not now, because Rita could have broken the plate on her face and instead she's just dumped it on her, her lap is a bowl of fish broth and soft potato, rings of onion slide down her torso, the mess, the heat, the foolishness, the shame. How sad Sofía is, alone now, covered in slop, no plate to bring to her lips. How sad the night is, really, how stupid, how strange, how gross. What a drag, everything stained like this. How loud the neighbor's door sounds when he finally scuttles inside his house, having witnessed the asinine fight between the sisters. It's an orphanage kind of night, futile and all for nothing.

It could have stopped there. After a little more crying, Sofía should have gotten up and cleaned the mess. She should have showered off the glop. She should have ignored the explosion. As for Rita, she could have shut herself in her room; after all, she'd been doing that for days. She could have shut herself in her room without cleaning the floor or sweeping up the glass.

Instead, once a little time has passed, Sofía gets up and goes straight to her own bedroom, where she takes off her stew-stained clothes and puts on something clean. She doesn't shower. She quickly wipes down her trunk, belly, and thighs with a napkin. Her skin smells of cooked fish; her neck, like onion. On leaving her room, she passes Rita's door, which has been left wide open, and sees Rita furiously scrubbing the floor, the violent mop dragging the scraps of food back and forth across the room. She's left the broom and the dustpan with broken glass in the living room. Rita is cleaning. Sofía predicts she'll take to dusting, change the sheets, throw in a few loads of laundry at this inopportune time of night, as if Sofía was the one to blame for all the foulness of recent days, all because she threw a plate of food on the floor. Because she provoked Rita's fury.

She should get into bed, pull the covers over her head, take a sleeping pill, but she plants herself in her sister's doorway and watches her work. Rita sees her but says nothing. So, my life is shit. Since when do you think my life is shit? Rita keeps on cleaning, sticks the mop under the bed and pulls out sand and dust bunnies. Shut up, Sofía. You want me to shut up? What do you think, that I'm afraid of you? You tell me to shut up and I have to shut up, is that right? I have cooked for you every day and I've tried to make sure you're okay and now . . . Shut up, Sofía, please. I don't want to shut up, I want you to listen. So, my life is shit, right? And yours? Rita laughs, it's almost a real laugh, not just sarcastic. You want to go there? Yes, Sofía, my life is more shit than yours, it always has been, you don't even have to ask. What's more, don't worry, even though your life is shit now, mine is much worse and it always will be. You always do everything better. You're better at getting separated, better at being left, better at living off other people's money. Everything you do is completely justified! But not me, of course not, because, you see, I stop eating, I puke in the bathroom, I lock myself in my room and my big sis has to take care of me like I'm a spoiled little girl, I'm so pathetic, even though I'm fine, even though all I am is sick of you, fuck, I'm so sick of you all. All of us? Who's all of us? Mama, me, who else? Julio? Ah! Maybe you're implicating Julio in this. Why don't you call him and tell him how sick you are of me? Rita has put down the mop but she doesn't approach her sister, she remains in the center of the room, thin arms hanging limp, still wearing that mix of laughter and rage on her face, her face is a threat, nobody knows an angry look the way Rita does, there's nobody more prepared for battle, her nostrils flare, if she could only breathe smoke, if she could make it all burn: What are you saying, imbecile? What are you insinuating? I am not going to allow—You won't allow what, Rita? Just get the fuck out of here, Sofía, get the fuck out. Go, you cunt. And Sofía cuts loose at last: You want me to leave? Why don't you leave? You wanted to sell this house, you have somewhere else to live, you don't give a shit about this place and you've been here all summer and you almost lost my child, and now you retreat into your fucking shell and I don't know what's wrong with you and I make you food and you won't even speak to me and now you tell me to go? I'm sick of you, of this situation, of calling mama and telling her you're fine when you're not but maybe nothing's really wrong, you're just bored, fuck, because in the end that's what always happens to you, everything bores you, but it's so easy to make people worry with your fucking secrecy, easy to make everyone bend over backward for you, like you're the only person in the world, it's always the same, fuck, always worrying us with whether you're okay, *in case, supposing that Rita, in case,* in case what? What's wrong with you now? Wasn't it all a long time ago? Still you and your issues? You don't talk, you don't eat, you close up and make everything so difficult, why can't you act like a normal person? What, couldn't I be the one to have a crisis this time? Does it always have to be you? What, you almost lose my child in a fucking Portuguese village and I'm still the one who ends up apologizing?

Rita observes her sister in fake paralysis. Her eyelids quiver slightly, her hands are balled into fists, surely she's hurting her palms with fingernails she hasn't trimmed in days. It's then that she takes a small step forward, then another. She's still far from Sofía, but Sofía is unsettled by her movement, it seems unnatural. Why is she moving? Rita's eyes glide toward her, they trap Sofía, they've broken the fever dream. She opens her mouth to speak and out comes a voice at odds with her eyes, with the tremor, with the night that covers them both. Sofía, she says, and her voice is a whistle slowly taking form, I can't take it anymore, and her words acquire substance, consistency, of course you don't owe me an apology for anything, of course not, sis, after how badly I've behaved. Sofía is poised to turn, to escape the mouth speaking to her, but she can't, she's riveted in the doorway and she must hear it: Do you know why I want to sell this house? Why I don't ever want to have to come to this town again? Because I want to forget. No, don't make that face, I don't want to forget papa, I want to forget other things. Sofía tries to articulate some word, her lips move soundlessly, but Rita continues to speak. I'm going to tell you, I think it's time, I can't take it anymore, because maybe it's your business, too; the voice continues to be a battle, she even comes a little closer, grabs the mop handle and leans on it, it seems as though everything depends on that handle, without it everything would collapse, even the violence, but it's there, it holds, it only takes a second to go from a word to a scream and Sofía is waiting for the scream, the confirmation of madness, yet it doesn't come. You remember what happened? Sofía knows exactly what she's referring to but she doesn't confirm or deny, she simply waits. You remember what happened with our cousin and . . . Sofía stops her, yes, fuck, I remember. Well, when I told you and you told mama, he stopped. He never came near me like that again. But the other one started. Sofía is about to clap her hands over her mouth, about to cry, stunned, but she stops. She is still, she holds out, because that is her duty, she deserves that surprise. What do you mean, the other one started? And Rita speaks smoothly, spins her yarn, a thread wet a thousand times by that droll mouth, between those strong, perfect teeth, pink gums like strawberries in water. Rita speaks with the consciousness of one who has lived, not one who is forced to listen. I mean just what I'm saying, I've always believed he was there when they hauled his older brother over the coals, and he took up the baton, I suppose they gave him the idea, he realized that *with me* he could do *that*. Do what? Sofía's tongue is heavy in her mouth, there's a whirring sound, but Rita doesn't answer, there is nothing to say, it's all there between them, dirty fish gasping for air, and she asks: Since when? Well, since then. Since then? Yeah, four or five. *Whir.* Until when? Ten, eleven, I don't really remember. Rita smiles, because the onslaught isn't over. Sofía holds her stomach, but manages to speak: And why didn't you . . . ? Why didn't I what? Why didn't I say something? Why would I? I told once, and what came after was worse, much worse, actually, and it lasted for years. Rita is still clutching the mop, and Sofía clutches the doorjamb, her back bent in a slight twist, chin down, she can't look at Rita now and she doesn't know if Rita is looking at her. Worse? What did he do to you? She has to ask, it's her obligation, although there's that hellish whirring in her head, did he kiss you? Yeah, he kissed me. And touched you? Of course he touched me. And . . . ? He kissed me and he touched me. The whirring is no longer in Sofía's ears, now it climbs decisively from her stomach to her throat. Four, five years old. The other cousin, nine years older.

Until she was ten, eleven. The other cousin, the one with the machete, nine years older. She still manages to hear her sister, who says: Now you know, and Sofía runs to the bathroom and lifts the toilet-seat lid and everything leaves her body, cooked white fish, onion. Rita waits a few minutes, a ceasefire, Sofía cleans her mouth, flushes, *whir, whir, whir*, she gets to her feet, around her it's a blur, and the ceasefire ends: Now get out of here. There's an unreal quality to Sofía's wet face, it isn't even the leftover trace of shock, yeah, I want you to go, because we aren't going to fix anything, the older sister makes out the younger one there, at the bathroom door, and reaches out to her, she reaches out, not in consolation, but defense, justification, I didn't know, how am I guilty for . . . And Rita laughs, unburdened now and alert. You see? she screams, that's what you have to say to me? That you aren't to blame? Get out of here, fuck, go to hell, I don't want to look at you, go. Sofía can finally react and leaves the bathroom and grabs the keys to her sister's car off the mantle, her phone and her wallet, and sticks them in the first bag she finds, and with her sister still screaming she manages, in a rush of dignity, to get a jacket from her room, leaving the house at last, crossing the patio, the daisies closed for the night, the sad lemon tree, and she gets in the car and inserts the key and even though she can't recall the last time she drove she takes off, unafraid, courageous, and disappears into the development, steps on the gas, and goes.

She doesn't get very far. On the highway, the tears, anxiety, typical dizzy sensation, she doesn't want to meet another car, doesn't want to have to pass anybody or let anybody pass her, she doesn't dare. She turns around as soon as she can and heads toward the beach. She's only been gone half an hour, she never even got out of the car. The sea rumbles there before her, sinks her. She doesn't have tobacco, though she could go into town to buy some—she did grab money. It's dark in among the pines. She starts the car again and drives home. She parks and gets out of the vehicle, her legs shake as she walks across the patio. But she can't get in, because she didn't take her keys. The house is buttoned-up tight, the windows shut, her sister's blinds drawn, lights out. The house is as empty outside as if it were empty inside. Where has her sister gone? Is she in there? She considers ringing the doorbell, but she knows it would be futile. She thinks, too, of pounding on the front door, on her sister's window, but she knows she won't dare. In fact, she doesn't even raise her voice: Rita, open the door, she says as if in a whisper, as if her sister were pressed against the other side of the door, listening to her, their faces so close, forehead to forehead. Rita, fuck. I don't have my keys. And suddenly it dawns on her that her sister knows she doesn't have keys, and that's precisely why she locked the house up, so Sofía can't get in, and she breaks into tears again, she wants to scream, scream as loud as Rita screamed before, but she doesn't, of course, she holds it in, stoic big sister, shattered, and she turns around, gets back in the car, and drives off to that dark spot among the pines from where she will watch the sea at dawn, where she can hear the sea, braying to be remembered, and there she sinks.

I REMEMBER MANY YEARS PASSED. I left home to study and be independent, and my sister stayed. I remember that everything had already changed by then. I had waged my battles and it seemed she was stuck inside hers. We weren't little girls anymore, I was a young woman and she was a teenager. I remember her body, fragile and resolute, the rounded flesh of her cheeks, still hot at the slightest touch. So many things had happened, as many as happen in families until they are no longer the same. We no longer lived with the organizing nucleus, we were distinct clusters by then, separated but laden with the same milk. Our grandparents were still alive, we didn't speak with the other half of the family, and our parents were still together. Rita was the one left milling around our house during the final phase of my parents' life together, the one who bore the prelude to grief, the tension. My room was turned into a stagnant mausoleum to return to some weekends. Those days, I called my mother from the other city once in a while, talked to her like we were girl-friends. Our family was about to blow up, and honestly that's what life was for us, tip-toeing through a minefield, a series of bombs buried in warm sand. We had grown up, and our parents were actually old; presumably, we were the shiny promise of the future, but my sister was in the midst of a crisis and nobody knew what was wrong with her. I expect nobody wanted to know.

And then came the psychologists, whom no one paid much mind. And the calculated, concerned whispers, the suspicion that something we'd all seen happen in other families could happen in ours: a sickly piece of fruit drops from the family tree, a sour grape shrivels on the vine, a wayward bird falls away from the flock. Is that what we believed? What Rita believed? I suppose she did. I suppose we were the ones who stood on the sidelines, despite the fact that there was nothing in the world we loved more than her.

But that period passed, and rather quickly. The truth is, now I recognize that I was the only one outside of it, only I was free. My occasional phone calls weren't sufficient means to take part. Did I call my sister at some point during that strange doctor-filled, silence-filled year? Did I ever come right out and ask what was going on, did I ever take her side? In conversations with my mother, did I delve into what mattered, did I have enough compassion to hear the confession? I imagine that's how they found out, how my mother found out, too late and to no effect, and so they kept quiet. I wasn't told, maybe to save me from pain, maybe because some things are impossible to tell. And I didn't ask. After all, we were a normal family. I was older but I was scared to talk to my sister about the thing we never spoke of, not since that first time. She had always held that power over me, the command of the conversation; although she was the youngest, she was the one with the right to be angry, the one who shut doors. I always tread with caution, a caution that didn't pertain to me, because of course she would have been willing to talk if I had tried to draw her out, if I had coped with her fear, and hers was the fear that mattered here, not mine. I could have stood with her in her shame. Hers was the shame that mattered.

I can remember her now, thin as a wreck, a lovely, limp bird, arboreal little face. Four, five years old, I don't know. She didn't know. I didn't know, either. The other cousin. The one with the smile, the machete. The cousin who disappeared from our lives, but not for the right reason. The one we had always humored, the one whose shouts, insults, boasts we bore, the one who taught us violence. The handsome boy, the winner, the favorite. The tribal chief, contemptible brain, sickly heart. The one who had been my friend. Nine years older than her. How long did it go on? Of course he kissed her, and touched her, but when? When did he touch her? Well, when they were alone, when we left them alone, so many times throughout the story of our large family, and now I remember a winter afternoon in my grandparents' house, his mother sent him back home for something and he asked my sister to go with him, and she did, and I remember now because it was rather odd that he asked, she was older than ten, she wasn't a small child. She would have been with him at our aunt and uncle's house, they must have been in his room, on the bed, and then they came back to our grandparents'. Of course she went if he asked her, how could she avoid it? Because weren't they together somehow? Hadn't he chosen her in tender childhood, sealed it with his will as a man? How smoothly the executioner makes an accomplice of his victim.

Why didn't she tell us? Why didn't you tell us? I asked her. Because I told once, and what came after was worse. That's what she said to me, the person she went to for help the first time, many years before, and for nothing. That's what she said to me, the person who left her by herself every afternoon, every night I was able to, already an absent adolescent, luminous star out in the street, always deserting my obligations, the love at home. That's what she said to me, the sister who didn't save her, who left her alone. And she said it without resentment. And without regret. I didn't live it, I let it be hers to live. Sure, I was a little girl too, but how black the weight of childhood can sometimes be. My sister said what she said without resentment and now dawn is breaking among the pines at the beach, and here before the dunes that herald the sea, inside this car that is hers, I remember her, I bring to my mind that which we have all shaped into forgetting, all of us, even her, I bring that girl to my memory and I remember her soft pink face, her eight years and her big T-shirts and her leave me alone, everyone saying that child can be so unsociable sometimes, and her grown-up expression, so serious and rocked by the wind, a seriousness that sometimes ensnared her, in spite of her surefire laughter, crystal laughter, in spite of the other face she still retains, a face full of joy and ease, the face of a soaring bird. I remember that little girl who—even when she was very young—didn't want to take off her bathing-suit top at the beach, that girl who covered herself up as if she had something to hide, that girl who sometimes suffered fits of embarrassment, sudden and exaggerated, that I—proud and skinny and shameless—made fun of. I also remember that girl one afternoon at our grandparents' house, picking up a present he gave her when he got back from a high-school trip, he who had never given a present to anyone, and suddenly here he is bringing a package for my little sister and we all looked on with satisfaction, the smiles of a harmonious family, where an older cousin brings a present for the littlest one, little straight-haired girl of six or seven, the present is a stuffed toy, a friendly worm that lights up in the dark, a gift as slippery as viscera, which my sister picked up very quietly, the plush worm, the trophy, the possession. I remember this now as the day breaks among the pines and I feel my body start to shake again and it's not because of the cold. I grab my phone and call my sister, but hers is off. I stop thinking then and call my mother. Many rings later she picks up and I'm crying and I know she's going to be really worried but I can't help it, I can't do anything, just hiccup and say mama, and it's normal for her to shout what happened, what happened until I finally manage to make myself intelligible and explain that nothing happened, mama, nothing happened, but Rita locked me out of the house, and we fought, mama, and I don't know what's happening, what's going to happen. I cry harder with each breath and I see the sea before me and I'm frightened, the sea is so big, and I tell my mother yes, mama, I'm going to head over there, don't worry. I don't tell her that I know everything, that she told me, I don't tell her that now I know it occurs to me that there are pills in the house, the pills I stopped taking and kept just in case, and I don't say anything about that but all of a sudden I don't want to keep talking to her, I want to hang up and start the car, but then my mother is saying I don't know, what about the first flight out? she's going to start packing and I can still locate enough inertia somewhere to tell her not to worry, to wait until she hears from me, that she's getting ahead of herself, and she replies was I unaware that I called her crying at seven in the morning to say my sister is locked inside the house, at which point I shoot back and respond that she isn't locked inside the house, I just left my keys, and I'm no longer crying and I want to end this, my chest hurts from stifling my heart, I could hang up on my mother and start the car already but I don't do it because I know that, somehow, everything is frozen, nothing is happening at the house, and now it's my mother sobbing on the other end of the line, and suddenly I can't help but feel immense tenderness, painful tenderness, toward her, a tenderness full of thorns, a rush of remorse mixed with love, and I continue to speak words of comfort as I think about how I only found this thing out just hours ago, or did I know before and choose not to see? Shouldn't I have known without anyone telling me? Were the signs not there? Was the wolf not dressed in his snazzy wolfskin, tough, surly wolfskin, never hiding in sheep's clothing, but always a wolf with his hackles up? Did the wolf not howl at the moon in front of all of us, did he not insolently bear his fangs? At any point in my intense life did I allow my mother to tell, my father to disclose, my sister to talk about this with me? And now, spending the night in a car after a fight, beside the pines, before the sea, I gather my sister's words and line them up and now every memory fits, pieces of a puzzle, one-off memories, concise. I suppose I closed my eyes one day and never opened them again, but my mother, will my mother have been able to forget for a single night in her life? Can a mother ever detach, for an instant, from a fact like that? Will my mother have rested, just once, for a few minutes, from her conscience, her own terror? And my father? Did he know? Was he possibly able to forget for one day, while he was alive? But I say nothing and my mother finally hangs up so I can go start the car, and I do, I start the car and back up and leave by way of the sandy trail leading toward the houses. I feel dizzy when I turn onto our street; I see our house at the end, exactly as I left it, solitary and mute, and I manage to park but I don't lock the car, I simply pull the key from the ignition and get out. There are cramps in my legs, I spent the night in the driver's seat, the air is cold and the sky is dark and I shake as I walk through the gate, shake as I cross the patio, pass the vestiges of dinner on the small table, dinner interruptus. I'm still shaking when I reach the front door but in that moment it's like the shadows of exhaustion under my eyes disappear, my mind is clear and my heart stops beating, I can only shake and imagine that it's all over, that these things happen, that it's finally happened to us, I can't help it, I imagine her body drained, still and vanquished, bird taken in the hunt. Now I'm the dog that will retrieve her, jaws gently closing so as not to cause pain, although it doesn't matter now, the bird's body is still hot between my teeth, obedient dog that always arrives late, and then I see a crack between the door and the frame, I put my hand on the knob and cautiously push and the door opens, because it's open, the door has been open for how long and there I was at the beach, sleeping in the car. I enter the living room still holding that vision of the valley of death and see my sister on the couch, thin and curled under a blanket, eyes closed in sleep, head on a pillow, her hair tucked to one side and her whole face open, pale, in repose. I go to her like I wasn't able to go to her before and I sit beside her, my hand alights on hers, warm, rough, bone, the beautiful hand of my sister, my friend, and she opens her eyes, so suddenly, so dark, so girl-like, and she says I was waiting for you, you didn't have your keys, I left the door open, and I don't know if she can understand me because I am crying, though not as hard, I sense the river slackening, stalling at last, I slept in the car, I tell her, on the beach, and my sister doesn't pull away, it's almost imperceptible but I think I even feel her hand shift so her palm grazes mine. You're so dumb, she says, you are really dumb, and I say but why didn't you call me and she replies, I left the door open. You just had to come in

LARA MORENO (1978) was born in Seville and raised in Huelva. She lives in Madrid, where she works as an editor and teaches writing. She has published the collections of short fiction *Casi todas las tijeras* (Quórum, 2004) and *Cuatro Veces Fuego* (Tropo, 2008), as well as several books of poetry, which have been collected, along with new and unpublished poems, in the recently published *Tempestad en víspera de viernes* (Lumen, 2020). She was awarded the FNAC New Talent Award upon the publication of her first novel, *Por si se va la luz* (Lumen, 2013). *Wolfskin* is her second novel.

KATIE WHITTEMORE is a graduate of the University of New Hampshire (BA), Cambridge University (M.Phil), and Middlebury College (MA), and was a 2018 Bread Loaf Translators Conference participant. Her work has appeared in *Two Lines*, *The Arkansas International*, *The Common Online*, *Gulf Coast Magazine Online*, *The Los Angeles Review*, *The Brooklyn Rail*, and *InTranslation*. Current projects include novels by Spanish authors Sara Mesa, Javier Serena, Aliocha Coll, Aroa Moreno Durán, Jon Bilbao, and Juan Gómez Bárcena.

**OPEN
LETTER**

**OPEN
LETTER**

WWW.OPENLETTERBOOKS.ORG

OPEN LETTER

CPSIA information can be obtained
at www.ICGtesting.com
Printed in the USA
JSHW052141020622
26573JS00004B/5